DESIRE AFTER DARK

GANSETT ISLAND SERIES, BOOK 15

MARIE FORCE

Donna,

Enjoy Slim + Erin!

Marie Force

Desire After Dark
Gansett Island Series, Book 15

By: Marie Force
Published by HTJB, Inc.
Copyright 2016. HTJB, Inc.
Cover Design: Diane Luger
Print Layout by Isabel Sullivan
E-book Formatting Fairies
ISBN: 978-1942295532

marieforce.com

View the McCarthy Family Tree here. marieforce.com/gansett/familytree/

View the list of Who's Who on Gansett Island here. marieforce.com/whoswhogansett/

View a map of Gansett Island. marieforce.com/mapofgansett/

The Gansett Island Series

Book 1: Maid for Love (*Mac & Maddie*)
Book 2: Fool for Love (*Joe & Janey*)
Book 3: Ready for Love (*Luke & Sydney*)
Book 4: Falling for Love (*Grant & Stephanie*)
Book 5: Hoping for Love (*Evan & Grace*)
Book 6: Season for Love (*Owen & Laura*)
Book 7: Longing for Love (*Blaine & Tiffany*)
Book 8: Waiting for Love (*Adam & Abby*)
Book 9: Time for Love (*David & Daisy*)
Book 10: Meant for Love (*Jenny & Alex*)
Book 10.5: Chance for Love, *A Gansett Island Novella* (*Jared & Lizzie*)
Book 11: Gansett After Dark (*Owen & Laura*)
Book 12: Kisses After Dark (*Shane & Katie*)
Book 13: Love After Dark (*Paul & Hope*)
Book 14: Celebration After Dark (*Big Mac & Linda*)
Book 15: Desire After Dark (*Slim & Erin*)
Book 16: Light After Dark (*Mallory & Quinn*)
Book 17: Victoria & Shannon (Episode 1)
Book 18: Kevin & Chelsea (Episode 2)
A Gansett Island Christmas Novella
Book 19: Mine After Dark (*Riley & Nikki*)
Book 20: Yours After Dark (*Finn McCarthy*)
Book 21: Trouble After Dark (*Deacon & Julia*)
Book 22: Rescue After Dark (*Mason & Jordan*)

More new books are alway in the works. For the most up-to-date list of what's available from the Gansett Island Series as well as series extras, go to marieforce.com/gansett.

AUTHOR'S NOTE

Sometimes we have to go back to go forward, and that is the case with *Desire After Dark*, which picks up the Gansett Island timeline the day after Big Mac and Linda's anniversary party in *Celebration After Dark*. In that book, Slim Jackson came home to Gansett for his friends' party—and to pick up where he left off the previous autumn with Erin Barton, the island's new lighthouse keeper.

Desire After Dark covers the weeks between the anniversary party and Evan and Grace's destination wedding. You'll see a few things that were mentioned in *Celebration* from differing points of view. The next book, *Light After Dark*, featuring Big Mac's daughter, Mallory Vaughn, will jump forward to the spring and the long-awaited arrival of the Lawry twins, among other exciting events on Gansett Island.

I know I say this same thing every time, but I can't believe we're at book 15 with Gansett and still going strong, with no end in sight. I've got lots of ideas for upcoming books, and I thank my faithful readers for continuing to support the Gansett Island Series five years after *Maid for Love* debuted.

When you're finished reading *Desire After Dark*, join the Reader Group. Remember that spoilers are allowed and encouraged in the reader group, so don't join until after you read.

Thank you, as always, to my amazing behind-the-scenes team, led by my majordomo, Chief Operating Officer Julie Cupp, CMP, along with Lisa Cafferty, CPA, Holly Sullivan, Isabel Sullivan, Nikki Colquhoun, Cheryl Serra, Ashley Lopez and Courtney Lopes. I couldn't do what I do without their support and hard work, as well as that of my husband, Dan, who runs the home front while I write. Thank you to my fantastic editorial team of Linda Ingmanson and Joyce Lamb as well as my beta readers Anne Woodall, Kara Conrad, Ronlyn Howe and Holly Sullivan. Big thanks to Sarah Spate Morrison, family nurse practitioner, for keeping me straight on medical details and for not telling her mom that she gets to read the books early.

Most of all, thank you to my extraordinarily supportive readers, who make everything possible. I appreciate you more than you'll ever know.

xoxo

Marie

CHAPTER 1

*O*n the morning after Slim Jackson came home to Gansett Island, Erin Barton awoke to the scents of his cologne and starch on the dress shirt he'd worn to the McCarthys' anniversary party. At some point, he'd discarded the suit coat he'd been wearing when he arrived.

She didn't remember falling asleep with him on the sofa, or how they'd ended up snuggled together under a blanket. His chest made for a comfortable pillow, and his arms around her had kept her from tumbling off the sofa during the night. The last thing she recalled was kissing him—soft, flirty kisses that hadn't gone much beyond lips stroking lips, with the promise of more to come.

The thought of that promise had her skin tingling with awareness of the man sleeping next to her. After they'd connected last fall, he'd left the island to work in Florida during the off-season. She'd been counting the days until she could see him again, which wasn't something she did very often. In fact, she couldn't recall the last time she'd looked forward to seeing any man.

Before he arrived last night, she'd tried to prepare herself for disappointment. Maybe the connection they'd forged months ago in person and maintained through texts and phone calls and FaceTime chats would've waned in the many weeks they'd spent apart. But it took only a few minutes in his magnetic presence to know the opposite was true.

Their connection was alive and well, and they had twelve days together to explore where it might lead. Though she'd enjoyed their many entertaining conversations over the last few months, Erin didn't know where she wanted their "flirtation" to lead. She hadn't been seriously involved with a man in years and wasn't sure she had what it took to be in a relationship anymore—or if she even wanted a serious entanglement at this point in her life.

The last man she'd been serious about had been during law school, before she lost her twin brother in the 9/11 attacks on New York City, and her carefully crafted life fell apart in the aftermath of unimaginable loss. By the time she came up for air, the man she'd once planned to marry was long gone, not that she could blame him. The poor guy had tried, Lord knows he'd tried, but there had been no consoling her.

Thinking about those dark days was never a good idea, especially today when she had something far more positive to focus on. She moved carefully to disentangle herself from Slim's embrace, hoping he would sleep awhile longer. He'd been tired last night from the long day in the air, flying from Florida to Rhode Island for the McCarthys' party—and to see her.

Erin went upstairs to make herself presentable. She also couldn't recall the last time she'd spent the night with a man. It had been a while, long before she moved to Gansett Island hoping to jumpstart her stalled life.

If the first few months on Gansett were any indication, the move had been a good one. Thanks to her close friend, the former lighthouse keeper, Jenny Wilks—now Jenny Martinez—Erin had been introduced to an amazing group of new friends. And she'd met Tobias Fitzgerald "Slim" Jackson Junior, the sweet, sexy pilot who'd come to her rescue after she sprained her ankle on a dark island road last September.

Thinking about that night made her feel giddy and breathless, which was silly, really. At thirty-eight, she was far too old for such foolishness. Regardless, he'd charmed his way into her life that night. He'd been dropping in regularly ever since, mostly via phone, text and FaceTime, until last night when he showed up in person, sparking more of that giddiness that seemed to happen any time he was around.

He'd met her parents at Jenny's wedding in October, and they'd immediately adored him and tuned in to the crackling attraction between them. That had been a great night, capped off by a magical good-night kiss when he brought her home. But then he'd left the island for three months to work in Florida, and Erin had been surprised by how much she'd missed him.

He'd been a terrible flirt from that first night. Thinking about what he'd said to her the second night could still make her shiver all these months later. After she'd agreed to have dinner with him—once she was off the crutches—he'd stated his intentions rather boldly.

"I'm also persistent. If you're going to make me wait until the crutches are gone, I guess I'll have to come by to visit every day and make a pest of myself so you don't forget about me."

"You're going to drive me crazy, aren't you?"

"Baby, that's the very least of what I want to do with you."

Thinking about that now made her smile. In addition to his sexy good looks, she loved how easygoing he was, how funny and confident. She loved calling him out when he got too cocky, and he made her laugh—a lot.

The thing she found most attractive about him, however, was his kindness, especially during the days leading up to Jenny's wedding. He'd understood how difficult it was for Erin to see her beloved brother's fiancée marry another man, even though she was thrilled for Jenny and Alex. Slim had provided the kind of support she would've expected from a longtime friend rather than a new one, and he'd helped to get her through what might've been a crisis otherwise. No matter what else happened between them, she'd always be thankful to him for that.

She took her hair out of the messy bun it had been in last night and brushed it until it fell in soft waves past her shoulders. After brushing her teeth and putting on a bra under her T-shirt, Erin crept down the stairs, taking a subtle glance at the handsome man still sleeping on her sofa, before continuing on to the kitchen to make coffee. While she waited for the coffee to percolate, she gazed at the collage of family pictures on the fridge, zeroing in on Toby's smiling face. He'd be gone fifteen years later this year, but to her it might've been fifteen minutes. She missed him desperately, even after all this time.

It had taken a while, a couple of years, actually, for her to realize she would simply never get over losing him. So she'd stopped trying, which had freed up the emotional energy she'd spent railing at the circumstances under which he died. She smiled back at him now, thankful for the photos, the memories, the reminders that he'd once existed and had been closer to her than anyone, other than Jenny, of course.

Though the photos were displayed in a tidy arrangement, Erin straightened them as she did every morning, in a pattern of left to right. Left side first. Always. Keeping up that ritual and many others was the only way to prevent further catastrophe, or so she told herself. Her obsessive routine was interrupted when an arm slid around her from behind and whiskers scraped against her neck.

"Morning."

A shiver of sensation traveled down her backbone. "Morning."

"You forgot to kick me out last night."

"So I did. You were tired after flying all day. I didn't have the heart to kick you out."

"That's awfully nice of you to say since you haven't even let me buy you dinner yet."

Erin gave his belly a playful poke with her elbow. "I'm beginning to think this dinner date is never going to happen."

"Oh, it's happening. Tonight, in fact."

"I have plans tonight." She poured two cups of coffee. "How do you like it?"

"Black is good."

With his hands on her hips, he turned her to face him. "What are these plans of which you speak?"

She handed him the mug and looked up at him, dazzled by his gorgeous face, the warm brown eyes, the sleep-ruffled hair, the scruff on his jaw and the lips that had kissed her so tenderly the night before. "Alex and Jenny are having everyone over."

"Then we'll do dinner tomorrow night, yes?"

"Sure, but I'll believe it when I see it." Erin loved to goad him, something she'd never felt comfortable doing with other men. But Slim was nothing if not comfortable to be around.

His eyes lit up with amusement as he took a drink of coffee. "I believe you're underestimating me."

"Would I do that?"

"Yes, I believe you would. But that's okay. I do my best work when the expectations are low." He wrapped a strand of her hair around his finger. "Your hair has gotten long since the fall."

"I decided to grow it out. You've seen that on FaceTime."

Shaking his head, he said, "You always have it up." He ran his fingers through the long strands. "I like it."

"Thanks," she said, unnerved by the intense way he looked at her.

"I need to head over to my place and see about getting the water turned on and firing up Big Bertha, the temperamental furnace that takes three hours to warm up."

"Oh, well… Um, you could stay here if it's easier than opening up your place." The words were out of her mouth before she could take the time to consider what she was offering.

A raised brow was his only immediate response. While she held her breath, waiting to hear what he would say, he took another sip of coffee.

"Unless you'd rather—"

He laid his index finger over her lips. "I'd rather be wherever you are, but I don't want to impose."

"It's no imposition. I have hot water and heat and everything you'd need."

"You left out one very important feature of your lovely offer."

"What?" she asked, genuinely confused.

He touched his lips to hers. "*You're* here, and since you're offering twelve days of all Erin, all the time, I gratefully accept your kind offer."

"Do I need to spell out what I'm offering and what I'm *not* offering?"

Smiling down at her, he said, "No need. We'll go with the flow and see what transpires."

Erin laid her hand on his chest, feeling the strong beat of his heart. "It's been a long time since I've done anything like this."

Covering her hand with his, he quirked that sexy eyebrow again. "Like what?"

"This. You, me, us. Hours on the phone, looking forward to seeing someone, *dating*."

"You make that sound like a dirty word."

"It has been for me."

"Well, you haven't had the supreme pleasure of dating Tobias Fitzgerald Jackson Junior. He's in a whole other league from all other men you've had the misfortune of knowing."

Erin rolled her eyes. "And he speaks of himself in the third person, because that's *so* attractive."

A rakish grin lit up his face. "You know it, baby." He put his coffee cup on the counter. "I'm going to grab my bag out of the car and then borrow your shower, if you don't mind."

"A daily shower is part of the lighthouse bed-and-breakfast package."

"Oh yum, what's for breakfast?"

Erin groaned. "Aw, *jeez*, I walked right into that one, didn't I?"

"You don't have to cook," he said, chuckling at her comment. "I could take you out somewhere."

"No need. I have stuff here. I'll scrounge up something edible."

"You sure about this, sweetheart? If you're having second thoughts about your spontaneous offer, I can get out of your hair for now and come back later. Totally up to you."

Erin *loved* that he called her sweetheart and appreciated that he'd given her an out, but she didn't want out. She wanted him to stay. She wanted to spend every minute of the next twelve days *with* him, not waiting for him to come back. That didn't mean she wasn't scared senseless of how attached to him she might be when it came time for him to leave again.

"I'm not having second thoughts about you staying," she said.

"Then what?" He touched the furrow between her brows that she hadn't realized was there.

"I'm concerned about what happens when the twelve days are up."

"That's easy. You come back to Florida with me and hang out for the rest of the winter."

Erin wondered if her shock registered on her face. "I'm not going to Florida with you."

"Why not? What've you got to do here that would be more fun than hanging out in the warm sunshine with me?"

Nothing. There was nothing here that would be better than spending the rest of the winter with him in Florida. But she couldn't do that. "I do have a life here, you know, and a job."

"That takes five minutes a day, and Jenny could do it for you since the landscaping business is shut down for the winter."

"They're not completely shut down. They're still plowing snow and selling Christmas trees."

"She would do it for you, Erin. You know she would."

Yes, Jenny would do it for her, but running the lighthouse wasn't the only reason she couldn't go.

But before she could fall down that particular rabbit hole, he came to her rescue once again. "Let's not worry about that today when we have so many better things to do, such as getting a tree for this place. It's four days before Christmas. Where's your tree?"

"I didn't bother to get one." Since her brother died, she hadn't bothered with a lot of things that used to bring her joy. A tree always seemed like more trouble than it was worth.

"We need to rectify that immediately. We can't very well spend the holidays together and not get a tree. I have needs that must be met."

The double meaning wasn't lost on her. "Is that right?"

"Absolutely! It's *Christmas*. That means we have to bake and cook and wrap presents. Lots to do and not a lot of time left to do it before the big day." He was still talking as he headed down the stairs. "Be right back!"

Erin watched him go, oddly elated by his overabundance of Christmas spirit when that would normally annoy her. She couldn't remember the last time she'd given a crap about the holidays. Well, that wasn't entirely true. The holidays were one of many things she'd stopped giving a crap about after her brother was cruelly murdered along with three thousand other innocent souls.

Erin couldn't help but wonder what a lighthearted, happy-go-lucky man like Slim would think of the darkness that dwelled inside her. What would he think when he found out that she hadn't stepped foot on an airplane in nearly fifteen years and, if she had her way, never would again? There were a lot of things about her that would probably be a huge turnoff to a guy like Slim, but that didn't mean she couldn't enjoy this interlude with him while it lasted and then pick up her regular life already in progress after he left.

CHAPTER 2

She had erected walls in front of her walls, barriers intended to keep anyone from getting too close, which was why Slim was completely shocked that she'd asked him to stay with her. Not that he was complaining. Not at all. He was thrilled but shocked, too. Standing before the mirror in the lighthouse's tiny bathroom, he shaved his face and puzzled through the unexpected turn of events.

During their many phone calls, FaceTime chats and texts over the last few months, she'd let him see her witty side as they bantered back and forth. Other than the night last summer when she'd asked him about his real name and she'd told him about the twin brother she'd lost, they hadn't delved too far beneath the surface. They talked about the winter weather in Florida versus Rhode Island, about his customers and flights, the places he went with his plane and the activities that kept Erin and her band of friends busy on the island during the cold winter months.

They talked about the TV shows they were watching, and had watched much of the last season of "The Voice" together, rooting for the same contestant to win.

Not once had they talked about where all those conversations might be leading. He'd asked her where she planned to be during the holidays, and when she said she was debating between staying on the island or going home to Pennsylvania, he asked if he could see her after the McCarthys' party. When he touched down on the island's runway yesterday, he hadn't known whether he would be here for one day or twelve days or what. He'd cleared his schedule in Florida through the holidays, hoping the longer visit to Gansett would materialize.

She'd seemed genuinely thrilled to see him last night, as thrilled as he was to see her after counting the days for weeks. And kissing her had been... He blew out a deep breath. That had been incredible, if also unexpected.

This entire situation with her was unexpected. He'd spent his adult life chasing the sun and the work. He flew out of Gansett Island in the summer and Palm Beach in the off-season, taking people where they needed to go while studiously avoiding anything that smacked of commitment in his personal life. That just wasn't his style—or it hadn't been before the September night when he rescued Erin on a dark road and found himself on the business end of a hook, getting reeled in slowly but surely by a woman for the first time ever.

It was funny, really, when you considered how much pleasure he'd taken in mocking his friends Mac, Adam, Grant and Evan McCarthy, who'd fallen one by one in the last couple of years, along with Owen Lawry, the Martinez brothers, Luke Harris and even Seamus O'Grady. His Gansett Island friends had gone to the "dark" side of love and marriage, and if a happier bunch of bastards had ever lived, Slim hadn't yet met them.

And now here he was, inordinately delighted by an invitation from the emotionally remote but incredibly sexy, beautiful lighthouse keeper who wanted him to stay with her for the next twelve days. The lighthouse was charming but tiny, with a bedroom, a small bathroom, a galley kitchen and a cozy living room. It had some of the best views of anywhere on the scenic island. But the one thing it didn't have was a second bedroom.

As he combed his hair and cleaned up the bathroom, he couldn't wait to see what bedtime might bring. Would he be spending another night on her comfortable sofa, or would he get to sleep with her? The thought of sleeping with her again, of holding and kissing her, not to mention the many other possibilities, had his skin tingling with anticipation. Though he'd studiously avoided commitment and anything that smacked of a relationship, he'd found himself craving more of this particular woman after spending time with her last fall.

Now that he was finally here, in her home, where she seemed to want him as much as he wanted to be there, he didn't care what they did—or didn't do. Knowing he had twelve long, cold winter days to snuggle in with her was the best Christmas gift he'd ever received.

DRESSED IN JEANS AND A SWEATER, SLIM CAME DOWN THE STAIRS TO find the table set with blue plates with white anchors in the middle of them. Erin was in the kitchen, wearing an apron, and he had the highly inappropriate thought that he'd like to see her in *only* the apron sometime. He forced that thought from his head so he wouldn't have to deal with an embarrassing situation.

"Something smells good." His stomach let out a loud growl to make his point.

"Don't get too excited. It's just pancakes and sausage."

"Too late. I'm excited."

"Clearly it doesn't take much to get you excited."

"That's not true at all. It takes a lot. Like a gorgeous woman making me a delicious breakfast while wearing a sexy apron. What's not exciting about that?" He helped himself to another cup of coffee and topped off her mug, too.

"How do you know it's going to be delicious?"

"Because you made it." He kissed her cheek and left her to finish cooking, because what he really wanted to do was kiss her senseless. There'd be time for that later, after she lost the wariness that remained in her expression when she looked at him. Was she wondering if he was sincere in his interest in her? How could she still be wondering about that after all the hours they'd spent talking over the last few months?

He'd never spent that much time talking to any woman without sex as part of the equation. But how could she know that lengthy conversations weren't part of his regular routine? He'd have to find a way to let her know that nothing about their "friendship," or whatever you wanted to call it, was regular *or* routine for him.

The breakfast was, in fact, delicious, and he scored more points by offering to do the dishes while she showered. As he worked, he noticed the family photos on the refrigerator, zeroing in on the smiling dark-haired young man who looked so much like Erin, right down to the dimple in his cheek and the devilish look in his eyes. He had to be Toby, and seeing a picture of him for the first time, Slim ached for her loss.

She came down the spiral stairs a short time later with her hair in a ponytail, wearing a red wool sweater adorned with white snowflakes, and faded jeans, looking far more like a college co-ed than a thirty-eight-year-old woman. He'd been shocked when she'd once referred to herself as an old lady because she was in her late thirties. Before she told him her age, he would've guessed thirty at most. He was thirty-nine and amazed to be having genuine feelings for a woman for the first time since high school.

"Ready?" he asked, stashing his phone in his back pocket.

"Whenever you are."

They took his truck to the Martinez Lawn & Garden retail store, where they spent half an hour picking out the perfect tree.

Jenny Martinez was working the cash register when they went inside to pay. "Hey, guys," she said, clearly surprised to see him with Erin. "What brings you out on this freezing-cold day?"

Slim produced the price tag the guy working in the yard had given him. "Erin needed a Christmas tree."

"Erin doesn't do Christmas trees," Jenny said with a questioning look for Erin.

Erin shrugged. "I guess I do this year."

"Very interesting," Jenny said with a grin for her friend.

Slim handed over three twenties for the tree.

"Hey, wait!" Erin said. "I want to chip in."

"You can buy the lights. We also need a wreath and some of that red stuff over there."

"The winterberry?" Jenny asked.

"Yeah, that. It'll look good in a vase on the table, don't you think, sweetheart?" He went over to pick out a bundle of sticks they didn't really need—and gave her a chance to talk about him "behind his back."

"HOLY SHIT!" JENNY SAID IN AN EXAGGERATED WHISPER. "WHAT GIVES?"

"Not sure what you mean," Erin said, though she knew exactly what her friend was getting at.

"You. Him. Buying a tree. Together. He called you *sweetheart*. Any questions?"

Erin laughed at Jenny's recitation. "He's hanging out with me for the holiday and wanted a tree. And winterberry, apparently." She glanced at him on the other side of the store where he was having an animated conversation with Paul Martinez.

"Hanging out," Jenny said, making air quotes. "Is that a metaphor?"

"For what?" While she tried to avoid Jenny's probing stare, Erin arranged and rearranged things on the counter.

Placing a hand over Erin's to refocus her attention, Jenny waggled her brows suggestively.

"Not yet it isn't."

"But it might be?"

"We're taking it hour by hour. So far, it's been fun. That's all I can tell you."

"You're still coming tonight, right?"

"Wouldn't miss it."

"Bring him. Alex and Paul adore him. They'd love to have him there, and so would I so I can gauge his intentions toward my sweet sister-friend Erin."

For many years after Toby died, she and Jenny had struggled to define their relationship to outsiders. Somehow "friend" didn't seem adequate when they should've been sisters-in-law. Over time they'd settled on sister-friend, but it had been a very long time since either of them had used the term. Hearing it now brought special meaning to a day that was already shaping up to be pretty special.

"I'm sure he'd love to come. I'll ask him."

"You're still bringing your famous seven-layer dip, right?"

"Yep."

"Good, because Alex asked me to make sure. I think he'd eat it with a spoon if I'd let him."

"I'll make extra for him."

"He would love you forever for that."

Slim rejoined them, carrying a huge bundle of winterberry. "Are you done talking about me?"

"Could he *be* any more full of himself?" Erin asked Jenny.

"Did she talk about me? Tell me the truth."

"She didn't say a word about you," Jenny said with a straight face.

"*Nothing at all?* I'm gutted, crushed, *devastated.*"

"You're also very dramatic." Amused, Erin handed over a twenty to pay for the winterberry and took the ten in change. "Let's get going. We've got a tree to decorate."

"I'll see you tonight," Jenny said.

"See you then."

"Don't do anything I wouldn't do in the meantime," she whispered to Erin. "Which means anything goes."

"Shut it!" Erin said, leaving Jenny laughing.

While Slim put the tree in the back of his pickup truck, she got into the cab that smelled of his distinctive cologne. If rakish sex appeal, quick wit and sharp intelligence could be captured in a scent, whatever he wore did the trick for her.

He got into the truck and fired it up, blasting the heat. The frigid day was overcast and stormy, the kind of winter day she loved and the majority of sane people hated.

Erin never used to love winter as much as she did now, but the older she got, the more she enjoyed hibernating in the winter. Although on Gansett Island, an endless array of social events kept everyone busy during the off-season, making hibernation difficult. It was probably just as well, or she'd be a total hermit by now.

"Where to?" she asked as he pulled the truck onto the main road.

"Now we go to find some lights and ornaments for the tree."

"I saw some stuff at the pharmacy last week. Not sure if it's still there or sold out by now."

"We'll start there. If necessary, we'll go beachcombing for ornaments."

Erin liked the way he operated, how he didn't sweat the small stuff and made the most mundane things, like eating breakfast, fun. In that way, he was her polar opposite. She sweated everything—big stuff and small. She was an obsessive over-thinker, which was why she'd shocked not only him but herself with the spontaneous invitation to stay with her.

For once, she hadn't taken the time to think the plan through from every possible angle and outcome. She'd just acted, and the look on his face had been priceless and well worth the lack of dithering that would normally precede such a decision.

She hadn't always been this way. At one time, she'd driven her parents insane with the number of times she'd changed her major before settling on pre-law. Her spontaneity had gotten her in trouble on more than one occasion, never more so than when perpetrating pranks with her equally mischievous twin. That side of her had died with him.

She'd read once about a man who'd detested chocolate until he had surgery and awoke from the anesthesia craving chocolate. Similarly, Erin had emerged on the other side of her tremendous loss a completely different person. Even all these years later, she was still getting to know that new person—and new Erin was someone else altogether when Slim Jackson was around.

Rediscovering the lighthearted girl she used to be had been an interesting side effect of her friendship with him. She'd nearly forgotten that girl had once resided inside her, but finding her again after all this time was like a revelation in and of itself. And that, more than anything, was why she'd asked him to stay. She liked how she felt when he was around—unburdened, hopeful, giddy, aroused, breathless, off-balance.

Those feelings also made her nervous for what would happen after he left again. His invitation to join him in Florida had stunned her. But what had stunned her even more was how much she *wanted* to take him up on it.

He was slowly but surely dragging her out of the shell she'd crawled into long ago, hiding from the parts of life she found too painful to deal with. Inside that shell, she was safe and protected from things that could hurt her. The thought of a life outside the shell made her shudder in fear of what happened when you loved someone too much and they were ripped from your life suddenly and without warning.

"Are you cold?" Slim asked, turning up the heat.

"Little bit," she said, rather than confess to the fears that had her shuddering.

Being on the island had helped to crack the shell somewhat. It was impossible to be around the people who lived here and not engage in meaningful relationships and new friendships. They simply wouldn't allow anyone to wallow by themselves for too long, and now there was a man who wasn't going to allow her to wallow either. At some point, she'd have to decide how far out of the shell she was willing to venture.

Slim parked the truck at the pharmacy and turned off the engine. "You okay over there? You're awfully quiet."

"Just thinking."

"What I wouldn't give to know what goes on inside that head of yours."

Erin laughed at the way he said that. "It's probably better that you don't."

"I don't know about that. Wait for me."

At first she didn't know what he meant, and then he was opening her door and helping her out of the truck. "While I appreciate your manners, I'm perfectly capable of getting out by myself."

"You get me, you get my manners, too, sweetheart." He also held the door to the pharmacy for her and ushered her in ahead of him with a hand to her lower back.

As a fully self-sufficient woman, she wanted to argue some more about his need to play the role of protective alpha man. But she enjoyed the courtesy too much to protest. She'd never been with a man who was so consistent about holding doors, and though it would take some getting used to, she decided she could live with his brand of gallantry.

They found a picked-over display of Christmas decorations in the front of the store. There were six boxes of white lights left, and he grabbed all of them.

"Why do we need so many lights?" Erin asked.

"My rule is, until it hurts to look at the tree, you don't have enough lights. Six boxes ought to do it."

"That's ridiculous, but if you insist..."

"I do." With the lights tucked under one arm, Slim reached for a box of gold ornaments.

Erin stopped him. "I like your beachcombing idea. It's much more original than generic gold balls."

"It'll be cold out there today."

"I can handle it if you can with your thin Florida blood."

His rich, wicked-sounding laugh sent a bolt of heat rippling through her body. He was sexy all the time, but when he laughed or smiled, his sexiness reached incendiary levels. "You're on, babe."

And she liked when he called her that and sweetheart. She liked it an awful lot.

CHAPTER 3

*W*hen they went to pay for the lights, Grace Ryan was working the register with another woman who was also wearing a white pharmacist's coat.

"What're you doing up here and not doling out drugs in the back?" Slim asked.

"This is what happens when you own the place and someone calls out sick," she said with a wry smile. "This is Fiona Connolly, also a pharmacist. Fiona, meet Slim Jackson, resident summer pilot, and Erin Barton, lighthouse keeper."

"Nice to meet you." Fiona shook hands with both of them. She was tall and fair-skinned with reddish brown hair and pretty brown eyes.

"Another pharmacist on Gansett?" Slim asked.

"She's covering when I'm away for the wedding and possibly longer if I can talk her into staying."

"Where're you going?" Slim asked.

"Evan has decided to make a go of his music with Buddy's label, and I'll be traveling with him. Fiona is one of my pharmacy school friends. She's thinking about holding down the fort for me here while we're on the road."

"I'm spending a few days here before the holiday to see how I feel about the isolation," Fiona added.

"That's amazing news about Evan and the plans to tour," Slim said. "I wondered what he'd do after his song hit number one."

"He's doing what he should be doing, and I'm going with him. So we need to show Fiona how much fun we have here on Gansett, even in the off-season, so she'll want to stay for longer than a week," Grace said, smiling at Fiona.

"Are you coming to Alex and Jenny's tonight?" Erin asked.

"Wouldn't miss it."

"Bring Fiona. Jenny won't mind. The more the merrier."

"That's our motto on Gansett," Grace said for Fiona's benefit. "Which is why our circle of friends seems to expand exponentially."

"Sounds like fun," Fiona said. "I'd love to go, if you're sure your friend won't mind."

"I know she won't," Erin said, "but if you'd feel better, I'll text her to tell her I invited you."

"That'd be nice. Thank you."

Grace rang up the sale of the lights, which Slim paid for before Erin could get her wallet out of her purse. He was too quick for her.

"Are you counting down to the big day?" he asked Grace as he pocketed his wallet.

"I can't wait." To Erin, she said, "You should come with Slim. We'd love to have you."

"Come where?"

"Oh, sorry—to my wedding in Anguilla. It was supposed to be in Turks and Caicos, but our resort was damaged by a storm, so they moved us to Anguilla. Somehow we will make do."

Slim laughed at the way she said that last part.

"I'd love to have you there, Erin. Please think about coming. It's going to be a blast. I think half the island is coming."

"Now that you mention it, I remember Jenny saying that she and Alex are going. Thanks for the invite. I'll have to see what's going on."

"No pressure, but it's a chance to escape this freezing weather for a few days."

"That does sound tempting," Erin said as her heart pounded with anxiety at the thought of flying to Anguilla—or anywhere else, for that matter.

"Could I trouble you for an extra bag?" Slim asked Grace.

"Sure, here you go." She gave him a plastic bag with the words *Ryan's Pharmacy* stamped on it in blue letters.

"Thanks, see you tonight," Slim said as he ushered Erin out the door with the proprietary hand on her lower back. He held the door to the truck and waited until she was settled to close the door.

"Should we hit the grocery store while we're in town?" he asked after he got into the driver's seat.

"I have plenty of everything, but if there's anything in particular you want, we can."

"I need my Ketel One. And beer."

"I got your favorite vodka, but we can stop at the liquor store for the beer on the way home."

"Thanks for thinking of me." He directed the truck to the town beach and parked in the deserted lot. "Let's go see what we can find."

While indulging his need to come around and help her out of the car, Erin pulled on gloves and tied her scarf tighter around her neck. Then she tied and untied the scarf again, making sure the left side was knotted over the right. Why that mattered, she couldn't say. It just needed to be that way or bad things might happen.

Carrying the bag he'd gotten from Grace, Slim took hold of her hand to help her over the sea wall and kept his hand wrapped firmly around hers while they walked. She was almost sorry she'd put on gloves, but she could still feel the heat of his bare hand warming hers.

They went down close to the water, where a long strip of seaweed made for fertile beachcombing. As was her routine, Erin stepped over the seaweed with her left foot. The right foot could never go first.

He stopped to pick up a scallop shell and held it up for her inspection.

Nodding in approval, she took advantage of the opportunity to remove her gloves, hoping he'd hold her hand again.

They walked the length of the beach, filling the bag with shells of all shapes and sizes as well as tiny pieces of driftwood and a long-dead starfish. With the wind whipping around them, it was hard to hear each other, so they didn't say much. They didn't need to. They kept up a steady communication with expressions and shared smiles over a particularly good find.

He ran ahead of her, stopping to scoop up an object that defied description. At one time it might've been a shell of some sort. Now it had barnacles growing on it and a starfish stuck to one end. Slim held it up high and shouted, "Topper?"

"Works for me!"

Smiling, he added it to the bag, which was nearly full. He took hold of her right hand for the walk back to the truck against the cold wind that brought tears to their eyes. Erin wanted to switch hands so he'd hold the left one instead. It took effort not to ask if they could switch, but she withheld the obsessive urge, hoping he wouldn't notice the way she favored her left side, even though she was right-handed.

She'd given a lot of thought to the question of why the left side and had come to the conclusion that it was because when they were photographed as children, Toby had usually been on the left and she on the right. That was the best explanation she—and many therapists —had for the odd left-side fixation she'd developed after his death.

Back in the truck, he blasted the heat and rubbed his frozen hands together. "This is going to be the coolest Christmas tree ever."

"It'll certainly be the most unique."

"I just thought of something we need from the grocery store," he said as they drove away from the beach.

"What's that?"

"Bleach. Unless we want your cute little lighthouse to smell like a bait shop tomorrow."

"Um, no bait shop, please."

"Not to worry. I gotcha covered." He told her to stay warm in the car while he ran into the store, emerging ten minutes later with three big paper bags in his arms. "Saw a couple of other things we needed to get into the Christmas spirit."

"Like what?"

"Hot chocolate, steak, baked potatoes and candles for the table. I'd rather make you dinner than take you out when it's freezing."

"You might be the best houseguest I've ever had."

"You just found me out. My goal is to get invited back."

Erin could tell she surprised him when she reached for his hand. "You have a standing invite."

His smile lit up his eyes, and he leaned in to kiss her. "God, I've been dying to do that for hours now."

"So why didn't you?"

"Afraid to scare you off. You're kind of skittish about all this, aren't you?"

"I guess you could say that."

"How come?"

Erin drew in a deep breath and released it slowly. "It's been a long time, a very long time, since I allowed anything like this to happen."

"And what exactly would you say is happening?"

His intense gaze made it impossible for her to look away. "I don't know yet, but today's been fun so far."

He reached out to drag his fingertip over her cheek, which made her want to lean into his touch. "Best day I've had since the last time I saw you." Keeping his eyes open, he kissed her again, softly, fleetingly. Too fleetingly for her liking. It only left her wanting more, which was probably another one of his goals.

After a quick stop at the liquor store, they headed to the lighthouse, where Slim wrestled the tree up the spiral staircase. "Whoever had the big idea to put spiral stairs in here wasn't thinking about Christmas," he muttered, holding the tree over his head as he navigated the tight curves.

"And now you see why I didn't bother with a tree."

"It'll be worth it. You'll see."

Thankfully, the tree came with a built-in cross stand that made it easy to position in a corner of the living room. Next, he saw to soaking their "ornaments" in bleach in a bucket he unearthed from the mudroom.

Entertained by his industriousness, Erin brewed a cup of tea and offered him some.

"No tea for me, thanks. I'm a coffee guy, and only in the morning."

She filed away the information along with the other things she was learning about him as they spent more time together. Taking her tea to the sofa, she watched him string the lights until he was satisfied with the coverage.

"Does it hurt to look at?" he asked.

Smiling, she said, "Downright painful."

"Perfect."

Using fishing string and superglue he found in a kitchen drawer, Slim created hooks for their ornaments and handed them to her for placement, until the only thing left was the topper that was so ugly it was beautiful. Slim surprised her when he placed his hands at her hips and lifted her so she could do the honors.

He brought her down slowly and gently and then turned her, his hands resting on her shoulders. "It's beautiful," he said of the tree, but he was looking at her.

"Yes, it is. I love it. Thank you for talking me into getting a tree."

"Thank you for letting me talk you into it."

He stared down at her, and then raised his hands to frame her face.

Erin couldn't breathe as she waited to see what he would do, and he didn't disappoint.

His lips came down on hers, and there was nothing tentative about this kiss. This one was all about desire and passion and the desperate need that had been building between them for months.

She wrapped her arms around his neck and opened her mouth to his tongue. Then they were falling, landing on the sofa in a tangle of arms and legs and hot, sexy kisses that left her breathless and yearning for more. Too fast. This was happening way too fast, but damn if she could summon the wherewithal to slow it down.

In reality, it'd been happening for months with hours of conversation and flirting building to the kind of spontaneous combustion she'd only read about and heard others talk about. She'd certainly never experienced anything like it herself. Until now, until him.

When he pushed her sweater up, he pulled back from her only long enough to remove it before recapturing her lips, which were now stinging from the intensity of their kisses.

"Ah, Christ," he said, drawing back for a better look at the black bra she'd bought at Tiffany Taylor's store last week "just in case" something like this happened with him. The dazzled expression on his face was worth the exorbitant cost of the bra. Wait till he got a look at the matching panties. "You're so fucking sexy, and you don't even realize it." His words were uttered in a low growl that had her tingling all over from what he said as much as how he said it.

He made her feel sexy, not only with how he looked at her now, but with the way he flirted with her constantly, letting her know how interested he was in being with her. A woman could get caught up in a man who made her the center of his attention.

He placed soft, strategic kisses along the tops of her breasts, which were overflowing the confines of the bra.

Erin squirmed under him, pressing against the thick erection that rested against her leg and drawing a deep groan from him. Finding the hem of his sweater, she worked it up and over his head, desperate for the feel of his skin against hers. His back, chest and arms were ripped with muscles that flexed as he moved above her.

He tugged on the bra. "Where's the hook?"

She reached between breasts that had always been too big for her liking and released the front clasp. His gaze burned with lust as her breasts sprang free of the bra and into his waiting hands, making her thankful for the overabundance for the first time ever.

"So, so hot," he whispered as he took her right nipple into his mouth and sucked hard, making her cry out from the shock as much as the powerful sense of need that had her arching into him, asking for more.

She grasped handfuls of his hair and held on as he tended one nipple and then the other.

His cell phone rang, but he ignored it as he kept up the sensual assault that had her on the verge of release, and he'd barely touched her. If he could do that with his hands and tongue…

God, this was crazy. She'd never reacted to any man the way she did him, and she was about to give in to the overwhelming attraction when his phone rang again.

Slim groaned and dropped his head to her chest. "Don't they know I'm very busy at the moment?"

She laughed at the frustration she heard in his tone, because it more than matched hers.

The phone went silent, and he smiled down at her, keeping his gaze fixed on hers as he kissed her softly. "One minute we're topping off the tree, and the next..."

She ran her hands over his back. "Not sure how we got all half naked."

His smile was positively wolfish. "Do I need to give you a recap?" The phone rang again, making him groan louder than the first time. "This had better be a fucking code-red emergency, or someone is a dead man." Raising himself up and off her, he went to get his phone from his coat pocket while she took in the sight of his spectacular chest and back. *"What?"* His scowl immediately morphed into concern. "Hey, take a breath. Say that again?" After a long pause, he said, "Yes, of course. I'll meet you there in ten minutes. No, it's fine. Just keep breathing, okay? Yeah, I know. I'll see you in ten."

Erin sat up, found her sweater inside out on the floor and put it back on. "What's wrong?"

"That was my buddy Luke. His wife is pregnant and having some issues. The clinic here recommended she get to the mainland, so he asked me to fly them over. It's faster than the ferry."

"Oh God, poor Sydney."

He pulled on his sweater and ran his fingers through his hair to bring some order to it. "I know."

"I hope she's okay."

"Sorry to leave like this."

She stood and went to him. "Don't apologize. Your friend needs you. You have to go."

"You want to come?"

"Oh. Ah… No, thanks. I've got some stuff to do here. I'll see you when you get back."

He kissed her quickly. "Don't wait for me to go to Jenny's. I'll catch up."

"Okay," she said, oddly disappointed by the interruption in their time together, even though she wanted him to help Luke and Sydney.

He started toward the stairs but then turned back, wrapping his arm around her waist and drawing her into another deep, sensual kiss that started her motor running all over again. "I don't want to be anywhere but right here." And then he was gone, his footsteps echoing off the metal treads of the spiral staircase as he ran for the door.

CHAPTER 4

*E*rin watched his truck go up the lane that led to the main road, noting he was driving much faster than he normally did. She hoped that whatever was going on with Sydney was minor and that she and the baby she and Luke wanted so desperately would be all right.

Reaching under her sweater, Erin refastened the clasp on her bra, gasping when the fabric rubbed against her sensitive nipples.

With his electric presence gone, the lighthouse was strangely silent, and Erin was slightly bereft in the wake of his hasty departure. She who had no problem staying busy on her own found herself at loose ends, unable to decide what to do with the rest of the afternoon she'd expected to spend with him.

She was brewing another cup of tea when she heard a plane fly over the lighthouse. She went to the window to watch until it was out of sight. Though she knew he was an expert pilot with thousands of hours of experience, her heart still leapt into her throat at the thought of him in that tiny metal box hurtling through the sky.

The thought of flying made her feel physically ill. It hadn't always. She used to love to travel and had spent time in Europe and Asia during the summer between college and law school. At one time, going to Australia and New Zealand had topped her to-do list. But after seeing those planes fly into the buildings where her beloved brother had worked...

Those images had haunted her for years. To this day, she avoided TV and the Internet in the weeks surrounding the anniversary out of fear of encountering them again. She'd gone so far as to delete her social media accounts because of the random way the photos and videos would show up out of nowhere, sending her spiraling for days. There was no way to prepare herself to experience the horror all over again, so she went out of her way to avoid it—and airplanes of any kind.

Which made for a cruel dilemma for her and the sexy pilot who had turned her comfortable existence on end since he came into her life, making her wish for things she'd given up hoping for a long time ago.

The phone rang, jarring her out of the pensive thoughts. Erin took the call from Jenny. "Hi there."

"I'm not interrupting anything, am I?"

"You would've been about twenty minutes ago."

"*Really?*" Jenny asked in a high-pitched squeal. "Do tell."

"There was some kissing. And stuff. Before he got called out on a job." Though Jenny and Sydney were close friends, Erin didn't mention Luke's frantic call to Slim. Until they knew more, Erin didn't want Jenny to worry.

"I love that kind of *stuff*," she said with a sigh. "He's *so* sexy." A deep voice in the background said something Erin couldn't make out. "Oh be quiet! I'm married, not blind."

Erin laughed at the banter between Jenny and her husband. "I can't disagree about his sexiness. But he's also very sweet and funny and..."

"You like him."

"I like him. A lot."

"He's crazy about you. He was watching you the whole time we were talking in the shop. This is so exciting, Er!"

"Don't lose your mind just yet. It's still very new."

"But it has potential."

"Maybe." As they talked, she arranged and rearranged the magazines on the coffee table, aligning the edges and then redoing it when she wasn't happy with how they looked.

"Why're you doing that thing you do any time someone gets a little too close?"

"What thing? I said *maybe*. How's that a dirty word?"

"You know exactly what I'm talking about. This guy could be perfect for you, and you're already battening down the hatches to keep him out."

"I am not! That's not true at all." Her hatches had been anything but battened down when he'd been sucking on her nipples. The thought nearly made her laugh out loud.

"Then what is it?"

"You know." Jenny was one of the few people in Erin's life, including her parents, who knew about her unwillingness to fly since the attacks. "Think about what he does for a living. He's already asked me to go to Florida with him and to Evan and Grace's wedding in Anguilla. How do I do that stuff?"

After a long pause, Jenny said, "Maybe it's time to put that fear aside and get back to traveling again. You used to love it, and Toby would hate that you lost that part of yourself because of him."

"It wasn't because of him," she said more sharply than she'd intended.

"I know, honey," Jenny said gently, "but you get what I mean. Slim is an excellent pilot. Everyone says so. If there's anyone who can get you past this, it's him. All you'd have to do is ask him to help you try."

She began to rearrange the magazines once again. "I have no desire to put myself through that."

"I understand better than most people would. It took me a long time to get back on an airplane. You know that."

"Yeah. I remember the first trip you took and how hard it was."

"It will be for you, too, and then it'll get a little easier every time."

"I just don't know if I can."

"You're interested in a wonderful man who happens to be a pilot, and you have a very real and very understandable fear of flying that's going to cause a problem in your new relationship if you don't try to address it somehow."

"Jeez, when you put it that way, I sound like I need to be committed."

"Shut up," Jenny said, sputtering with laughter. "You do not!"

"What if…"

"What? Just say it."

"What if I can't get past it? What if I decide it's better for me to never fly again? How do I manage whatever this is with Slim when flying is his life?"

"First of all, flying is his *livelihood*, not his life. And you'll find a way to work around it if you and he are meant to be. If he cares about you as much as I suspect he already does, he'd probably tell you that he'd never want you to be afraid or uncomfortable, even if it means making some changes in his own life."

"You're awfully certain of that."

"I have a good feeling about you two, and so do Alex and Paul. They both said so this morning after you were here."

"You guys are talking about me behind my back?" she asked, amused by the island gossip machine.

"Nah, nothing like that. We're happy for you."

"I know."

"Still coming tonight?"

"I told you I wouldn't miss it."

"You're allowed to miss it if you get a better offer for more of the *stuff* that got interrupted earlier."

"I think I can control myself long enough to attend your party."

Laughing, Jenny said, "See you soon. And think about trying the flying thing once to get that first time out of the way. You know Slim would be great about it."

As she ended the call with Jenny, Erin wondered how she would think about anything other than the dilemma that threatened to derail the promising relationship with Slim before it even got started.

~

OWEN LAWRY PULLED THE CRUMPLED LETTER OUT OF HIS BACK POCKET and looked at it again. Although one sentence could hardly be called a "letter." It was blackmail. Emotional blackmail. The page he'd wanted to rip to shreds the minute he opened it said only, *Take my call and I'll give your mother a divorce.*

In the two days since the "letter" had arrived at the Sand & Surf Hotel that Owen owned with his wife, Laura, he'd ignored two collect calls from the Virginia prison where his father now resided after pleading guilty to abusing Owen's mother. Owen hadn't even known that collect calls could be made to cell phones, and how had his father gotten his number? No one in his family would ever give it to him, so it must've been one of the lawyers who didn't know the full history between father and son.

They couldn't know that the last person on God's green earth that Owen wanted to talk to was Mark Lawry, which of course his father knew. Thus the emotional blackmail. He hadn't felt this wound up since the weeks before the trial, when he'd had to prepare himself to see the son of a bitch who'd raised him. He'd thought it was over now that the trial was done, but with his father, it was never over.

Of course, Laura had tuned in to the fact that something was up with him, but he hadn't told her about the letter or the blackmail. She had enough to contend with carrying their twins, taking care of Holden and helping to run the hotel, which was booked with holiday-week reservations. Their life, as always, was busy and fun, except for when his father dropped in to remind him that Owen could run but he couldn't hide from his past.

His coffee had gone cold while he stared out the window at the ocean. He loved the view from the hotel his grandparents had owned for fifty years until they gave it to him and Laura as a wedding gift. He loved the life that he and Laura had here with Holden and was eagerly anticipating the twins, who'd arrive in March. Everything was going so well, which made this latest volley from his father so poorly timed.

A gurgle from Holden's room let Owen know the little guy was awake. He poured the remains of his coffee down the sink and went to fetch him. This was Owen's favorite time of day with the baby he was raising as his own, even though his biological father was Laura's first husband, Justin. He came to the island once a month to see his son and contributed child support, but Owen got the rest of the time with Holden, including moments like this when the baby's cute face lit up with delight at the sight of him.

Owen scooped him up and held him close, breathing in the sweet baby scent that he'd become addicted to since Holden was born. "Hey, buddy. You sleep good?"

"Dadadadada."

His heart melted any time Holden called him that, and for the millionth time, he wondered how anyone could expend their rage on a helpless child who was completely dependent upon them for everything. He discarded Holden's heavy overnight diaper and changed him out of his pajamas into tiny jeans and a red sweater. He was so damned cute with his dark hair and eyes, the picture of his biological father, not that Owen and Laura cared who he looked like.

Owen was blessed to have Laura and Holden in his life, and he gave thanks for them every day. At times like this, when his emotions were stirred by memories he'd sooner forget than relive, he was extra thankful for Laura and the baby, who reminded him of how far he'd come from where he'd started out in life.

He brought Holden into the kitchen and put him into his high chair with some dry cereal. They had the same routine every morning, and Owen loved it. He took the morning shift with the baby so Laura could sleep in. As her pregnancy progressed, she couldn't seem to get enough sleep.

A soft knock on the door preceded his mother ducking her head into the apartment.

"Come in," Owen said, smiling as she came in the door with her fiancé, Charlie, trailing behind her. They were nearly inseparable these days, and Owen couldn't be happier for them.

"Morning." Sarah went past her son to kiss her grandson's forehead.

Holden squealed with happiness at the sight of two of his favorite people.

"I see where I rate around here," Owen said, amused by his mother's focus on the baby.

"Grandchildren always bump children." Sarah leaned in to kiss Owen's cheek. "You should know that by now."

"Wait till the twins come," Charlie said. "You'll be lucky if she says hello to you."

Owen laughed, because he knew that was true. His mother was almost as excited about the new babies as he and Laura were. She was excited about everything now that his father's trial was behind them, and he was finally exactly where he belonged. Which was why Owen was so tormented over his father's latest cruel volley. His mother and Charlie wanted to be married but were content to live together forever if his father refused to let her go.

After everything they'd both been through before they found each other, they should have everything they wanted, and Owen hated being the one thing standing between them and a happy future. Intellectually, he knew it was his father standing between them, not him, but he could fix that. If only he could bring himself to accept a call from the person he least wished to speak to.

"We're on our way to Uncle Shane and Aunt Katie's for breakfast," Sarah said to Holden. "You want to come with us?"

At the words *Uncle Shane*, Holden began kicking his feet and trying to break out of the high chair.

"I'll take that as a yes," Sarah said, laughing. "Is it okay with you?"

"Sure," Owen said. "He loves his time with Shane." Laura's brother was happily engaged to Owen's sister, Katie, and living a few doors down the street from them. Having his sister nearby and seeing her settled with Shane was another thing to love about his life on Gansett Island.

Sarah expertly removed Holden from the high chair, got him cleaned up and into his hat and coat. "We'll be back in a little while."

"Take your time. We're not doing anything today."

"Maybe we'll come back at naptime, then," Sarah said with a smile that lit up her eyes.

"Just let me know," Owen said.

"We will."

"Give Dada a kiss," Sarah said.

Holden came stumbling across the room on legs that wobbled under him. He and Laura called him the "drunken sailor" since he'd begun walking a week ago—at only ten months old. Owen bent to receive a wet, sloppy kiss from the little guy. "Be good for Gram and Gramps."

"Dadadadada."

"Let's go see Uncle Shane and Auntie Katie," Sarah said as she picked up Holden.

Owen saw them out and then went to look in on Laura, who was still sound asleep. He stretched out on the bed next to her, staring up at the ceiling and filled with anxiety as he waited for the phone to ring again. He'd been there about thirty minutes when Laura turned over, cuddling up to him as best she could with the huge baby bump between them. March couldn't come soon enough for either of them. Her hand landed on his chest, which helped to calm and settle him.

The calming effect she had on him was one of the things he loved best about being married to her.

"You gonna tell me what's wrong?" she asked in a sleepy, sexy-sounding voice.

"Nothing's wrong. Holden's with my mom and Charlie, so I'm taking advantage of a lazy morning with my wife."

"I'm not talking about right now. I mean in general over the last few days. You're brooding over something."

They'd been living together for more than a year, but the way she paid attention still took him by surprise.

"You don't have to tell me if you don't want to, but I'm right here if you need me."

He covered the hand she'd put on his chest. "I know."

"And despite the two linebackers you've graced me with, I'm pregnant, not fragile."

"I definitely know that. You're Superwoman."

"Talk to me, O. Tell me what's on your mind."

Because he hated having distance of any kind between them, he pulled the folded piece of paper from his pocket and handed it to her.

"What's this?"

"Read it."

He watched as her eyes skimmed over the single sentence and widened with shock. *"Oh my God! Is he for real?"*

"Unfortunately, yes."

"Has he called?"

"Twice so far. I haven't accepted the call. Yet."

"Owen, your mother would *not* want you to do this for her. She and Charlie are perfectly content the way they are."

"How can I live with being the reason they aren't able to get married?"

"You are *not* the reason."

"You know what I mean."

"He wants you upset and riddled with anxiety waiting for the phone to ring. You're not going to give him the satisfaction."

"I'm tired of running in fear from him. What if I take the call, see what he wants and buy my mother's freedom in the process?"

"What if he says something that sets you back twenty years? Have you thought of that?"

"He doesn't have that kind of power over me anymore."

"Doesn't he?"

Owen sighed deeply, filled with feelings of defeat that he'd thought were in the past. "I hate that he does. I hate it more than anything."

"I know, honey, and that's why I don't want you to talk to him. You've been so unburdened since the trial ended. I can't bear to see you go back to how you felt before it."

"And I can't bear the idea of my mom not being able to move forward with Charlie because of me."

"Owen…"

"I know it's not technically because of me, but I can do something about it."

After a long pause, Laura pushed herself up to one elbow to look down at him. "What if I take the call? His note doesn't say it has to be you."

"No way. Not happening."

"Why not? He's nothing to me. He can't hurt me."

"You don't know him. You don't know what he's capable of."

"Sure, I do. I was here when your mother arrived on the island after he beat the hell out of her. I've witnessed the wounds you carry with you. Don't tell me I don't know what he's capable of. I do know, and I'm not intimidated by the idea of taking a phone call from him."

"I can't let you do this. It's just… I can't."

"Would you do it for me? If the shoe were on the other foot?"

"Yes, but—"

"No buts. I'll take the call. I'll see what he wants, and I'll take care of it."

"Laura…"

"I'll take the call, Owen."

"Okay," he said, hating the relief he felt at knowing he didn't have to talk to his father. What kind of man did it make him that he was letting his pregnant wife do his dirty work for him?

"There," she said with a big victorious smile, "was that so hard?"

He couldn't help but return the smile. "You're such a hellcat when you want to be."

"Why thank you. I may be a hellcat, but I'm also a wife who loves her husband too much to let anyone hurt him ever again."

"I love you, too, babe. I want you to promise that if he says anything offensive, you'll hang up immediately."

"I will. I promise. Now help me out of this bed so I can pee and brush my teeth and then fool around with my husband while our son is otherwise occupied."

"I do love your agenda, Mrs. Lawry."

"I do love you, Mr. Lawry."

CHAPTER 5

*T*hough he wanted to get back to the island—and Erin—as soon as possible, Slim went with Luke and Sydney to Women and Infants Hospital in Providence. He hoped he could provide some support to his buddy, who was silently freaking out about the possibility of a problem with Syd's pregnancy.

The doctors asked Luke to wait outside while they evaluated Sydney in the hospital's emergency department. When Luke put up a protest at being separated from her for even a few minutes, Slim was glad he'd come along. He took his friend by the arm and led him to the nearby waiting room, forcing him into a chair.

"You need to breathe," Slim said.

"I can't do anything until I know she and the baby are okay."

"If there's anything wrong, they're in the best possible place."

"She can't lose this baby, Slim. She'll never survive another loss."

He wanted to assure Luke that Sydney wasn't going to lose the baby, but he couldn't know that for sure. "I know it's hard not to go to worst-case scenario, but at the first sign of trouble, you got her here as fast as you could. There's nothing else either of you could've done that you didn't do."

Luke sagged into his chair. "She's been so happy, making plans, talking about names. It's like she's finally allowed herself to hope again."

Slim ached at the thought of that hope being ripped away from someone who had already had more than her share of heartache, having lost her first husband and her children in a drunk-driving accident several years ago.

"I talked her into trying for the baby. If she loses it..."

"Luke, buddy, you gotta be positive for her."

Luke bent his head and dropped it into his hands.

Slim rested a hand on Luke's back, offering what comfort he could and knowing it was nowhere near enough.

"I'm so glad you were on the island and able to bring us over."

"So am I."

Taking a deep breath, Luke sat up. "I hope I didn't mess up your day too badly."

"Don't give it a thought. What I was doing will keep until later." He couldn't wait to get back to Erin, to resume where they'd left off, to kiss her and touch her. Okay, enough of those thoughts, or he was going to have an embarrassing situation to contend with.

"So you're sticking around for the holidays?" Luke asked while staring at the door to the exam rooms.

Sensing his friend was desperately seeking something to take his mind off what might be happening with Sydney, Slim said, "There's this lighthouse keeper, you see."

Luke tore his gaze off the doors to look at Slim. "You and Erin? Really?"

"Seems that way."

"I wondered if anything would come of that after Alex and Jenny's wedding, but then you left."

"And I've talked to her almost every day since."

Luke returned his attention to the doors that stood between him and the woman he loved. "Wow, that's awesome. She seems really great."

"She is, but she's really guarded, too. She's been through a lot in her life. You know that Jenny's fiancé, who died on 9/11, was Erin's twin, right?"

"Yeah, I did know that."

"From what I can gather, her life has been in somewhat of a tailspin since then. I'm trying to take it slow, but whenever I'm with her, I seem to forget about that plan."

"It was like that with me and Syd when we first got together, too. After losing her family the way she did, she wasn't sure she wanted to risk her heart again. I'm glad she finally decided to take the leap."

"She is, too. You guys are great together."

As if he couldn't bear to stay seated any longer, Luke got up and began to pace. "What could be taking so long?"

"I'm sure they're just being thorough."

Luke rubbed his chest. "I feel like I'm having a heart attack."

"It's probably anxiety. Try taking some deep breaths."

Luke was still rubbing his chest fifteen minutes later when a nurse came through the doors.

"Mr. Harris? You can come on back."

Luke bolted for the doors.

Slim watched him go, hoping and praying he'd get good news on the other side. While he waited to hear more, he sent a text to Erin.

At the ER with Luke and Syd. Waiting to hear what's up before I head back. Do you miss me yet?

She replied right away: *Who is this?*

Ha-ha. You're very funny!

Hoping for good news for Syd. It's nice of you to wait with them.

Luke is losing it. I'm glad I came.

Did they say what's wrong?

Not really, and I didn't want to ask. I'll give it another hour or so and see if they need a ride home.

No problem. My other boyfriend is here entertaining me while you're gone.

So wait, I'm your boyfriend?

No, the other one is. You're my fling.

You're so going to pay for that when I get back.

39

I'm very scared...

I'll give you a heads-up when I'm on the way back so you can get the BF out.

That's very sporting of you. See you soon! Be careful in that tin can you fly around in.

Sweetheart, I'm an ace in that tin can. You ought to let me show you sometime.

Slim chuckled with amusement at her witty retorts. He'd become addicted to their conversations over the last couple of months, mostly because of her delightful sense of humor. She made him laugh more than any other woman ever had, but it hadn't escaped his notice that she didn't seem to have any desire to take off with him to Florida or Anguilla, or anywhere else for that matter. In the time they had left together, he'd have to see if he could get her to talk to him about why she didn't want to spend more time with him.

YOU OUGHT TO LET ME SHOW YOU SOMETIME...

Ugh. Erin stared at the text on her screen. If she let this relationship with him continue on the current path, eventually she'd have to tell him how she felt about flying. Talking about it with Jenny earlier had been hard enough. She didn't want to consider how hard it would be to tell him.

The conversation with Jenny kept cycling through her mind as she waded through her overflowing email in-box, looking for fresh ideas for the Ask Erin column she wrote for a Philadelphia newspaper. The column was on hiatus for the holidays, but with the afternoon suddenly free, she'd decided to try to get a jump on some material for the new year.

She'd initially been hired to write high-profile obituaries and other death notices for the paper—and hadn't that been a good time? She'd stumbled into the writing of the column, filling in for someone who was on maternity leave. The original columnist had chosen not to return to work, and Erin was offered the column full time. When she had the chance to move to Gansett, she'd arranged to continue writing the column remotely. So far it was working out well, and the change in scenery had been good for her. Not to mention the amazing new friends she'd made since moving to Gansett.

It was nice to live close to Jenny, too. Having her nearby was like being with family, and Erin couldn't wait for when Jenny and Alex started a family so she could dote on their kids. She tried not to think too much about the children her brother and Jenny might've had together. Toby and Jenny had wanted to be young parents, so their children would have been approaching high school age by now.

Erin couldn't think about that, or she'd send herself spiraling. It had happened far too often for her not to recognize the signs. She'd gotten through Jenny's wedding in the fall, in large part thanks to Slim's support, and she'd find a way to deal with the emotional wallop that the eventual birth of Jenny's first child was sure to bring. Erin had no doubt she would be treated as a beloved aunt to Jenny's children, but she was painfully aware that they wouldn't actually be her nieces and nephews.

"Enough of that," she said out loud, as if saying the words would steer her thoughts away from the perilous path to nowhere good. She clicked on an email and tried to lose herself in someone else's problems, a practice that had been strangely cathartic since she'd been writing the column.

> *Dear Erin,*
>   *I'm not sure if you can help me, but I don't know where else to turn.*

So many of her letters were from teenage girls who were afraid to tell anyone else their problems. Even if she didn't feature their questions in the column, she replied to every one of them, hoping her words might make some small difference to a struggling teen.

> *I caught my brother stealing from a local store and confronted him. He said his friends dared him and it was a one-time thing. Then I saw him do it again. We were at the drugstore, and he put things in his pocket and walked*

out without paying. His friends weren't there. It was just the two of us. I want
to find a way to stop him without getting him into trouble with the police, and
I don't want him to hate me for ratting on him. Please help me. I can't sleep or
eat or do anything but picture my brother in jail.
    Sincerely,
    Tara

Dear Tara,
    Your brother is lucky to have a sister who cares for him as much as you
do. I understand your desire to protect him, but you can only do so much. If
you're unable to speak to one or both of your parents about what your brother
is doing, I urge you to talk to another adult you trust, a teacher, school
counselor, neighbor or coach, someone who can help you navigate this
situation. Tell them what you've told me and ask for help. Your brother may
be angry at first, but one day he'll thank you for keeping him out of big
trouble. Please write to me and let me know how your situation resolves itself.
    Hugs,
    Erin

She had a team of experts on retainer whom she could call on to advise her on how to answer questions when needed, but some, like Tara's, were more clear-cut. The girl needed to tell someone she trusted and allow them to relieve her burden. She hoped Tara would write back to let her know the outcome.

Sometimes people wrote back to say her advice had backfired and made a bad situation worse. Erin tried to learn from that kind of feedback, but the disclaimer at the bottom of each column and email absolved her of any binding responsibility toward the people she corresponded with. And the paper's legal team vetted every answer before it went live online or in the paper.

Dear Erin,
    My life has been destroyed by the discovery that my husband is having an
affair—with my friend. I'm devastated, angry, hurt and so many other things
I can't begin to put into words. Having been betrayed by two people I loved is

ruining me. I can't find a way out of this unbearable pain. Please tell me how to make myself feel better and how to live without these two people who were so important to me.

Debbie

God, what to even say to this one?

Dear Debbie,

I'm so sorry this has happened to you. Sometimes there are no words that can bring comfort in a situation like this. But I will say that over time, you'll find a way to go on, even if that seems impossible right now. It's important to change your routine, to meet new people who interest you and to make new friends. New hobbies and new activities, such as joining a gym or taking a dance class, can lead to new people. Some would say that forgiveness can help you find the path forward. That may or may not work for you, but I put it out there as a possibility you might want to explore. You won't ever forget what happened, but perhaps if you can forgive them, you can set yourself free in the process. In the meantime, rely on the people who bring you joy and please let me know how you're doing. I'll be thinking of you and wishing you well.

Hugs,

Erin

She answered three more inquiries—one from a woman coping with the loss of her mother, another from a bride-to-be who'd changed her mind about getting married and was looking for a graceful way out, and a third from a young man who wanted a certain girl to notice him as more than a friend. Though she hadn't personally experienced any of these situations, she'd known her fair share of grief and found that approaching her replies with empathy and compassion went a long way toward helping the people who wrote to her. That the column had been picked up for national syndication thanks to her hard work counted as her greatest professional accomplishment since she left law school.

Erin loved the work, the challenge of sinking her teeth into meaty dilemmas, and she appreciated the distraction of helping other people deal with their problems. By the time she crafted her fifth reply, she looked up to notice the sky getting darker. It was time to make her dip for tonight, along with an extra batch for Alex to eat with a spoon.

She checked her phone to see if Slim had texted, but there was nothing new. Thinking about Sydney and hoping for a positive outcome, she got busy in the kitchen while also continuing to ruminate over the idea of whether taking one flight with Slim would help her over the hurdle that was keeping her grounded.

CHAPTER 6

For Mac McCarthy Junior, the day after his parents' anniversary party had been long and trying. He'd awoken far too early and was tired, cranky, hungover and sexually frustrated. Somehow, a night that was supposed to be kid-free thanks to Maddie's parents had turned into two kids with fevers in bed between him and his wife. He'd been kicked in the head and the gut—twice each—and Hailey's foot had just missed the family jewels.

Enough was enough.

He'd dragged himself out of bed, taking his feverish little girl with him. Better to hold her while she slept than to risk being unmanned by a sharp elbow or foot. And Maddie had suggested getting the kids a dog for Christmas. *As if!* That would be just what he needed—two kids *and* a dog in his bed.

Thomas had woken up feeling worse and had clung to Maddie, while Hailey was all about Daddy. Usually, that was more than fine with Mac, but after a restless night, he was tired and expecting more of the same tonight.

"I guess we should call Jenny and tell her we're out for tonight," Maddie said late in the afternoon.

Thomas was asleep in her arms, and Mac worried about her

catching whatever the kids had. She was still in her first trimester of pregnancy, and he didn't want anything going wrong this time. They'd bounced back from losing their last pregnancy, but thinking of the baby they'd lost could still bring tears to his eyes—and hers.

"I suppose so." Though he was disappointed about missing the night out with friends, their children came first. "You want me to put him to bed?"

"You can try."

"Let me put her down first. I'll come back for him." Mac went upstairs and got Hailey settled in her crib, watching as she popped her thumb into her mouth. Her cheeks were red from the fever, but it was lower now than it had been earlier. He went down to collect Thomas and got him tucked into bed, too, returning to Maddie, who was stretched out on the sofa. "You feel okay, hon?"

"Yeah, just tired. Been a *long* day." Only yesterday, she'd confessed to feeling unattractive to him as her pregnancy had progressed. He'd shown her just how attractive she would always be to him, but he'd looked forward to showing her again last night.

It worried him that she could think he would ever fall out of love —or lust—with her. That would never happen, and he wanted to be sure she knew how much she meant to him. She held out a hand to invite him to lie with her on the sofa.

He gladly accepted the invite, snuggling up to her. "Whatever shall we do with this night we now get to spend at home?"

"We could sleep like sane people would after the day we've had."

"We could, but what fun would that be?" He ran a hand down her back to cup her ass, tugging her in tight against him.

"Is there ever a time you're not interested in sex, Mac?"

He pretended to think about that for a second. "When you're in the room? No, not really."

"You should've come with a warning label," she said, a teasing smile making her eyes sparkle with amusement.

He nuzzled her neck. "What would the warning label have said about me?"

"Whoever marries this man must be prepared to put out morning, noon and night, even after a full day of tending to whining, sick kids."

"That sounds about right, and I'm glad to hear you're prepared to put out morning, noon and night."

She nudged him with her elbow, making him laugh.

"I can't help it that I love you so much I can't stop touching you."

"Don't try too hard to help it."

Mac grunted out another laugh as he kissed her. "How about a sofa quickie?"

"Do I have to do anything?"

"Nothing other than be your amazing, sexy self."

She groaned dramatically. "There is nothing sexy about me right now. I have kid drool on my shirt."

"I told you yesterday that I don't want you talking shit about my wife, and I meant it. Everything about her is sexy."

"I think you may be delusional or under some sort of spell."

"I'm under the Madeline McCarthy spell. She just *does it* for me."

She placed her hand on the face he hadn't bothered to shave. "Remember when you were single and unencumbered and living it up in Miami? A different hot babe every day?"

He knew she was teasing him, as she often did about his former life. "I never think about Miami or being single. Why would I wish for that when I have you and our kids and my work and my family and a great life here?"

"It's a better life than the one you had there?"

"You can still ask me that after everything we've had together?"

"I wonder sometimes. That's all."

Dropping his forehead to rest against hers, he said, "Let me put your mind at ease. There is *nowhere* I'd rather be than right here with you."

"Even with sick babies who whine and cry all day?"

"Especially then. I got hours of Hailey snuggles today, which are hard to come by now that she's on the move." A strand of Maddie's caramel-colored hair had broken loose from her ponytail. He tucked it behind the fragile shell of her ear and traced a fingertip over the line of her jaw. "I never wish for my old life." He kissed her, starting with soft, sweet touches of his lips to hers, which became hotter, deeper kisses when her mouth opened and her tongue teased his. "And I can't bear that you think there'll ever be a time when I don't want you."

Being with her made the difficult day with the kids fade away. She always had that effect on him, making him forget everything else but her when they were together this way.

Working her leg between his, she pressed her thigh against his erection, making him groan. He thought about suggesting they move this upstairs but didn't want to take any chances that they'd wake the kids.

Determined to see this through to the finish, right here on the sofa if that was what it took, he worked Maddie's T-shirt up and over her head. His own shirt went sailing across the room as he knelt to help her out of the yoga pants that had been feeding his fantasies all day as she tended to their children. He *loved* the way her ass looked in the clingy pants.

Her skin was flushed and rosy from the heat they generated together, and knowing she wanted this as much as he did had him moving faster to get rid of their clothes. The overly large breasts that she hated and he loved were sore from her pregnancy, so he was extra gentle when he held them and ran his tongue over each nipple, making her squirm beneath him. That little squirm ramped up his urgency, and while he would've loved to spend more time on foreplay, time alone was one thing they hadn't had much of today.

He came down on top of her, her arms wrapping around his neck to bring him back for more kisses. Being naked with her was his favorite thing in the entire world. "Missed you," he whispered as he captured her lips for another tongue-twisting kiss.

"We did this yesterday, Mac. You haven't had time to miss me."

"I missed you today when I had to share you with the other man in your life."

Smiling, she tilted her hips in invitation, and that was all the encouragement he needed to enter her in one smooth thrust that made him gasp from the overwhelming pleasure.

"God," he whispered, "that's so good. It's always so good."

"Don't go slow, Mac. Not tonight." She wrapped her legs around his hips and pushed into his thrust, making him see stars. Between that and the way she dug her fingers into his ass, tugging him deeper into her—

A cry from upstairs made him freeze mid-thrust.

"*Mommy!*"

Mac wanted to wail—and he wanted to finish.

Maddie pushed at his shoulder. "Let me up."

"*Maddie…*"

"I'll meet you in bed after I settle him."

Though it was the very last thing he wanted to do, he withdrew, helped her sit, found her T-shirt and handed it to her.

She kissed him before she headed for the stairs. "Sorry."

With his cock throbbing and his heart beating furiously, he fell back on the sofa, trying to calm himself and taking a measure of comfort from one small thing—at least Thomas hadn't caught them in the act this time.

Luke brushed the hair back from Sydney's forehead, gazing down at her as she slept in the hospital bed. Dried tear tracks marred her otherwise flawless complexion.

Thank God. Thank God. Thank God. The two-word phrase cycled through his mind like a chant, because the baby was fine. Syd was fine. Earlier, when she'd looked at him with those big doe eyes and told him she was bleeding, he'd had to force himself to keep it together for her when he was freaking out on the inside at the thought of losing the baby they both wanted so badly.

He had to keep reminding himself that she was fine. The baby was fine. Everything was okay. Sydney had worn herself out, worrying and crying and stressing. They'd given her something to settle her and had decided to keep her overnight because her blood pressure was higher than it should be.

Gee, I wonder why.

Then he remembered that Slim was still here, waiting for word about Syd's condition before he left.

Luke bent to kiss her pale cheek and went to find his friend, who was right where he'd left him in the waiting room, flipping through a copy of *People* magazine. He jumped up when he saw Luke coming. "How are they?"

"Fine, thank goodness."

"Oh," Slim said, heaving a huge sigh of relief. "That's great news."

"They're going to keep her overnight, so you can split. Sorry to have messed up your day. Send me a bill for the flight."

"No apologies needed, and Merry Christmas on the flight."

"Slim—"

He waved off Luke's protest. "That's the end of it. I'm so glad everything is okay."

"Thank you. I'm glad, too. So damned glad. If anything ever happened to her... I can't even imagine it."

"I don't know how all you guys do it."

"Do what?" Luke asked.

"The wife and kids and home and hearth thing. It's so fraught with peril everywhere you look." He shuddered. "The thought of giving someone that much power over me... It's frightening."

Luke smiled for the first time in hours. "It's also the best thing to ever happen. To be loved the way she loves me... There's nothing else like it in this world."

"If you say so."

"When I saw you with Erin at Jenny and Alex's wedding, I thought maybe something might come of that. The sparks were flying. Everyone saw it."

"I'm spending the holidays with her at the lighthouse."

"Oh, wow, I hadn't heard that."

"It was just decided this morning."

"I hate to tell you, but spending the holidays with a woman smacks of serious."

"It does not. We're hanging out, having fun."

"Just be careful," Luke said with a teasing grin that belied his exhaustion. "You might find yourself with a shackle around your ankle in the new year."

"Bite your tongue," Slim said, smiling.

Luke extended his hand. "Thank you again for everything today— the ride and the support. Much appreciated."

Slim shook his hand and gave him a bro hug. "Any time. Give me a ring when you're ready to head home. I'll pick you up."

"You're the best, but don't worry about us. We'll take the boat back when Syd's ready." Luke sent Slim on his way and returned to Sydney's room in the ER. They'd be moving her upstairs to the OB ward in the next hour or so. He sat by her bed, took hold of her hand and rolled his head, seeking to relieve some of the tension in his neck and shoulders.

She squeezed his hand.

He raised his head to find her watching him with concern.

"Are you okay?"

"If you are, I am."

"Sorry to put you through such an ordeal."

"Don't be sorry. I have a feeling this won't be the only time our little princess puts us through the wringer."

She smiled. "What a way to learn what we're having."

"At least we'll never forget the first time we saw her."

"No, we won't. Do you want to go to a hotel for the night? No need for both of us to be stuck here."

"I'm not going anywhere without you and the princess."

"Are you sure?"

He raised her hand to his lips. "I'm very sure."

ON THE FLIGHT BACK TO GANSETT, SLIM THOUGHT ABOUT THE conversation he'd had with Luke. He'd spoken the truth about being fearful of giving anyone that much power over him. But even as he'd said the words, he knew he'd already given Erin the power to hurt him, which was a sobering thought. When, exactly, had that happened?

At the very beginning, if he was being honest with himself. He thought about the night he'd come upon her sitting outside the lighthouse, tending to a fire and crying about her dead brother's fiancée marrying someone else. Her grief had broken his heart that night, and her fortitude had impressed him ever since.

Not only had she gotten through Jenny's wedding, she'd positively sparkled as one of her bridesmaids, tending to the woman who should've been her beloved brother's wife. That took some kind of guts, and he admired her tremendously for the way she'd put aside her own pain to rally for her friend.

But seeing Luke so undone over Sydney earlier had given him pause. Caring that much about someone else was a scary thing, and something he'd gone out of his way to avoid. Soon he would be forty, and he was no closer to settling down than he'd been at twenty.

Regardless of how attracted he was to Erin—and he was incredibly attracted to her—he wasn't sure the family-man life was for him, and he had no idea at all what she wanted. They hadn't "gone there" in their many conversations. He might be getting way ahead of himself—and her—by asking questions about home and hearth and family.

A shackle around his ankle would give him hives. No doubt about that. But the idea of spending more time with Erin made him happy and excited for what might be possible. Enjoying a woman didn't equate to being shackled. Did it?

As the island came into view, he turned his full focus toward landing safely, relying on the runway lights to touch down in the dark. Slim couldn't wait to get to her, to be with her, to kiss her some more, to… Damn, maybe he was more shackled than he'd thought.

He went through the methodical routine of securing his plane—speaking of shackles—by attaching the clips to the metal rings built into the tarmac to ensure that the gusty winds expected over the weekend wouldn't damage his livelihood.

The second he was in the cab of his truck, he sent Erin a text to find out where she was.

At Jenny's. Are you back?
Just now. On my way.
See you soon.
Can't wait.
He couldn't wait either. Shackled had never felt so good.

CHAPTER 7

"Check out that big smile," Jenny said after Erin stashed her phone in the back pocket of her jeans and resumed chopping red peppers for Jenny's veggie tray.

"What big smile?"

"The one that stretched across your face when you heard from your sexy pilot."

"He's not my sexy pilot," Erin said, beginning to feel uncomfortable with Jenny's certainty that something would come of her friendship with Slim.

"Is he or is he not a sexy pilot?"

"He is."

"Is he or is he not shacking up with you over the holidays?"

"Have you always been this much of an ass pain, or did it start when you were happily married?"

"She's much more of a pain since she got married," Alex said as he came into the room, grinning at his wife.

"Listen to him," Jenny said, scoffing. "I'm the best wife he's ever had."

"You know it, baby." He hooked his arm around her from behind and kissed her neck until she giggled like a schoolgirl.

Erin was taken by surprise when her heart began to ache. By now, she ought to be used to seeing Jenny in love with someone else. But until she'd come to the island over the summer, Alex had existed in the abstract for her, the new guy Jenny was seeing. Now he was a flesh-and-blood man who was obviously crazy about Jenny. Toby's Jenny…

"Er?"

Erin looked up from the pulverized peppers to realize Jenny had been talking to her. "Sorry, I was spacing."

Jenny sent her a dirty smile.

She thought Erin was thinking about Slim. That was for the best. The last thing Erin would ever want to do was crap on the happiness Jenny had waited so long to find. Toby, who'd been madly in love with Jenny, would tell Erin to get over herself and get on board, especially while she was a guest in Jenny and Alex's beautiful new home.

Paul and Hope came in a few minutes later with Hope's son, Ethan, who was full of pre-Christmas excitement.

"I set you up with the Xbox in the bedroom," Alex said to Ethan.

"Nice!"

"One hour and then it's bedtime," Hope called after her son.

"Mac and Maddie's kids are sick, so they're out tonight," Jenny said. "But they invited everyone to their house on the twenty-sixth."

"Sure, sounds fun," Hope said.

"You guys never quit with the partying," Erin said.

"That's all there is to do around here this time of year," Hope said.

"Need me to give you some pointers for passing the time, bro?" Alex asked, a cocky grin making his eyes gleam with mischief.

"Oh, sorry, honey," Hope said, wincing. "I tossed him a softball, didn't I?"

"And he hit it right out of the park." Paul smiled at Hope and put his arm around her. "You should know better by now."

"I really should."

"Alex's dirty mind and mouth are the thing of legend," Jenny said for Erin's edification.

"You love my dirty mind, and you positively *adore* my dirty mouth."

Jenny stuffed a roll in his mouth, making everyone laugh hysterically.

"I love you *so* much, Jenny." Paul wiped laughter tears from his eyes. "So, *so* much."

"You love that I manage him for you," Jenny said to her brother-in-law.

"Yes, I do."

"Manage me, my ass," Alex said around a mouthful of bread.

"Your ass is one of the best parts of you," Jenny said to groans.

Jared and Lizzie James arrived with another man Erin hadn't met before. They introduced him as Jared's brother, Quinn. Like Jared, he was blond, but unlike his brother, Quinn didn't smile easily and was polite but quiet. Lizzie more than compensated, telling them how Quinn had come to see the building she and Jared had bought to house a health care facility for the island's elderly.

"What do you think of our fair island so far, Quinn?" Paul asked over cocktails.

"It's, um, small."

"You live in New York City," Lizzie said. "Anything would seem small to you after that."

"There's small and then there's Gansett small," Quinn said with a small grin.

Watching their back-and-forth, Erin could see how hard Lizzie was trying to convince her brother-in-law to embrace her project. She wanted him to be the staff physician at the new facility. While Quinn resembled his older brother in looks, he had none of Jared's easygoing charm or wit. Quinn was more buttoned down, somber.

Though intrigued by the James family dynamic as talk turned to holiday plans, Erin found herself watching the door, waiting and anticipating. Any minute now. God, she was like a silly teenage girl waiting for her boyfriend to arrive. Could she be any more ridiculous? Except, that was how she felt. Her skin prickled with awareness of him, and he hadn't even arrived yet. Knowing he was on his way had her heart beating faster. Her face felt warm, and she was probably flushed, giving away her secrets to the room full of friends.

Eager for a moment alone to get ahold of herself before he got there, she went into the kitchen for a glass of ice water.

Naturally, Jenny followed her and insisted on getting the water for her.

Erin took a sip, the cold liquid soothing her parched throat.

"You going to be all right?" Jenny asked in a teasing tone.

"I don't know. I'm all wound up inside over him, and I shouldn't be. He's here for a short visit, and then he's going back to Florida for the rest of the winter. What can possibly come of it?"

"Erin... Really? You're honestly asking that? You're not indentured to the island and the lighthouse. You could go *with* him."

"I don't know. Nothing has been decided."

"You should go and see what happens. What do you have to lose? If it doesn't work out, you can come back here for the summer."

"I have everything to lose. I can't... I don't know if I'm ready for what this could be."

Jenny left her perch by the sink and crossed the room to where Erin leaned against the counter. She put her hands on Erin's shoulders, forcing her to make eye contact. "I've been right where you are. When Alex and his ghastly lawn mower came roaring into my life, I wasn't in any way prepared to contend with him and all the things he wanted from me. In fact, neither was he with everything that was going on with his mom. But look at what we would've *missed* if we hadn't found the courage to take a chance."

Oh God, Erin thought, *I'm going to cry*. She blinked furiously to keep the tears contained.

Jenny hugged her. "It's so frightening to risk more than we can afford to lose. I get that. I get it better than anyone else ever could. But Toby would want us to be happy, Er. I have to believe that, or I wouldn't be able to get through the day."

Clinging to Jenny and her wisdom, Erin nodded.

"If I can do it, so can you."

Erin laughed and drew back from the woman who'd become her

touchstone after they lost Toby. "I never would've survived without you."

"Ditto. But we can do better than survive. We can *thrive*. And someday, after we're done here, we'll see him again. I want him to be proud of me when that day comes."

"So do I." Erin took a deep breath, trying to pull herself together. "I admire you more than anyone. I hope you know that."

"The feeling is definitely mutual. And… I think your guy is here."

Erin was on the verge of reminding Jenny that he wasn't her guy when Slim came into the kitchen and made a liar out of her. Her heart nearly leapt from her chest at the sight of his handsome, smiling face as well as the windblown hair and the rugged leather jacket he wore. He was like a fantasy come to life, and his dark eyes drank her in.

"Is that Alex calling me?" Jenny asked, scooting from the kitchen to give them a moment alone.

"She's nothing if not subtle," he said.

"Always has been her strong suit."

He came over to her, making her entire body go haywire in reaction to his nearness. *What. The. Hell.*

Unsure of what he expected, she looked up at him, trying to anticipate his next move. But when he merely hugged her, she sagged against him, breathing in the bewitching scent of man and leather and soap.

"Missed you," he whispered, close enough to her ear to set off another series of unprecedented responses that converged in an insistent throb of desire between her legs.

Dear God. What was it about this man? How did he reduce her to a quivering pile of *want* simply by walking into a room and hugging her?

When she came up for air, she realized her arms were inside his coat and wrapped around his waist. If this was how she reacted when he was gone for a few hours, how would she feel when he left again to resume his winter life in Florida? She didn't want to think about that, especially not while he was standing right in front of her, sizing her up with those sexy dark eyes that *saw* her a little too well for her liking.

"Did you miss me?"

"Did you go somewhere?"

His eyes glimmered with amusement, his smile transforming his face from handsome to ridiculously sexy. "You hurt me with your nonchalance."

"Yes, I missed you. Feel better now?"

"I've never felt better in my life."

"*Never?*" she asked, relying on humor to hide her emotional reaction to his heartfelt words.

"Not that I can recall."

With his fingers on her chin, he tipped her face up for a soft, sweet kiss that left her dizzy and dying for more.

"To be continued," he said, releasing her.

It was too much and not enough at the same time. How was that possible? All he had to do was walk into the room to put her on full alert. Her nipples were tight, her belly quivering, her palms sweaty, and the tingle between her legs had become a full-blown throb from one simple hug and kiss.

Nothing about him was simple, especially the way she reacted to him. If he could turn her on so completely with nothing more than a hug and a kiss, what would happen later when they were alone again at the lighthouse? She needed a fan to cool her face and a stiff drink to calm her nerves.

Erin poured herself a vodka and soda on ice, hoping for some liquid courage to deal with a situation that was rapidly spinning out of her control. She made the same drink for him, and they joined the others. Slim sat next to her on the sofa, his leg pressed tight against hers, his arm stretched out behind her.

While the others laughed and talked about the McCarthys' anniversary party, plans for the upcoming holidays, Lizzie's health care facility project and other island gossip, Erin tried to find the equilibrium that had deserted her when Slim arrived. As exciting as it had been to be on the receiving end of his affection, it was still possible to stop this before it went any further. They hadn't made each other any promises. They hadn't done things that couldn't be undone.

Yet.

If the heated make-out session earlier and her reaction to seeing him again after a few hours apart were any indication, the status quo wouldn't last much longer. This was happening, and she'd encouraged it by asking him to stay with her. She'd encouraged it with every hour she'd spent flirting by text, on the phone and FaceTime with him over the last few months.

But now that he was here, sitting right next to her and obviously wanting more of what they'd had earlier, she was scared to cross that invisible line between flirty fun and seriously committed. With the exception of her family and a few close friends like Jenny, she'd made being noncommittal an art form, living her life on the surface without delving below to see what she might find.

The surface had worked fine for her. No one got hurt on the surface. Everything was simpler there, cleaner. This situation with him was getting complicated and messy, and she already ached at the thought of him leaving. So what would it be like when he actually left and they were forced to go back to texts, phone calls and FaceTime to stay in touch? Would he want to stay in touch if they had a hot and heavy fling while he was here? Maybe a fling was all he wanted anyway.

This, right here, was why she avoided entanglements at all costs. So how had she found herself firmly entangled in this enigmatic man?

It had happened the night he told her his real name. Nothing had been simple after hearing he shared a name with her beloved brother.

"Hey," he said, nudging her with his shoulder. "Where'd you go?"

She emerged from her thoughts to find that Evan McCarthy and Grace Ryan had arrived with her friend Fiona, Evan's brother Adam and his fiancée, Abby Callahan.

"Nowhere," she said in response to Slim's inquiry.

"You're not overthinking things by any chance, are you?"

"What? No. I'm not doing that." Scalded by his insight, she tried to escape, mumbling something about helping Jenny in the kitchen.

He took her hand, stopping her. "You want to go?"

"I…" She wanted to go, and she wanted to stay, to buy herself some time to figure out what was happening to her and how to get it under control while she still could.

He watched her with those knowing eyes that saw right through her bullshit and found the heart of her more easily than any man before him ever had. "Let's go."

"I, um, Jenny…"

"She'll understand."

And she would. Erin had no doubt about that. "Okay."

They made their excuses to Jenny, who was far too pleased about the development for Erin's liking.

"Call me in the morning and tell me everything," Jenny said as she hugged her. "Take notes so you don't forget anything."

"Stop it."

"You stop it."

"What am I doing?"

"Other than freaking out?"

"I'm not doing that."

"No?"

Erin could fool some people but not Jenny. Never Jenny. "Maybe a little."

"It's going to be okay. I promise."

"You can't know that for certain."

"None of us can, but one thing I know for certain is that a life half lived is no life at all."

And what, really, could Erin say to that?

After shaking hands with the McCarthy and Martinez brothers, Slim held out a hand to Erin, who was still reeling from Jenny's pronouncement. "Ready?"

Eyeing his hand the same way she might an unpinned grenade, she nodded and let him help her into her coat and lead her from the house.

"Leave your car here," he said. "We'll get it in the morning."

"Oh. Okay." Relieved not to have to drive, she let him help her into the passenger side of his truck and tried to put on her seat belt. Her fingers were like a bunch of thumbs, refusing to behave, which was why she was still fumbling with the seat belt when he got in and clipped it for her.

He turned on the engine and cranked the heat. "What's wrong?"

"Nothing."

"Could you not do that? Could you not say it's nothing when anyone who knows you even a little can see it's something?"

Remember that thing about the way he saw her? Yeah. So…

"Have you changed your mind about this, Erin? If you have, all you've got to do is say so. I'll be disappointed, but I'll leave you alone if that's what you want."

Suddenly, that was the very *last* thing she wanted. "I don't want you to leave me alone. But I also don't want…"

"What?" His hand was warm upon her cheek as he caressed her face so tenderly it brought tears to her eyes.

"I don't want you to hurt me. And you could. You could so easily."

"Erin, sweetheart… God, that's the last thing I'd ever want to do." The seat belt he'd just clipped was released, and he lifted her right out of her seat onto his lap and into his arms.

"How'd you do that?" she asked, stunned by his strength and how quickly he'd reacted.

"I will not hurt you. I promise."

Moved by the ferocity behind his words, she said, "You can't promise that."

"I can promise I'll do everything I can to make you happy if you give me the chance. That's all I'm asking for. A chance, and that's more than I've wanted from anyone, if that tells you anything."

"I'm afraid."

"Why?"

"I don't do things like this. Not anymore. It's been so long, I… I may have forgotten how."

"You're doing fine so far." He kissed her softly and sweetly, making her head spin with awareness and desire and a craving need for more that took her by surprise. How could she be trying to wiggle her way out one minute and craving more the next?

"We should probably talk before this goes any further," she said.

"We probably should." He kissed her again, drawing her bottom lip into his mouth and running his tongue over it.

Erin gasped and fisted handfuls of his coat, needing to hold on to something. "That's not talking," she said when he released her lip.

"It's communication of a different sort." Holding her close to him, he said, "We've done a lot of talking in the last few months, but we haven't talked about what it is we're doing here."

"No, we haven't. And we need to. Before anything else happens."

"*Anything else.* Is that what the kids are calling it these days?"

Erin laughed at his predictably witty reply. His humor had attracted her from the first night they met, and it made whatever they were doing easier than it would be otherwise. "You've got to let me go so you can drive us home."

"In a second." He held her for another full minute before he released her to climb back to her own seat. "Jenny probably thinks we're getting busy out here."

"Hopefully, she's entertaining her guests and not paying attention to what we're doing."

He steered the truck toward the long driveway that took them past the greenhouses on the way to the main road. "Oh, she's paying attention."

"What do you mean?"

"She watches over you like a mother hen. No harm shall come to you under her watch."

"She's more my sister than my friend. I think she'd kill for me."

"So noted. I vow to never give her a reason to kill for you."

Though his tone was joking, she believed the underlying sentiment was sincere.

CHAPTER 8

They rode the rest of the way to the lighthouse in silence tinged with anticipation, at least for Erin. She had no idea what to expect. Would they pick up where they'd left off before Luke's call, or would there be awkwardness now that they'd had hours to think about what'd nearly happened earlier?

As if he knew she was spinning, he reached for her hand.

The heat of his hand around hers calmed and soothed her. He released her only so she could open the gate for him when they arrived at the lighthouse property. After he drove the truck through, she closed and locked the gate, sealing them off from the rest of the island for the night.

"I can't remember the last time I did this," she said.

"Did what?"

"Brought a man home with me for the night. It's been... years."

"I'm honored to be spending tonight and this week with you."

"I'm far too old to be nervous, but I am. I don't want to be, but I can't seem to help it."

"There's nothing to be nervous about. We're just hanging out, having fun."

"That's what I thought, too. Until..." Whatever truth serum had her spilling her guts to him dried up at the thought of telling him everything.

He parked the truck outside the lighthouse and shut off the engine, casting them into darkness. "Until what?"

"You walked into Jenny's tonight, and I was so incredibly happy to see you. It... It stopped being casual for me. I'm not sure that's what you want—"

With his hand on her face, he turned her toward him. "I'm exactly where I want to be tonight, with the woman who's worked her way so far under my skin in the last few months that I can no longer imagine a day without her being part of it."

His gruffly spoken words made her heart leap and her blood race. She could feel the throb of her pulse in her neck and between her legs.

"Let's get out of the cold," he said.

In the time it took Erin to gather her belongings, he was around the truck, helping her out and guiding her over a patch of ice that she would've missed if he hadn't been there. They removed their coats in the mudroom and hung them on the hooks one of the previous tenants had installed.

Erin felt his gaze on her as she went up the spiral stairs ahead of him. The enhanced sense of awareness she experienced when he was near made her feel out of sorts and off her game, but not necessarily in a bad way. How had she made it to thirty-eight without having experienced anything that could compare to the way she'd felt when he'd walked into Jenny's earlier?

Mitch, the man she'd lived with in law school, had been handsome, sexy, intelligent and funny, but he'd never made her blood boil the way Slim did simply by walking into a room. At one time, she'd expected to marry Mitch. That seemed like such a long time ago now, so far in the past as to be part of someone else's history rather than hers.

Slim poured two vodka cocktails, handed one to her and took a deep drink of his, all without taking his eyes off her. "You're a million miles away. What're you thinking about?"

She forced herself to meet his gaze. "I'm thinking about the last man I was seriously involved with. It was a long time ago. During law school. I thought I was going to marry him and have it all—a family and a career and a home."

He took her by the hand and led her to the living room.

Drink in hand, Erin curled her legs under her and sat on the sofa while he plugged in the tree lights and killed the lamp before settling next to her.

"What happened?"

"9/11 happened. He tried. God knows he tried. He stuck it out for more than a year afterward, but…" She sighed, the weight of the difficult years that followed her brother's death still heavy on her soul after all this time. "I've avoided anything that smacked of entanglement ever since."

"Whatever became of him?"

"He graduated from law school, and last I heard he's a partner in a firm in Philadelphia. He married one of our law school classmates, and they have a bunch of kids. Four at last count."

"So you keep in touch?"

"I get Christmas cards with pictures of his beautiful family."

"That must be hard to see."

"It's not, really. When I look at him and his family, I don't feel anything other than happy for him that things worked out."

"That's awfully generous of you."

She shrugged off the praise. "I don't care about him. Not anymore. I stopped caring about him the day my brother died. It was like every emotion inside me died with him, and it took years—literally *years*—to feel anything other than numb. What guy wants to be around that?"

"If he truly loved you, he would've stuck it out."

"I think he truly loved me, but I don't blame him for leaving. I never have. It was almost a relief when he finally pulled the plug. There was one less thing that needed my attention when my grief required all my energy. I had nothing left to give him or anyone else. It was all I could do to be somewhat available to my parents." She looked directly at him. "I'm not numb anymore. Not like I was. But I still don't know if I have what it takes to do something like this, because I haven't tried again since then."

He brought her hand to his lips, and the caress of his skin against hers set off a reaction she felt everywhere.

"I'm not looking to pressure you, Erin. And I can't possibly understand or even fathom what you've been through losing your only sibling—your twin, no less—in such a horrible way. But when I look at you, I don't see grief or loss. I see resilience and fortitude and a stunningly beautiful woman who deserves to be happy after all she's been through. I don't know if I'm the guy to make you happy, but you make me want to try—and that's a big deal for me, too, in case you were wondering."

Erin smiled at his adorably vulnerable expression. "So what you're saying is you want to try to make a go of this?"

"I think I do, but only if it's what you want, too."

"And what would 'making a go of it' entail? We're not exactly babes in the woods here. We've got established lives that don't intersect for a big part of the year."

"A, you are most definitely a babe, and B, those are details that can be worked out later if it comes to that. God knows I'm no expert on relationships, but it would seem to me that two people who are relatively new to them might want to take it slow and not get ahead of themselves worrying about what happens down the road."

"I can't help but worry about that. In eleven days, you're headed back to Florida for months."

"And I'll remind you again that you're more than welcome to come with me."

"What if you're sick of me by then?"

"That won't happen."

"How do you know?"

"Because."

She raised a brow. "Care to elaborate?"

"I couldn't wait to get back to you tonight. Every minute I was gone felt like pure torture."

Okay, that was a pretty damned good answer.

Before she could formulate a reply to such a stark statement, he said, "What if I forget to put the toilet seat down or leave my wet towels on the floor? And the underwear… That could end up anywhere. You might be ready to give me the heave-ho days before I'm due to leave."

Erin shook her head.

"You seem awfully certain."

"I was awfully glad to see you at Jenny's."

He leaned in, his intentions clear, and even though she knew what it was like to kiss him, this felt like the first time all over again now that they'd declared their intentions to give it a whirl. He kept his eyes open as he kissed her, so she did the same, watching him watch her.

Outside, the frigid wind howled and the waves crashed against the rocks below, but inside the cozy confines of her lighthouse, it was getting warmer by the second. His lips were soft but insistent, his eyes closing when their tongues met in a sensual caress.

Though the last thing she wanted was to stop what had only just begun, Erin broke the kiss. "Let's go upstairs where it's more comfortable."

"I'm perfectly happy to sleep right here if you're not ready for that."

"If I wasn't ready to sleep with you, I wouldn't have asked you to come upstairs with me."

"Well, all righty then. After you."

Once again, Slim followed her up a spiral staircase, his eyes drawn to her sexy ass in the tight jeans she'd worn to Jenny's party. Those jeans were a thing of beauty, but they had nothing on the woman who wore them. She was beautiful inside and out, and the more time he spent with her, the more hooked on her he seemed to become. Her brutal honesty about the end of her last significant relationship had touched him deeply.

And earlier, when she'd let him know he had the power to hurt her… *Whoa.*

"I'll be right out," she said. "Make yourself at home."

"Thanks."

The bathroom door closed behind her.

As he unbuttoned his shirt, it amazed him to think of how far they'd come from the night in September when he'd rescued her and then slept next to her in a chair so he could be nearby if she needed him during the night.

Everything since then had been leading to this moment. From finding out he shared a name with her late brother to attending Jenny's wedding and meeting her parents to hours on the phone and FaceTime to their reunion last night, they'd been building something rare and fragile, something to be treasured and nurtured.

His worries about shackles now seemed foolish in light of what she'd shared with him. This, the way he felt when he was with her, was why men allowed themselves to be caught. He sat on the foot of the bed, waiting for his turn in the bathroom and debating whether he should leave his shirt on or take it off. To hell with it. She'd seen him shirtless earlier. He shed the shirt, laying it over a chair when he might've dropped it on the floor at home.

Returning to the foot of the bed, he propped his elbows on his knees and dropped his head, rolling it from side to side to relieve the tension in his neck. He felt like he was on unsteady ground with her, which was rare. Usually there were few mysteries in his dealings with women. They went out, they had fun, sometimes they had sex, sometimes they didn't. That routine had worked for him. But now… Everything was different, and this situation reminded him of being with the only girl he'd ever loved, back in high school, when he hadn't the first clue what she expected from him.

Unlike then, when the uncertainty had led to anxiety, now it turned him on. Being with Erin felt brand-new, like he was just waking up from a nearly twenty-year nap to find a whole new world waiting to be discovered. And now she had him waxing poetic, he thought with a grunt of laughter at the direction his thoughts had taken.

She came out of the bathroom wearing an oversized T-shirt that left her long legs bare for his perusal. "I don't own anything that might be considered sexy," she said, her expression so vulnerable his chest ached with longing.

"Yes, you do. You're wearing it." He stood and went to her, kissing her forehead on his way into the bathroom, where he splashed cold water on his face and brushed his teeth. Then he took a minute to catch his breath, to calm the rapid beat of his heart. His attraction to her was unprecedented.

This whole situation was unprecedented for him. He didn't go out of his way for women, and he certainly didn't *stay* with them. One of his cardinal rules of dating had always been never to spend the night, and here he was planning to spend *twelve* nights with Erin—and more if she agreed to come home with him.

Rather than feeling constrained by the idea of a real relationship, he couldn't wait to see what would happen next. And he couldn't wait to kiss her and hold her and…

Stop. Don't get ahead of yourself. One step at a time.

He took a deep breath and left the bathroom. Since he hadn't planned to stay with her, he hadn't brought anything to sleep in, which presented another unique dilemma.

Erin was in bed, head propped on her upturned hand, watching him as he made a snap decision to leave his jeans on—for now—and stretched out next to her, turning on his side. He traced a fingertip along the V of her T-shirt, which ended just above the deep valley between her breasts. "How can you say you don't have anything sexy?"

"This is just a T-shirt. I used to have some slinky stuff, but it didn't make the cut when I downsized to the lighthouse."

"You like the slinky stuff?"

"I used to love it, but I haven't had much use for it lately."

"Now I know what to get you for Christmas."

"Oh. Are we doing that?"

"What fun is Christmas if you don't have a present under the tree to open?"

"Don't go crazy, you hear me?"

Keeping up the subtle movement of his fingertip, he shifted closer to nuzzle her neck. "You make me all kinds of crazy. So crazy I have to remind myself that I shouldn't tell you all my dirty thoughts about you."

"Why not?" she asked, sounding as breathless as he felt.

"Because you'd stop thinking I'm a charming gentleman."

"When did I think you're a charming gentleman?"

"Ha-ha."

"I won't stop thinking that."

"Yes, you will. You'll think I don't respect you when that couldn't be further from the truth."

"Tell me one thing." Her eyes glittered with excitement and desire that made him hard as a rock.

"Mmm, how to choose just one when there're so many to choose from?"

"Try."

"Your lips."

"What about them?"

"When we would FaceTime, I became obsessed with your lips." He rubbed his finger over her lips. "I would think about your mouth and how badly I wanted to kiss you and how much I wanted..." No. Too far. Too much.

"What did you want? Say it."

"I wanted to see your lips wrapped around my cock. I wanted to see your mouth fall open in surprise when I made you come. I wanted to hear you screaming my name and leaving scratches on my back. I thought about your mouth obsessively. But not just your mouth."

"What else?" she asked, her voice a faint whisper.

"Your gorgeous breasts." He cupped them and teased her nipples, which were already hard and tight under his palms. "I wanted to see them and kiss them and suck on your nipples until you begged me to fuck you."

"Yes, I want that. I want you to do that."

"How much of it?"

The intensity of her gaze slayed him. "All of it."

CHAPTER 9

$\mathcal{E}$rin was done thinking about the many reasons it might not be a good idea to get swept away by him. It was far too late for such worries. She was already caught up, and hearing him speak so bluntly about what he wanted cleared her mind of everything other than the intense desire for the things he'd described.

He flashed a wicked, sexy grin. "Does this mean you like it when I talk dirty to you?"

"Find out for yourself."

"Ahhh…"

She fell to the pillow, laughing at his befuddled response. "I'd think that a man of your advanced years would know how to tell whether or not his dirty talk was having the desired effect."

"Sweetheart, are you laughing at me right now?"

She pinched her fingers together. "Maybe just a little. Mostly I'm trying to decide if you're all talk and no action."

Uttering a low growl, he pounced, kissing her face off with deep, sweeping strokes of his tongue. Gone were the tentative touches and the light caresses. They'd thrown gas on a fire that had been set to simmer for months, and the flame scorched her from within.

The T-shirt disappeared over her head, baring her breasts to his greedy gaze. As he watched, her nipples tightened to the point of pleasurable pain.

She rested her arms on either side of her head, giving him tacit permission to take what she offered.

"So fucking sexy," he said as he drew her left nipple into the heat of his mouth.

Erin gasped and raised her hips, colliding with the rigid length of his erection against her sex.

"*Erin.*"

"Hmmm?"

"You're so hot. I can feel how hot you are."

"You made me that way with your dirty talk."

He kissed his way down her body, then looked up at her, his chin propped on her belly. "Just to be completely clear, this isn't the only thing I want from you or with you."

"No?"

"Definitely not."

The emphatic way he said that made her heart leap, and that was before he resumed his journey toward the waistband of her pink bikini panties.

"These need to come off," he said, tugging at them.

Tentatively, Erin raised her hips and let him slide them down her legs, which quivered madly.

"Still okay?"

She bit her lip and nodded, even though alarms were sounding in her head. *This will change everything. Are you ready to change everything? Will you be able to cope when he leaves again?*

"Are you overthinking again?" he asked, watching her carefully as he ran his hands over her legs, subtly moving them apart.

"I'm trying not to."

"You know what the advantage of being our age is?"

Perplexed by the odd question, she said, "Um, not really."

"Wisdom," he said, kissing her inner thigh. "Perspective, patience." Each word was punctuated by another kiss. "We're smart enough now to know that when we click with someone, really click the way you and I have, it's something to hold on to, something to value."

His words of wisdom were almost as much of a turn-on as the dirty talk had been. Before she could formulate a response to the profound insight, he opened her to his tongue. Erin buried her fingers in his hair and held on tight. He played her like a maestro with his tongue and fingers, taking her up so fast she had no time to prepare for the climax that rocked her.

"Yes," he whispered. "So beautiful, so hot."

She whimpered when he withdrew, but he was back a second later without his jeans and rolling a condom over his erection. Erin took a long look at his sexy body, noting the muscles, the scars, the tan lines and the big cock that stretched to above his navel. She held out her arms to him, and he came down on top of her, capturing her lips in a passionate kiss that started the tingling between her legs all over again.

He pushed into her slowly and carefully, watching for signs of distress, but there was no distress, only desire.

No one had ever made her feel the way he did—in bed and out. No other man had ever made her laugh the way he did, turned her on the way he did or made her feel sexy and desirable the way he did. He was one of a kind, and he was right about the way they'd clicked.

She held on to his shoulders as he went deeper, both of them gasping from the impact.

He dropped his forehead to hers, seeming to collect himself.

Erin caressed his back and wrapped her legs around his hips.

"Wow," he whispered. "I knew you'd feel good, but this is a whole other level of good."

"Mmm, for me, too." She lifted her hips to encourage him, and he took the hint, pressing deeper while kissing her with soft, easy strokes of his tongue. The tenderness devastated her and brought tears to her eyes. God, what was he *doing* to her?

"Are you okay?"

"Yeah, so okay."

"You sure?"

She looked up at him and nodded. "Don't go slow. It feels so good."

He took her words to heart, picking up the pace while pressing his fingers to her core, the combination leading to a screaming orgasm that made her thankful for the isolation of the lighthouse. There was no one around for miles to hear how he made her scream.

Reaching beneath her, he gripped her bottom in his big hands as he drove into her to find his own pleasure, coming with a deep groan as he heated her from the inside with his release. When his arms gave out, he came down on her, his body heavy and warm from exertion.

"I think you might've just ruined me for all other women."

Wrapping her arms around him, she laughed. Leave it to him to make her laugh after *that*.

"No, really. That was… *Wow*."

"Yes, it was."

He raised his head to look at her. "Yeah?"

She nodded and then smiled when he kissed her.

"I knew you were going to be big trouble the night I picked you up by the side of the road."

Erin smacked his shoulder. "Don't say that like I was a hooker on the prowl or something."

His laughter rocked his big body. "So I shouldn't have told my mom that's how I met you?"

"You did not!"

Grimacing, he said, "Oh, um, is that going to be a problem?"

"Be serious. You did not tell her that."

"I had to tell her something when she asked what I was doing for Christmas. I said hopefully spending it with the woman I picked up on the side of a Gansett road last September."

She glared at him.

"After she got a flat on her bike and sprained her ankle in the dark. Of course I told her that part, too. What do you take me for?"

She poked her index fingers into his ribs, making him startle. "That was not funny."

"It was, too. You were about to laugh. Admit it."

"I'll admit no such thing." She pushed at his shoulder. "Get off me, you wildebeest."

"*Wildebeest?* Not even five minutes ago, you were screaming my name, and this is the thanks I get for that stupendous orgasm?"

"Oh my God! You're so full of yourself, it's not even funny."

"Was that or was that not a stupendous orgasm?"

"It was okay."

His eyes widened and his mouth went slack, but for only a second. "So you've had better?"

"I refuse to answer that on the grounds that your ego is on the verge of not fitting into my little lighthouse."

"My ego fits just fine in your little lighthouse, baby, and that was a stupendous orgasm. I don't care what you say."

She tried to contain the laughter but couldn't stop the gurgle that seemed to explode from her throat.

"See, I *am* funny."

Rolling her eyes, she pushed on his shoulder. "Let me up."

"Only if you come right back."

"I'll come right back."

"Because you want another stupendous orgasm."

She pinched his rear—hard—and got him to move, groaning as he withdrew from her. That was when she realized he was hard again.

His sheepish grin made her smile. "I can't help if he thinks you're ridiculously sexy."

Trying not to think about his eyes on her ass, Erin went into the bathroom and closed the door, needing a moment alone to contend with the emotional firestorm unfolding inside her. It *had* been a stupendous orgasm, but more than that, the connection she'd shared with him had been unlike anything she'd experienced before, not to mention the laughter afterward. She laughed more with him than with any guy she'd ever known, except her brother.

Toby would've liked him. She had no doubt whatsoever about that. Her brother had disliked most of the guys she'd dated, including Mitch, whom he'd declared not good enough for her. That comment had led to one of the few really heated fights she and Toby had ever had, the last time she ever saw him, no less. He and Slim... They would've been the best of friends.

After using the facilities, she washed her face and brushed her hair before putting on the robe that hung on the back of the bathroom door. She tied it tight around her waist and opened the door. He was lying on his side, watching for her. At some point, he'd disposed of the condom, and her eyes were immediately drawn to the fact that he was still hard.

She went to her side of the bed to stretch out next to him.

"What's up with this?" he asked, tugging at the knot at her waist.

"I was cold."

"I can warm you up a lot faster than a robe can." He untied the knot and pushed open the front of the robe. "Sit up."

Erin did as he asked and let him slide the robe from her shoulders and then draw her into his warm embrace under the comforter.

"There. Isn't that better?"

It felt so damned good to be held by him, to breathe in his alluring scent, to feel his chest hair under her cheek, his whiskers rubbing against her forehead and his hard cock against her belly. She loved it all.

"You okay?"

"Uh-huh."

"Don't be shy around me, Erin. I love the way you look, and I love looking at you. You've got nothing at all to be shy about. You're gorgeous and sexy, and I want to see you."

How did he go from outrageous humor to heartfelt sincerity without missing a beat? If she didn't know him so well, she'd wonder if he was for real. But after months of long conversations, she knew he was exactly what he appeared to be. "Thank you."

"I mean it."

"I know." She dragged a fingertip over his chest. "Did you really tell your mom about me?"

"She wanted to know what I was doing for the holidays."

"You don't go home for Christmas?"

"Home is Florida in the winter and here in the summer."

"You don't talk about your family. Ever." She looked up at him. "That's why I'm sort of surprised you told your mom about me."

"I talk about them."

"Not to me."

"Never?"

"Nope."

"Hmmm, well, what do you want to know?"

"Do you have siblings?"

"I have a brother, Jack, who's two years younger than me. He's married with a couple of kids and lives in Orange County, California."

"Jack Jackson?"

"His real name is Jonah, but his high school football teammates called him Jack, and it stuck."

"Are you close?"

"We don't see each other very often, but we text a lot and catch up whenever we can on the phone. I also FaceTime with his kids, who are the cutest kids ever."

"Were you close growing up?"

"Yeah, we were. Our folks split up when I was six and he was four. They fought over us for years, which was as fun as you might imagine. By the time they finally settled on joint custody after years of battling, we were all set with both of them."

Erin's heart broke at the thought of two little boys stuck between battling parents. "At least they both wanted you. That's something, isn't it?"

"They wanted us until they remarried and started new families. Then we were just a couple of teenagers in the way at both houses."

"So you have half siblings, too?"

"Yep. Two half sisters, two half brothers and three stepbrothers. I'm not really close to them, though. Jack and I were so much older that we didn't spend much time with them growing up. He was driving by the time the last one was born. They're all good kids, don't get me wrong, but they don't feel like siblings to us."

"What do you normally do for Christmas?"

"Hang with my friends in Florida, go to the beach, fly people to their families. Nothing special. Christmas stopped being a big deal to me years ago." He slid his hand from her shoulder down her arm to take hold of her hand. "Until this year. This year it feels pretty damned special."

"I'm glad you're here."

"Me too, sweetheart."

CHAPTER 10

*D*r. Kevin McCarthy sat at the bar at the Beachcomber and watched Chelsea work. Watching her was one of his favorite things to do, second only to being naked in a bed with her. She was tall and lean with curves in all the right places, lovely gray-blue eyes and a long blonde braid down her back, the sexiest woman he'd ever been with, hands down. Yes, he was a bit obsessed with her, but so what? Who was he hurting by indulging in a deeply satisfying relationship?

That he was also having the best sex of his life with a woman sixteen years his junior was no one's business but his—and hers. Nursing a beer, he thought about his sons, Riley and Finn, and the odd vibe of disapproval he'd been getting from them in the last couple of weeks. It was funny, in a way, when you thought about the many nights he'd sat up waiting for them to come home over the years. Now it was his turn, and they weren't happy about his new relationship—not that either of them had actually said so.

He was trying to be sensitive to how hard it was for them to see their father with someone other than their mother, but ending the marriage hadn't been his idea. Maybe they needed to spend some time with their mother so he wouldn't be the only one taking heat from them.

As much as he wished it didn't, their disapproval irritated him. He'd worked his ass off to support his family. He'd been a faithful, if sometimes inattentive, husband. His wife of nearly thirty years had left *him*, not the other way around. What right did his sons have to make him feel guilty for moving on with someone new?

They didn't. They had no right at all to make him feel this way when he was enjoying himself enormously with Chelsea.

"What's on your mind, Doc?"

He looked up to see her standing before him, eyeing the shredded mess of paper on the bar in front of him. He'd been tearing up a cocktail napkin without realizing it. Scooping up the scraps, he balled them into a wad. "Nothing. Sorry. Almost done?"

"Just have to clean up. You want one for the road?"

"Nah, I'm good, thanks."

She gave him another curious look before moving on to finish up.

Kevin rolled the ball of paper between his palms. If he were one of his patients, he'd be telling himself to talk it over with his sons. Except, he didn't want to. He didn't want to hear the reasons why his relationship with Chelsea was a bad idea, doomed to fail before it even got off the ground.

They'd been together a couple of months now, and it was working just fine, as far as he was concerned. And she seemed happy, too. They'd begun to talk about where they were going and how their relationship was about more than just sex, which was a step forward in his mind. What else mattered?

The final stragglers left the bar shortly after midnight, and fifteen minutes later, Chelsea was ready to go.

Kevin held her coat for her and then put an arm around her shoulders as they walked to his car. She rented a tiny, cozy house in town, so they didn't have far to go to get to her place. They'd fallen into a comfortable routine over the last few months, spending time together every night at her place, which gave his sons the full run of the house he had rented for the three of them.

He and Chelsea rarely spent a full night together, and sometimes he rolled in after three or four in the morning. Maybe his sons were pissed about that, too, since he'd made them come home at a reasonable hour until after they graduated from college and got their own homes. The three of them had been living together again since the fall, when they'd come out for Laura's wedding and ended up staying for the winter—Kevin because he'd needed to regroup after the split with Deb and his sons because their cousin Mac hired them to work for his construction company for the winter.

After a short drive, Kevin followed Chelsea into her house, removed his coat and went into the kitchen, where she poured a glass of wine for herself and opened a beer for him.

"Thanks, hon." Since he'd had only two beers much earlier and was still fine to drive, he downed a hearty mouthful and leaned back against the counter to look his fill at the gorgeous woman who'd captivated him so completely. He certainly hadn't expected that when Chelsea invited him to come home with her one night in September. At that time, he'd figured they might have a fun one-night stand, and that would be that.

But that night had turned into three of the best months of his life, and he was in no rush to see it end. As recently as last night, he'd tried to talk Chelsea into committing to more, but she wanted to wait until his divorce was final to make any decisions. After Christmas, his first order of business would be to get in touch with Dan Torrington about speeding up the divorce.

"You want to talk about it?" she asked as she worked her fingers through her hair, releasing the braid she'd worn to work.

"Talk about what?"

"Whatever's bugging you."

"Nothing's bugging me. I'm fine." He forced a smile for her benefit. "Tired."

"Just last night, you told me you want more than a hot roll in the sack, but when you're obviously upset about something, that's not my concern?"

He stared at her, stunned by the forthright statement. That sort of communication had been missing in the latter years of his marriage, and it was one of many things he appreciated about Chelsea. Kevin put down the beer and took a few steps toward her. Putting his hands on her shoulders, he looked into her eyes. "You are so much more to me than a hot roll in the sack. If you don't know that by now, I need to do a better job of telling you so."

"I'm not fishing for compliments, Kevin. You told me last night you want us to be about more than sex. You haven't been yourself tonight, and I'm asking why."

He appreciated the effort she was making and was encouraged that she'd taken what he said last night to heart. "It's nothing to do with you. It's the boys... I've been sensing a little pushback from them."

"About us?"

"Among other things."

Her brows knitted the way they did when she was thinking something over. "Hmm."

"What does that mean?"

"It's just... Don't take this the wrong way, but you know they aren't *boys* anymore, right? They're fully grown men, as are you, and all of you are free to do whatever you want, within reason, of course."

"I do know that, but old habits die hard. I've always called them 'the boys,' and I probably always will. And I do know that we're not doing anything wrong. Believe me, I know that. They're still getting used to their mom and I breaking up, and they're having a hard time processing it. That's all it is."

"The breakup wasn't your doing. They know that, right?"

"Yes, they do, but we're still their parents, and our split has had an impact on them. I see it all the time in my practice. I swear divorce is easier on little kids than it is on grown kids. It tilts their entire world out of alignment. Everything they believed to be true is challenged."

"And they get over it. In time. It's not fair for them to make you feel bad about doing something that makes you feel good, especially when it wasn't your decision to end your marriage."

"It was in some ways," he said with a sigh. "I knew she wasn't happy, and I didn't do a damned thing about it."

"Because you wanted out, too?"

"Yeah, but I was never going to leave her."

"I don't get that. If you were unhappy, why would you *stay*?"

"Loyalty, tradition, the boys... Lots of reasons."

"And not one of them is about being *happy*. Don't you have a right to be happy? Don't we all?"

"Yeah, we do. I'm happier than I've been in a long time. And that's all thanks to you." He raised his hands to her face and compelled her to look at him. "That's what I was trying to tell you last night when I said I want this to be more than just the best sex of my life."

"I thought about what you said. That's all I thought about today."

"Yeah?" His heart fluttered with hope. He was so gone over her and was looking for something, anything other than screaming orgasms to indicate the feeling was mutual.

She nodded. "I don't want you to think..."

"What, hon?"

"That I don't want the same thing you do. I do. More than I expected when we started this. I'm just wary, that's all. You're going through a huge life change, and as great as this has been—and it's been amazing—I don't want to get ahead of myself when you're not divorced yet."

"I understand that, and I thought a lot about what you said last night, too. I get it. In a few months, the divorce will be final, and we'll see where we are. Until then, no pressure, just fun. Okay?"

"Okay, but I still want to know if something's bugging you. Just because we aren't making declarations of forever together doesn't mean I want you to feel like you can't talk to me."

"I love talking to you. You've become my favorite person to talk to."

"About stuff that *matters*, Kevin. Not just surface things."

"I hear you, and I want that, too. I want it all with you, Chelsea Rose, and I'm going to keep telling you that until you believe me. In fact, I want you to join the boys and me for Christmas dinner, and I want you to come with me to my nephew's wedding in Anguilla."

She eyed him skeptically. "Seriously?"

"Dead seriously."

"Would your sons... They'd be okay with that?"

"Sure." As he said that, he hoped he was right, but he had a few days to smooth things with them before Christmas and weeks before the trip to Anguilla.

"You have no idea if they'd be okay with it, do you?"

"I don't care if they are or they aren't. Like you said, they're grown men, and I have to stop treating them like kids. You'll be there as my guest, and they'll be polite, or I'll ask them to leave. Okay?"

"If you're sure..."

"I'm sure I want to spend Christmas with you, and I'd love to have you with me in Anguilla."

She smiled, and his heart fluttered with more hope. Everything was new with her, like he was falling in love for the very first time. That thought stopped him cold. Was he *in love* with her?

Before he had a chance to process that possibility, she was kissing him, her mouth opening under his, their tongues meeting in a dance that had become so familiar and so *necessary* to him. God, he was in love with her. Had been for a while now, if he was being honest.

With her hands on his chest, she pushed him backward toward the living room, stopping him before he could sit. She unbuttoned his pants, and working together, they got rid of his pants and then hers. She helped him out of his sweater, and he was happy to return the favor. Then she gave him a gentle nudge that sent him into an uphol-stered chair with no arms. She straddled him, her wet heat against his cock making him harder than he'd already been. She was so hot and sexy and willing to do anything if it felt good.

He cupped her ass and pulled her in tighter. "You make me feel like the luckiest guy to ever live that I get to be with you this way."

"We're both lucky to have found this."

"Mmm." He nuzzled her neck as she moved on his lap with the deliberate intent of making him insane. "That's why we need to hold on to it."

She tightened her hand around his cock. "Hold on to it like this?"

Kevin gasped as he laughed. "Just like that."

Chelsea raised herself up and came down on him, taking him in slowly, torturing him with the tight squeeze. Since she was on birth control, they'd stopped using condoms after both had produced clean bills of health, and he loved the way she felt against his bare skin.

"Fucking hell, that's amazing," he whispered, teasing her nipple with his tongue, which only made the tight squeeze tighter. Being with her reminded him of experiencing sex for the first time, only hotter than ever. And when she began to ride him, tilting her hips back and forth, he nearly lost his mind. "Chelsea, baby…"

"Hmmm?"

"Don't act like you don't know what you're doing."

"What am I doing?"

He looked up at her and waited for her to meet his gaze. "You're making yourself essential to me."

Her smile lit up her eyes and had her picking up the pace until they were both coming with shouts of pleasure and a deep, satisfying sense of connection that was slowly but surely changing the course of his life.

He was most definitely in love with her.

CHAPTER 11

*C*hristmas Day dawned sunny and cold on Gansett Island. A light dusting of snow overnight made the lawn sparkle in the morning sun. The sea was choppy and a deep, vivid blue. Erin never tired of the view from the lighthouse and wondered how she'd ever go back to living in an ordinary house after having lived here.

After a series of late nights, Slim was still asleep, so she snuck downstairs to make coffee and check her email.

Her body ached in areas that hadn't ached in years, but it was a good kind of pain, the best kind. He was a creative, inventive lover who never ran out of ways to pleasure her. Erin's head was spinning from four nights of sensual pleasure that had her rethinking everything about what she wanted from him.

She plugged in the tree lights, made coffee and took a steaming mug to her desk to fire up her laptop to check her email. Scrolling through the latest messages to her Ask Erin account, she found one message that captured her attention.

Dear Erin,

I've met a wonderful guy who makes me feel like a princess. I've never been with a guy who listens the way he does and seems to truly care about

*making me happy. So what's my problem, you might ask. Well, thanks to all
the frogs who came before him, I'm having a hard time believing my prince is
for real. I keep waiting for the other shoe to drop and I'll see who he really is.
That's how I think, and I fear I'm sabotaging the best thing to ever happen to
me by saddling him with the sins of his predecessors. Maybe he is as great as
he seems, and I'm the one who needs to stop being so cynical. How do I get
past this dilemma before I ruin the best thing to ever happen to me?*

Sincerely,

Beth

Wow, Erin thought, *that strikes close to home.* When writing the
column, she often felt like a fraud since she hadn't been in a real relationship in years. In lieu of actual experience, she tried to come at
each situation from a practical standpoint. But this one got to the crux
of her concerns about Slim. How could he possibly be as awesome as
he seemed?

She kept waiting for him to be cranky or nasty or testy or anything
other than his usual witty, charming self. Surely he couldn't keep that
up indefinitely, could he? It had been four days since the first time
they slept together, and if anything, he'd only been more charming
since then. He wasn't like some guys who got what they wanted and
seemed to lose interest. No, the more he got, the more interested he
seemed to be.

Erin chewed on the end of a pen as she puzzled over her dilemma
and Beth's. The sex was stupendous, life-changing, mind-blowing.
Every superlative she could think of applied to sex with Slim Jackson.
The more they did it, the more she wanted. He was like a drug, the
best kind of drug, and she was quickly becoming addicted. Which led
her right back to what would happen when he left to finish out the
winter in Florida.

She'd be a hot mess. That's what would happen. Sighing, she
dropped her head into her hands. In just a few days, he'd turned her
world upside down, and she liked the view from down here. She'd had
more fun, more laughs and more sex than at any other time in her life.

It would be so easy to get hooked on a guy who made it so easy to like him, which was why she needed to tread carefully. Her free and unencumbered life had worked well for her and made it so she could do things like pick up and move to Gansett Island to be the lighthouse keeper without a hassle. She rented rather than owned. She dated rather than committing. She took jobs she could walk away from when they stopped being fun or beneficial. She had friends who didn't require daily care and feeding to stay in her life. She liked her life the way it was, and sexy Slim Jackson was the first significant threat to her freewheeling way of life.

Returning her focus to Beth's letter, Erin tried to separate her own situation from Beth's.

> *Dear Beth,*
>
> *Congratulations on finding a prince in a sea of frogs. Sometimes people are exactly what they seem, but you're wise to be cautious and to protect yourself from being hurt. What has he told you about his past dating history? Has he made a habit of commitment or is he a serial dater? What do his friends say about him when he's not around? What does his mother, sister, daughter say? How he treats the other women in his life says a lot about how he'll treat you when the blush wears off the rose—as it always does.*
>
> *By all means, do your due diligence, but don't make the mistake of projecting the actions of other men onto your new guy. Not all guys are the same, and it isn't fair to expect him to do the same things another guy did just because they have the same plumbing. It sounds to me like you've found a gem. When you've done all your research and the time comes to stop being cynical, I hope you'll open your heart to the possibility that he could be your happily ever after. Do let me know how things work out.*
>
> *Hugs,*
>
> *Erin*

She saved the letter and response in the file she was compiling for her next column and sat back to reread what she'd written. It was probably time to take her own advice and apply it to her relationship with Slim.

The sound of the toilet flushing upstairs let her know he was up.

Erin went into the kitchen to put on more coffee and start breakfast. He was always starving in the morning, and she loved cooking for him. She loved everything about having him around. Her small living space should've felt cramped with him underfoot, but it didn't. He was a courteous, easy guest, and she wished he could stay far beyond New Year's Day.

They had another week until then, and she planned to fully enjoy every minute while trying to decide her next move. When she wasn't wrapped up in his arms, she thought obsessively about his invitation to come to Florida.

Honestly, she thought as she cracked a half-dozen eggs, *you're a disaster over this guy, Erin, and it's getting worse with every passing day.* Take yesterday, for example. They'd gone into town to do some last-minute Christmas shopping, had lunch at Stephanie's Bistro, which was open for the holiday week, and were back home in bed by two. They hadn't left her bed again except to eat soup at midnight.

She didn't spend sixteen hours in bed with a man. Or she hadn't before he came along.

He snuck up behind her and wrapped his arms around her waist, dropping his head to her shoulder. "Morning, sexiest lighthouse keeper ever."

Her face flushed with heat that she assigned only partially to the burner she stood watch over. "Jenny might take issue with that."

"Jenny is beautiful, but she's got nothing on you." He rubbed his hard cock against her backside.

"I can't believe you've got any gas left in your tank after yesterday."

"My tank is fully recharged and ready for more of the same."

Erin cracked up laughing. "You're incorrigible."

"You love that about me."

Her heart staggered at his use of the word *love.* "And you suffer from a terrible lack of self-esteem. I worry about that."

"I know. It's a problem I'm trying to overcome." He nudged her hair out of his way and placed hot, openmouthed kisses on her neck that made her legs feel wobbly under her.

"Keep that up, and I'll burn your breakfast."

"We can't have that. I need all the fuel I can get to keep up with you."

"Keep up with *me*?"

"Aw, yeah, sweetheart. You're a wild woman. I had *no* idea."

"I'm going to punch you when you let me go."

Chuckling, he tightened his hold on her. "This is already the best Christmas I've had since I believed in Santa."

"Really?" she asked, ridiculously pleased to hear that.

"Really. I love being here with you."

"I love having you here."

"Mmm, there's a whole lotta love flying around this morning. And speaking of flying, why don't we go for a ride before we go visiting later? I can show you some of my *other* skills."

Erin hadn't been expecting him to say that and had no idea how to respond. After a long pause, she said, "We've already got a lot going on today. Maybe another day?"

"Sure, whatever you want." He let her go and began to butter the toast, leaving Erin to breathe a sigh of relief. She was on borrowed time on this issue, and before long, she was going to have to tell him she didn't do airplanes. Not anymore.

SLIM AND ERIN LEFT THE LIGHTHOUSE SHORTLY AFTER THREE TO GO TO dinner at Jenny and Alex's house. On the way, they stopped by to see Luke and Sydney, who were enjoying a quiet day at home.

"Thank God you're here," Syd said when they came into the living room where she was on the sofa, a blanket over her lap. "He's keeping me prisoner. I need someone to spring me."

Slim laughed at the way Luke rolled his eyes at his wife's complaints.

"She's doing exactly what the doctor told her to do—nothing."

"He acts like I was put on official bed rest. He's even carrying me to the bathroom! Erin, tell him this has to stop!"

"Umm, well..."

"Not you, too! I thought we were friends."

"We *are* friends," Erin said with a laugh, "which is why I want you to do what you're told and take it easy for a few more days."

Sydney scowled at her.

"Thank you, Erin," Luke said. "She's driving me crazy."

"*I'm* driving *you* crazy? That's a laugh!"

"Love you, sweetheart," Luke said with a big goofy grin that made all of them laugh, even Sydney.

"This sucks," she said. "We had all kinds of fun plans for today, and we're stuck at home."

Luke sat on the sofa and placed his wife's feet on his lap. "It's for a good cause."

"Yes, it is," Sydney said, smiling at him.

Slim and Erin sat on the love seat and kept the happy couple company for an hour before they had to leave to continue on to Jenny's.

"Tell everyone we said Merry Christmas," Syd said glumly.

"I will," Erin said.

"Did you hear we've got a New Year's Eve wedding to look forward to?" Slim asked Luke.

"Yes! Adam and Abby are tying the knot. Can't wait. What a fun night for a wedding."

Slim recalled Abby's tearstained face on the flight back to Gansett the day of the anniversary party and wondered if there wasn't more to the story of their impromptu wedding than anyone had yet heard.

On the way to Jenny's, he took hold of Erin's hand and brought it to his lips. "What're you doing on New Year's Eve?"

"I figured we'd hang out and watch the ball drop before you have to go back to Florida."

"How about coming with me to my friend's wedding?"

"Are you even invited?"

"Ha! Of course I am. This is Gansett. Everyone is invited. I have a great group of people I hang out with in Florida, but the people here, especially the McCarthys, they're my closest friends."

"I can see why. I love the people here. At first, when Jenny asked me about applying for the lighthouse job, I thought *no way*. I could never stand to be marooned on an island all year. But she encouraged me to come see for myself, and after one weekend here, I was packing my bags."

"I hate leaving in October, but there's nothing much for me to do here all winter. Well, there hasn't been in the past, but now there's this gorgeous lighthouse keeper who makes me want to rethink my plans for the rest of the winter."

"Don't tease me."

"I'm not." He looked over in time to see her brows furrow and her lips purse. "I'd much rather be here with you than down there without you. Have you given any more thought to coming with me?"

"Oh. You still want me to?"

"Erin," he said, laughing, "*yes*, I want you to. Haven't I spent days showing you how badly I want you?"

"Yes, but... I... I don't know about Florida. I have a commitment here and a contract with the town and... I just don't know."

"None of that sounds insurmountable if you want to come, but I won't push you if it's not what you want." He felt oddly disappointed by her noncommittal attitude. After the last few blissful nights in her bed, he was fully committed to her and them and seeing what might come next. Not knowing where he stood with her was making him crazy, but he was trying to give her space she seemed to need to come around in her own time.

But what if she didn't come around? What if this was nothing more than a holiday fling to her when he was getting in deeper by the minute? That would suck. He was damned if he did and damned if he didn't.

He drove into the driveway at Martinez Lawn and Garden and went around the retail store to hang a left toward Jenny and Alex's house. Other cars were in the driveway when they arrived. He parked in the road so they could leave when they needed to and shut off the engine.

"Slim."

"Yeah?"

"I'm sorry if I said the wrong thing just now. My head seems to be all over the place the last few days, but I'm thinking about your offer and trying to figure out what to do."

"I don't want you to think I'm pressuring you to decide something if you're not ready to, but I'd love to have you in Florida with me and at Evan's wedding in Anguilla. We'd have so much fun."

"I know we would, but I'm not ready to decide anything for sure yet. I thought my life was settled after I moved here, and then I met you and we've had this time together and now… Now I don't know what's what, and nothing feels settled anymore."

Her distress moved him. It made him realize how fragile she was and that he needed to be extra careful with how he handled the next steps with her. "There's no rush, sweetheart. I swear. I'm not going anywhere for another week, and we've got plenty of time to figure out what happens next."

"Okay," she said with a sigh of what sounded like relief.

"Don't stress out about me. There's no need for that. I promise." He leaned over the center console to kiss her. "We good?"

"Yeah, we're good."

"Let's go have some fun."

CHAPTER 12

*I*nside, Alex poured drinks for Erin, Slim, David, Daisy, Paul and Hope while Jenny put the finishing touches on dinner.

"Alex, why don't you show the guys what Santa brought you before dinner?" Jenny said.

"Is it something that's going to add to my emotional scars where you two are concerned?" Paul asked.

"You're going to love it, bro." Alex led the men to the basement, where a brand-new pool table was the centerpiece of the family room. "Is my wife the best, or what?"

"She's pretty damned awesome," Paul said, running a hand over the rich green felt. "Let's break this baby in!"

Alex called dibs on Slim for his team, which left David and Paul to play against them. "Jared and Quinn can play the winners," Alex said as he racked the balls.

"How did Jenny get a pool table out here without you knowing about it?" David asked.

"She recruited Joe and Seamus to help her get it on the ferry and then have it delivered here while I was out plowing snow. Best Christmas ever." As he said the words, Slim noted the hint of sadness in his friend's eyes and realized this was also the brothers' first Christmas without their mother, who was in a memory care facility on the mainland. He wanted to ask how she was doing but didn't want to ruin the festive mood.

David saved him the trouble by asking if they'd heard from Marion's caregivers.

"We talked to them yesterday," Alex said. "She's doing very well, adapting to her new surroundings."

"That's great news."

"It is until we show up and she begs us to take her home," Alex said, grimacing as he broke, watching a striped ball head for the corner and then groaning when the ball bounced short of the pocket.

"That's got to be rough," Slim said.

"It blows," Paul said bluntly. "We leave there feeling like total shit every time, and the kicker is that five minutes after we're gone, she doesn't even remember we were there."

"But we're a disaster for days afterward," Alex added.

"Have you thought about cutting back on the visits?" David asked as he eyed the orange number five ball and sank it in the side pocket.

"If we do that, we still feel like shit," Alex said. "It's a no-win situation no matter what we do."

David moved on to sink the yellow number one and the green number six.

"Um, Alex, the doc is kicking our ass here," Slim said. "Is it not enough that you're a freaking doctor? Do you have to be a pool shark, too?"

"I'm about to also be an engaged man," David said without looking up from the table.

"Say *what*?" Alex asked.

"I'm going to pop the question when we get home tonight. Daisy has no idea."

"Oh my God," Paul said. "That's awesome."

Whoa, that's big news, Slim thought. After David's spectacular breakup with Janey McCarthy, Slim had wondered if he would ever get married. But then he met Daisy, and the two of them had fallen hard for each other. He was glad to see David taking another chance on love. Based on the way Daisy positively glowed with happiness whenever David was nearby, Slim had a feeling this one was for keeps.

"Congratulations," Slim said. "Happy for you."

"Thanks."

"You're awfully sure she'll say yes," Alex said.

David shot him a disdainful look. "If I wasn't sure of her answer, I never would've told you yahoos."

"That hurts me," Alex said gravely.

"So guess what Hope got for Christmas." Paul said after David finally missed a shot and their team got a turn. He lined up to put the eleven ball in a corner pocket.

"What?" Alex asked.

"Airline tickets to Vegas. The three of us are leaving tomorrow for three days there and then a week in San Francisco."

"Hey, that's cool," Alex said. "Good time of year to get away."

"Great time of year to tie the knot, too," Paul said nonchalantly.

Alex stared at his brother, agog. "Wait. *What?*"

"You heard me," Paul said, amused by his brother's reaction. "We're going to Vegas to get married."

"Get outta here," Slim said. "That's awesome." If things kept up this way, he'd be the last single man standing before long.

"Very cool," David said. "Was she surprised?"

"About the trip, yes, but not about the getting-married part. We've been talking about doing it here, but I thought it would be more fun to get away. We'll have a party in the spring to celebrate."

Alex gawked at his brother, seeming stunned by his news.

"What?" Paul asked him. "You aren't mad, are you?"

"I'd kinda like to be there when you get married."

"Then why don't you and Jenny come with us?"

Alex seemed to think that over for about two seconds. "Don't mind if we do."

"I don't mind at all. We'd love to have you."

"All this talk of weddings is going to make Slim jealous," David said.

Slim's first impulse was usually to cringe when people used the words *wedding* and *Slim* in the same sentence, but after the nights he'd spent wrapped up in Erin's arms, the thought of it didn't seem as repulsive as it once would have.

"It's okay," Slim said, affecting a grave expression. "I think I can handle it."

His dad had told him a long time ago that someday he'd meet a woman who would make settling down seem like the most natural thing in the world. Slim had spent most of his life in skeptical disbelief that it would happen to him as women passed through his life without sticking.

Until now.

Was Erin the woman his dad had told him he'd find? He couldn't say for sure yet, but he felt more "settled" in her presence than he had with any other woman he'd known before her. That much was for certain. At times, he had to remind himself he'd known her only a couple of months and not years. He was so comfortable with her, it was easy to forget their relationship was still new in many ways.

Up until a few days ago, it had been a nice friendship with the possibility of more. Now it was so much more, and he still had no idea where it was leading. The good news was nothing had to be decided immediately, but a week from now when it was time for him to head south again, he hoped they'd be ready to make a decision or two about the path forward.

He wanted her in his life. It was that simple. And he wanted her badly enough to play by her rules for the time being.

Just as David sank the eight ball in the corner pocket, Jenny called them upstairs for dinner.

"We never stood a chance against him," Slim said to Alex. "We got hustled."

"I want to be on his team next time," Alex said.

"Now don't fight over me, boys," David said, grinning. "It's Christmas."

They trooped upstairs, still sparring about the pool game.

"Daisy," Alex said, "you ought to know that your boyfriend is a hustler."

Daisy put her arms around David. "Aww, did you kick their butts, honey?"

"I put a hurt on them."

"That's my guy." She kissed him square on the mouth.

"Ugh," Alex said. "Get a room."

"Can we choose any room we want upstairs?" David asked, waggling his brows at Alex.

"Not at *my* house. Gross."

"Alex, come help me with dinner and leave David alone," Jenny said.

"He humiliated me at my own pool table on the first day," Alex said. "I'd think you'd have more sympathy for your husband."

"I'll massage your wounded ego later. For now, I have people to feed."

Slim laughed at Jenny's saucy reply.

"He's still such a baby," Paul said.

"I heard that, asshole," Alex called from the kitchen.

"*Shut it*," Jenny said while the others laughed.

Baby, Paul mouthed.

Slim smiled at Paul while Hope placed a hand over his mouth. Their bickering made Slim miss Jack. He was long overdue for a visit with his brother's family, and he'd love to bring Erin with him.

"Leave your brother alone," Hope said.

"He invited himself and his wife on our trip," Paul told her when she'd removed her hand.

"Oh yay! That's great. We'll have so much fun."

Paul hooked his arm around her waist and drew her in close to him. "As long as I get to marry you, I'll put up with him crashing our party."

Hope's smile lit up her pretty face.

Jenny came rushing out of the kitchen and threw herself at Hope. "You're getting married! And we're going with you! Oh my God! This is huge! When were you going to tell me?"

"I was waiting for Paul to tell Alex."

"We're going to be *sisters!*" Jenny said, tears making her eyes shine. The two women clung to each other.

Slim glanced at Erin in time to see a stricken expression on her face. Ah, *damn.* Jenny was supposed to have been her sister, too. He crossed the room to Erin, put his arm around her and let her know he understood.

She leaned her head into his chest in a moment of silent unity that did funny things to his insides. What the hell was that? He was hungry, and the smells coming from the kitchen were making his stomach growl. That was all it was.

But when he looked down to find Erin gazing up at him with affection and appreciation and a million other things he couldn't easily identify, he knew it was far more than hunger. It was something else, something altogether new.

The moment was broken when Jared, Lizzie and Quinn came in the front door, apologizing for being late and bearing side dishes that they handed over to Jenny.

"You're not late," she said. "You're just in time for dinner."

Quinn handed Jenny a bottle of wine. "Thanks for having me."

"We're so glad you could join us. How are you enjoying the island so far?"

"It's beautiful, but a little quiet for my liking."

"Wait until summer," Paul said. "You won't believe it's the same place."

"That's what everyone tells me," Quinn said. "But how do you not go nuts out here in the winter?"

"Oh, we find ways to keep ourselves entertained," Paul said, smiling at Hope.

Her entire face turned bright red as she swatted him. "Knock it off."

"I see how it is," Quinn said, using his thumb to point to Jared and Lizzie, "living with these two. They 'disappear' frequently."

"We do not!" Lizzie said.

"Um, yeah, we do, babe," Jared replied, earning a glare from his wife.

"On that note," Jenny said, "let's eat."

Slim held a chair at the dining room table for Erin, who was far more subdued than usual. He reached for her hand and gave it a squeeze.

She sent him a grateful smile, but he sensed she was unsettled. He couldn't wait to be alone with her again later when he'd try to get her to talk about it.

ERIN FELT FOOLISH FOR ALLOWING SUCH A SIMPLE THING TO SEND HER reeling, but witnessing Jenny's joyful celebration with Hope had felt like a punch to the gut. Jenny was to have been *her* sister, and while Erin was truly happy for Hope and Paul—and Alex and Jenny by extension—the incident was just another reminder of what'd been lost.

And now she could feel herself falling into the black hole of despair that struck at the oddest of times, like today when she'd been having a really great day with people she adored. All it took was one sentence, one comment, one second to change the dynamic for her.

She ought to be used to it by now, having suffered through frequent mini-crises since Toby died, but she was never prepared for the darkness to swoop in to remind her that while her life and Jenny's had somehow moved forward, Toby was gone forever.

Slim's hand wrapped around hers was a comfort until he was forced to release her to take the serving dish that Paul passed to him.

Jenny served a delicious meal of tenderloin, red bliss potatoes, asparagus, mixed vegetables and freshly baked bread, but Erin couldn't get anything past the lump in her throat. She dabbed at her lips and mumbled an "excuse me" before she got up and went to the bathroom in the hallway to try to get herself together.

The last thing she wanted was to ruin Jenny's first Christmas with her new husband and family with reminders about a past they'd both sooner forget than dwell on, especially on a holiday.

Life is for the living. That was what Toby would say if he were here to see her melting down over him more than fourteen years after his death. They'd lost their grandmother a few years before he died, and when Erin said she felt guilty for rarely visiting her gravesite, that had been Toby's reply. He'd said their grandmother wouldn't want them to feel guilty about not going to the cemetery, because they'd been devoted to her in life, which was what really mattered.

Erin reached for a tissue from the box on the counter and dabbed at her eyes, hoping she could get this situation under control so she wouldn't have to reappear with red eyes. She took a deep breath, held it for a long count and then released it. Earlier in the day, she'd talked to her parents, who were visiting with her other grandmother for Christmas.

Over the years, they'd gotten out of the habit of making a big deal of holidays, because it was just too painful. They preferred to spend time together on regular days that weren't so fraught with memories and regrets and family expectations.

A soft knock sounded on the door. "Er? You okay?"

Erin checked her appearance in the mirror and took another deep breath before she opened the door to Jenny, forcing a smile for her friend's benefit. "Hey, sorry. I'm fine."

Jenny took a careful look at Erin, tilting her head. "No, you're not. What is it?"

"Oh, the usual holiday thing," she said, affecting nonchalance. "I just had a little moment, but I'm fine now."

"You don't have to pretend with me," Jenny said softly.

"I don't want to ruin our lovely day."

"You're not ruining anything. It sneaks up sometimes when we least expect it. Happened to me last night."

"Really?" Erin was ashamed to realize she'd assumed Jenny was so happy with Alex that she rarely thought of Toby anymore.

Jenny stepped into the room and closed the door. "I think of him every single day," she said softly in response to Erin's unspoken thought. "Nothing could ever change that."

"I didn't mean to imply—"

"Erin, honey, I know you didn't. It's only natural for people to think I've moved on with Alex. I'm happy again, so why would I dwell on the grief of the past? But you and I both know it's not that simple." As she rested her hand over her heart, her eyes filled with tears. "He will *always* be with me. Always." Jenny cleared her throat and took the tissue Erin handed her. "Do you remember at our wedding when Alex and I lit three candles and then the unity candle?"

"I can't say I noticed that."

"Well, we did, and the third candle was for Toby. Alex suggested it. He never loses sight of the fact that he got his happy ending because someone else died."

"That's… That's a wonderful tribute."

"His picture is still on the bedside table in the room I share with my husband." She took a small step closer to Erin. "And you, my dear, darling friend, will always be my *sister*, no matter how many new sisters I may acquire along the way."

"I'm a jealous cow," Erin said, sniffing through her tears. She should've known Jenny would tune in to what had set her off.

Jenny laughed. "No, you're the loyal and wonderful sister of my heart who understands my journey better than just about anyone else ever could."

"I love Hope. She's awesome."

"Yes, she is, and I couldn't be happier for her and Paul and Ethan. She's going to be a wonderful addition to my family, but she could *never* take your place in my family or my heart. You're right there next to Toby, two of the most important people in my life."

Erin hugged her, and they clung to each other the way they had during the horrible days, weeks, months and years that followed Toby's death. "I'm sorry to rain on your first Christmas with Alex. I've been a bit of a basket case lately."

"You're not raining on anything, and you're *not* a basket case.

You're falling in love with a wonderful man, and if I know you at all, you're fighting it tooth and nail."

"I'm *not* falling in love. I'm in lust. That's all it is."

"Funny, that's what I said about Alex, and now here I am with his ring on my finger and knocked up with his kid."

Erin gasped. "Oh my God! You are? You're *pregnant?*"

Smiling at her reaction, Jenny said, "Three months."

"You didn't tell me!"

"We haven't told anyone, but I wanted you to know."

Erin hugged her again. "This is such amazing news. I'm so happy for you guys."

"Thanks, we're thrilled. But don't think my news gets you off the hook on falling in love. I see the way you look at him and the way he looks at you. I've never seen you look at anyone else the way you look at him, not even Mitch."

"This... He... We..." Erin groaned in frustration while Jenny laughed.

"He's got you stuttering."

"Among other things," Erin muttered.

"Can I give you one teeny, tiny piece of advice?"

"Can I stop you?"

Laughing, Jenny put her hands on Erin's shoulders, compelling Erin to look at her. "When Alex and I were first together, I was a disaster. All I did was try to deny what was happening because it was too much too soon. I'd learned the hard way not to take chances, you know?"

"I know all too well."

"But there was something about him. Something different. And he refused to let me cop out of what was happening between us."

"Sounds like Slim."

"Letting it happen with Alex is the best thing I've done since I lost Toby. I want you to find your happily ever after, too, Er. And I think he could be it."

"I don't know if I'm ready for all the things he could be."

"You're never ready for something like this, but I'd hate to see you have regrets if you wimp out and let him get away."

"Wimp out?"

"Isn't that what you'd be doing if you don't at least *try* to make it work with him?"

"You don't pull any punches."

"When have I ever pulled punches? I want you to be happy, and in order for that to happen, you have to take a chance. *You have to*. Isn't that what you're always telling the women who write to you?"

"Don't throw my own words back in my face," Erin said, smiling.

"You know I'm right."

They were interrupted by another knock.

"Your guy or mine?" Jenny asked. "What do you think?"

"Probably yours."

"I say yours, but let's find out." Jenny opened the door to Slim and sent Erin a smug look.

"Everything all right in there, ladies?" he asked, his eyes laser focused on Erin.

"Yes, we're good," she said.

"Take a minute." Jenny kissed her cheek before she left the room, patting Slim's arm on the way by.

"Sorry," Erin said. "I just needed a minute. I'm okay now."

"You're sure?"

"Yeah."

With his hands propped on the doorframe, he said, "When Jenny said that to Hope about being sisters… I've only seen that expression on your face once before, the day Jenny married Alex at the lighthouse."

Unnerved by his assessment, she crossed her arms. "You're awfully insightful."

He flashed the irrepressible grin that she found so sexy. "Pilots and bartenders, sweetheart. I've been telling you that for months now."

Erin went to him, put her hands on his chest and kissed him. "Thank you for coming to check on me. Let's go finish dinner."

"You want to skip the McCarthys' later?"

"Not at all. I'm fine. I promise." She thought he would step back to let her pass, but instead, he wrapped his arms around her. Snuggled into his warm embrace, breathing in his appealing scent, Erin relaxed ever so slightly. He made her feel like nothing bad would happen if he continued to hold her this way. "Let's go finish dinner."

He kissed the top of her head and released her, but kept his hand on her back as they returned to the dining room, where the others carried on as if nothing had happened, which was exactly what she needed.

Erin loved these people. She truly did. And she was beginning to love Slim, too.

CHAPTER 13

Kevin cooked a turkey that turned out sort of dry. His sons would eat anything, so he wasn't too worried about impressing them. No, he was far more concerned about making sure Chelsea had a nice dinner.

She brought mashed potatoes and apple pie and wore a pale pink sweater that clung to her breasts. Her long blonde hair, which was usually braided for work, was loose around her shoulders. What in the world was a goddess like her doing with a schlep like him?

"Nice apron," she said, her eyes taking a slow, lazy trip down the front of him, making him thankful for the apron.

"You're not allowed to look at me like that today."

"My apologies."

"Ah, fuck it." He put his arm around her and was kissing her senseless when Riley walked into the kitchen, clearing his throat to let them know he was there. Kevin withdrew from the kiss, noting the way she diverted her eyes as her face flushed with embarrassment.

"Sorry." Riley got a beer from the fridge, cracked it open and went into the living room.

Chelsea glared at him. "You're not allowed to do *that*," she hissed. "Not here."

"Sorry."

"You are not."

"No, I'm really not. They need to get used to seeing me kiss you."

"Baby steps, Kev."

"Which one of us is the shrink, anyway?"

Chelsea stirred the gravy he had simmering on the stovetop. "Sometimes I wonder."

Placing his hands on her hips, he leaned into her to check the other pans.

"Get that thing off me."

"You like that thing."

"Kevin!"

"What time are we eating, Dad?" Finn asked as he made his first appearance of the day. Neither of his sons had been there when he got home last night. He had no idea what time they'd rolled in. Finn's dark hair was standing on end, and his blue eyes were rimmed with red, signs of a hangover.

"Half an hour or so. Rough night?"

"Fun night."

"You remember Chelsea, right?"

"Sure," Finn said. "How you doing?"

"I'm good," Chelsea said. "Merry Christmas."

"Yeah, same to you." He escaped to the living room with his brother.

"Awkward," Chelsea whispered.

Kevin began to question the wisdom of inviting Chelsea to join them for their first Christmas since he and Deb had split up. Maybe it was too soon to expect his sons to welcome his girlfriend, or whatever she was, into their home away from home for a holiday.

Since it was far too late to turn back, he decided to make the most of it. "Everything's ready." He gestured to the table he'd set earlier.

"It looks really nice," Chelsea said, taking in the table and the tree he'd put up to try to make the holiday festive.

His sons weren't feeling the Christmas spirit, but Kevin was determined to get through the day as best they could. They sat down to dinner, and the boys dove into the food, eating like they hadn't been fed in a month. Chelsea picked at the food on her plate, pushing the turkey around in the gravy.

"Did you get a chance to talk to your family today?" he asked her.

"I talked to my mom and stepfather this morning and my brother this afternoon. My niece and nephew told me every present Santa brought them."

Kevin was ashamed to realize he hadn't known she had a brother, niece or nephew. He wanted to know if her father was still alive, but he couldn't ask that now. "How old are the kids?"

"Three and five."

"I remember those days," he said, glancing at Riley and Finn.

"Mom called," Finn said.

"Oh. Good. How's she doing?"

"Fine. She's home by herself today."

Kevin had to bite his tongue to keep from saying that was what she'd wanted when she ended their marriage. "So she's at the house?"

"Uh-huh."

That was news to Kevin, who'd been told on her way out the door that he could have the house she never wanted to see again.

Riley polished off a second plate and stood. "I'll do the dishes."

"I don't mind doing them, son. Take the day off." They'd been working long hours to help Mac finish the addition at Seamus and Carolina's house in time for the holidays.

"Are you sure?"

"Yep."

"Okay. I'm going to go meet some friends for a beer."

"I'll come with you." Finn rose, plate in hand, to follow his brother.

"I'll see you at Uncle Mac's later?" Kevin asked.

"Yeah, I'll be there," Riley said.

"Me, too," Finn added.

The front door closed behind them, and silence fell upon the house. Kevin released a deep breath that he'd been holding and noted Chelsea watching him from across the table, wineglass dangling between her fingers. "Sorry about that."

"Nothing to apologize for."

"They're not usually so… quiet."

"Doesn't matter how old you are when your parents split up. It's always hard."

Kevin topped off her glass with more wine. "How old were you?"

"Seventeen."

"Ouch. Senior year?"

She nodded. "And to make it even better, my dad hooked up with the mother of one of my best friends, breaking up two marriages for the price of one affair. It was a huge scandal. We were the talk of the high school." Looking over at him, she added, "I get how your sons are feeling. Even if your breakup wasn't a scandal, it was the end of life as they knew it."

"I suppose so."

"It's hard to see your parents moving on with other people, even if you like the other people. I adore my stepfather, but I didn't at first. To me, he was part of the problem."

"What changed?"

"He makes my mom really happy, happier than she's ever been."

"That counts for something."

"It counts for a lot."

"What about your dad? Is he still with the other woman?"

"Yep, they're married and have more kids together."

"So everyone is happy. Do you see your father?"

"Occasionally. I didn't see him for years after it first happened. I couldn't bear to be in the same room with him. About five years later, he had a massive heart attack, and we thought he was going to die. Since then, my brother and I have tried to be a little more forgiving, but we can never forget what he did to our family."

After a long pause, Kevin said, "You know what kind of bums me out about my situation?"

"What's that?"

"I feel like they're blaming me, when she's the one who had the affair. She's the one who left me and wanted out of the marriage."

"They know that. Why do you think they're here with you rather than there with her today?"

"Hmm, I figured it was because they're working here for the winter and it was easier to stay."

"You sell yourself short, Kevin. They're here because they *want* to be. They've probably known for some time that she's back home, but they chose to stay—with you and the rest of their family."

"It'll be interesting to see what happens when this job at Seamus's is done. Mac has told them he wants them to stay, but I'm not sure they will."

"What were they doing before they came out here?"

"They work for a big construction company in Connecticut. They're both engineers, and when things happened with Deb and me, they took leaves of absence from work to come out here for a while."

"And it never occurred to you that they did that so they could help you through a rough time?"

"Not really," he said with a sheepish grin. "You sure you didn't go to medical school?"

"Nah, I'm a graduate of the school of hard knocks—and I'm a bartender. I get people, and I've seen them with you before we were together. It's obvious they think the world of you."

"Is it?" he asked, touched by her assessment.

"Yes, Kevin," she said, laughing. "They adore you. Just give them some time and space to get used to the new reality. They'll be fine and so will you."

"That's good to know." Before he could lose his nerve, he said, "Come to my brother's with me. You know everyone, and it'll be fun."

"It's a family thing."

"It's a *Gansett* thing. Everyone is welcome. My brother loves you. He'd want you to come."

"Your brother loves everyone."

"True, but he's got a soft spot for you, as you well know."

"He's adorable."

"Don't make me jealous."

"Now you're being ridiculous."

"So you'll come?"

"Sure, I'd love to." She took a sip of her wine. "But only because he's going to be there."

It took Kevin a second to realize she was joking, and then he laughed. Today hadn't gone as smoothly as he'd hoped, but she'd made him see that it was the first step in what would be a long journey for him and his sons as they adjusted to their new normal.

ON THE DRIVE HOME FROM ALEX AND JENNY'S, DAVID LAWRENCE relived the last six months of utter bliss with Daisy. After a couple of years spent putting his life back together from the mess he'd made of it, Daisy had come along right when he was beginning to feel normal again.

At that time, however, nothing had been normal for her. Her ex-boyfriend had beaten the hell out of her and might've killed her if Blaine Taylor hadn't gotten to Daisy's house when he did. David shuddered to think of what could've happened if Blaine had arrived even five minutes later.

He shuddered to think of what he would've missed out on with Daisy, whose sweet love had been a balm on the wounds he carried with him—most of them self-inflicted. The demise of his relationship with Janey McCarthy had nearly ruined him, not to mention the long and painful battle with lymphoma.

Those dark days were behind him now, and the most pressing thing on his mind lately was making his relationship with Daisy permanent. He'd been working for months with a jeweler on the mainland to create a one-of-a-kind ring for a one-of-a-kind woman, and he couldn't wait to give it to her.

His Daisy was a humble, no-frills woman. When he first met her, one of her prized possessions had been the sofa she'd found discarded by the side of the road. She'd brought it home, reupholstered it herself and turned a piece of junk into a treasure. Knowing she had zero expectations when it came to an engagement ring had made it that much more fun for him to design something he hoped would blow her away.

He'd asked the jeweler to help him create a ring that would remind her every time she looked at it that she was everything to him. The well-insured ring had been shipped to the clinic and had arrived three days ago. Victoria, his close friend and colleague, had burst into tears when he showed it to her.

"What?" he'd asked, alarmed by her reaction. "What's wrong?"

"Oh, David. It's *incredible*. Absolutely *incredible*." She'd hugged him and cried some more and oohed and aahed over the ring with such enthusiasm that David was even more confident that Daisy would love it, too. Her happiness was the only thing that really mattered to him.

Only a few years ago, he couldn't imagine life without Janey, but he'd done a spectacular job of screwing up that relationship beyond all repair. From the worst failure of his life, he'd learned what not to do this time around when the stakes were so much higher.

David had loved Janey. No question about that. But he was madly, deeply, insanely in love with Daisy, and he couldn't wait to make a lifetime commitment to her.

"You're awfully quiet," she said as they drove home to the place they now shared on the waterfront estate owned by Jared and Lizzie James. "What're you thinking about?"

Since he wasn't ready to tip his hand on what he had planned for when they got home, he said, "That this was a very nice day. A great Christmas."

"Best one I've ever had."

"Really?" He looked over and caught the big smile she directed his way. God, he loved that smile and went to great lengths to make sure he saw it frequently every day.

"Of course it was. I have you, and that's all I need to make this the best Christmas of my life."

And she hasn't seen anything yet… They'd exchanged gifts that morning, fun things, practical things and silly things. She'd loved the big box of lingerie he'd bought her at Tiffany's store, and he'd particularly loved the telescope she'd gotten for him after he'd expressed an interest in getting one. He'd let her think the gift-giving was over for the day, but his best gift was still to come.

David brought their joined hands to his lips and nibbled on her knuckles, making her laugh. He liked her laughter even more than the smiles. He liked absolutely everything about her. After he lost Janey, he'd resigned himself to a life alone, because what woman would ever want a man who'd cheated on his fiancée and girlfriend of thirteen years?

But Daisy hadn't held that transgression against him. Instead, she'd asked him if he'd learned from it. Not only had he learned from it, the experience had shown him what kind of man he didn't want to be. He swore to himself—and to her—that he would never make that mistake again. She believed him, she trusted him, and she loved him. David took none of those precious gifts for granted—and he never would.

At home, he ushered her upstairs to their cozy loft above Jared's garage. They'd talked about someday building a home of their own. Daisy thought that day was far off in the future, but he'd already talked to Mac McCarthy about putting them on the schedule for next winter.

The man who'd once been his future brother-in-law was now a friend, after David saved the lives of Mac's daughter and later, his nephew, both of whom might've died at birth without his involvement. Not to mention what he'd done for Janey, putting her back together in a clinic unequipped for such emergencies after PJ's chaotic birth.

He didn't like to think about that day or what a close call it had been. One thing he knew for sure was that he never would've gotten over being responsible for Janey's death. Thank goodness she and her baby had both come through fine, but it had been far too close for David's comfort. The only good thing to come out of that traumatic day was regaining the respect and admiration of a family he'd once planned to be part of.

Now that he and Daisy were home and it was go-time, David was suddenly nervous. He took Daisy's coat and hung it next to his. While she was in the bedroom, he turned on the gas fireplace, plugged in the Christmas tree lights and lit the candles they kept in the living room for what she called "romantic nights at home." He loved those nights when they cooked dinner together, opened a bottle of wine and watched a movie or played a game or made love on the sofa. It didn't matter what they did. They always had fun together.

David went into the bedroom to see what she was doing. The bathroom door was closed, so he took advantage of the opportunity to retrieve the ring from the velvet box in his bedside table. He put it in his pants pocket and went out to the living room to wait for her. On the way to the sofa, he checked to make sure the bottle of champagne he'd put in the fridge earlier was sufficiently chilled.

Everything was ready. All he needed now was her. All he'd ever need for the rest of his life was her.

As he waited, he thought about the night when she'd been bruised and battered at the hands of the man she'd loved. Her courage had touched him deeply that night when he'd treated her at the clinic. While she recovered at home, he'd fallen into the habit of checking on her after work each day. She'd insisted on sharing with him the abundance of food the island community had brought her, which began their habit of having dinner together each night.

It had taken off from there. One night at a time, one dinner at a time, his days began to be shaped around the hours he got to spend with her. And since she'd moved in with him, he got to sleep with her every night and wake with her every morning, and a life that had spun out of control was now firmly back on track, thanks in large part to the calming effect she had on him.

However, when she came into the living room wearing the peach silk nightgown and matching robe he'd given her earlier, the last thing he felt was calm. The color perfectly complemented her peaches-and-cream complexion. Her long blonde hair had been brushed until it fell in silky, shiny waves down her back.

David was speechless, which wasn't conducive to his plans for the evening.

She sat on the sofa next to him, curling her legs under her, as if she

115

hadn't just blown him away simply by walking into the room wearing peach silk. "This is nice," she said of the fire, the candles and the tree. "Very cozy."

"You're stunning," he said when he'd recovered the ability to speak.

"This old thing?" With a coy smile, she ran her finger down the front of the robe, hooking it in the belt that was knotted at her waist. "My boyfriend bought me this for Christmas. I thought he might like to see me in it."

That, David realized, was the last time she'd ever refer to him as her boyfriend. From now on, after he asked the most important of questions, she would hopefully refer to him as her fiancé, and then, before too long, her husband. He couldn't wait for either of those titles.

"Suffice to say your boyfriend thinks you look magnificent in it."

She caressed the spot between his brows. "You're pensive tonight. You're sure everything is okay?"

"Everything is as good as it has ever been."

"Wow, that's nice to hear."

"It's all because of you, you know." He'd rehearsed this moment a thousand times in his mind, but now that it was upon him, the words he'd practiced didn't seem adequate.

"What is?"

"Everything. Everything is perfect because of you and how much I love you. I was a wreck of a man when I met you, and slowly but surely, one day at a time, you put me back together. You gave me back my life, Daisy."

Her eyes filled with tears. "You did the same for me," she said in a hushed tone. "After everything that happened with Truck," she said of the ex-boyfriend who had abused her, "I couldn't imagine taking a chance with any guy again. But there you were, every night after long days at work, coming to check on me. You were so sweet and caring. You made me forget all my plans to stay single forever."

"Thank goodness for that," he said, smiling as he took her left hand and kissed the back of it. "You mean everything to me, Daisy. I hope you know that."

She moved onto his lap, straddling him and taking his face in her hands to kiss him. "I do. Of course I do. How could I not when you tell me every day?"

David drew her in closer and fell into the kiss, his tongue rubbing against hers and setting off a predictable reaction. He broke the kiss and redirected his attention to her neck. "Do I tell you too often?"

"No," she said, laughing as she tilted her head to give him better access. "I never get tired of hearing how much you love me."

"I hope you'll never get tired of that or of me."

"Never. No way. I love you so much. Sometimes I think you have no idea just how much. You say I put you back together. How about what you did for me? You were the first guy I ever dated who treated me with respect and kindness and sweetness. I'd never had any of that until I had you."

"You deserve all that and so much more. You deserve everything."

"As long as I have you and us, I have everything I'll ever want or need."

She had given him the perfect opening to pop the question.

"Could I get up for a second?" he asked.

"Oh, sure." She moved back to where she'd started out, legs under her as always.

For the rest of his life, he would never forget how her expression went from baffled when he moved the coffee table out of his way to astounded when he dropped to one knee before her.

"David," she said, gasping. "*What…*"

He took hold of her hand once again. "My beautiful, sweet, adorable, sexy Daisy. Would you please do me the huge, enormous, life-changing honor of being my wife?"

"*Yes!* Oh my God, yes. *Yes, yes, yes.*" She threw herself into his arms and kissed him.

"I was hoping you'd say that," he said when they came up for air.

"Was there any doubt?"

"Not really, but thanks for not making me suffer."

"I would never do that to you."

"Wait! I forgot the most important part." He hadn't forgotten, but now he couldn't wait to give her the ring. Still smiling at her enthusiastic response to his proposal, he retrieved the ring from his pocket and slid the three-carat stunner onto her left hand. A two-carat princess-cut diamond was framed by another carat of smaller diamonds that continued all the way around the platinum band.

"David. Oh my *God*."

"Do you like it?"

"Do I *like* it?" she asked, laughing as tears ran unchecked down her face. "It's the most beautiful ring I've ever seen! How did you do this? You never left the island!"

"A jeweler on the mainland helped me out. I told him I wanted something spectacular for the most amazing woman I've ever known. I said it had to be as special as she is. A hundred emails later, I think we got it." Her reaction made all the effort to get it right worthwhile.

She continued to stare at the ring, moving it this way and that to catch the light from the candles and the tree. And as she studied it, her smiled dimmed ever so slightly, enough that he noticed.

"What's wrong?"

"How could anything be wrong?"

"Daisy, I know you well enough by now to know when something is troubling you. Please just tell me what it is."

"You'll think I'm silly."

"Never."

She looked up at him shyly. "I worry that you spent too much money."

Knowing how frugal she'd had to be in her old life, he'd expected her to feel that way. "If I'd spent ten times more, it still wouldn't have been enough."

"Yes, it would!"

"No, it wouldn't. I don't want you to worry about money anymore. I make a very nice living, and so do you. We've worked hard and have earned the right to have nice things and enjoy life. It made me happy to buy this ring for you. It's the ring I wanted you to have."

"It's incredible, David," she whispered. "I can't stop looking at it."

"I'm glad you like it."

"I love it." She looked up at him with big eyes gone liquid with emotion. "I'll never forget this night. Not ever."

He moved back onto the sofa and took her into his arms, kissing her. "And we haven't even begun to celebrate. How about some champagne?"

"I'd love some—after you kiss me some more."

"I can do that," he said, thrilled to have the rest of his life to kiss her and love her and have everything with her.

CHAPTER 14

$\mathcal{N}$ ext door at the Jameses' house, Quinn's four-month-old puppy, Brutus, had the full attention of three adults, all of whom were on the floor playing with him. He was a mixed breed of some sort, with floppy ears and huge feet that he constantly tripped over. Expecting him to be a big dog, Quinn had given him what he called a "man's" name.

"He's adorable," Lizzie declared as she tugged one end of a rope while Brutus pulled from the other end.

"He thinks he's so fierce," Quinn said, amused by everything Brutus did, which Lizzie took as a positive sign that her brother-in-law was coming out of the fog he'd been in since his last deployment overseas. Something had happened over there. Something he didn't talk about to anyone, even Jared.

After asking his family to give him time and space to deal with some things, he'd fallen off the radar for months. He hadn't said what he was dealing with or where he'd been, and they hadn't asked. The one thing Jared had asked of her before Quinn arrived to spend Christmas with them was not to ask him about where he'd been or what he'd been doing.

That wasn't easy for someone who was curious by nature, but

she'd respected Jared's wishes. Besides, she wanted Quinn to love it here so much that he'd accept their offer to run their health care facility. Now that they were nearly finished with the addition to the O'Gradys' home, Mac McCarthy, his cousins, Riley, Finn and Shane, as well as Luke Harris, would begin gutting the interior of the former school building in January.

They had promised to have the construction finished by June, which would give her and the team she planned to hire over the summer time to furnish and equip the facility with everything they'd need to begin accepting patients in September. The best news of all? They already had a waiting list of people interested, either on behalf of themselves or an elderly family member.

The one thing they didn't have yet was a medical director, and that was where Quinn came into play.

"Did you have a good time today?" Lizzie asked him.

"I did. They're a fun group of people."

"We do have a good time around here," Lizzie said, encouraged to hear he'd enjoyed the day. "There's always something going on, even in the winter."

Worn out from playing, Brutus curled up in Quinn's lap and started snoring a minute later.

Quinn stroked the dog's soft fur. "Do you ever feel confined or cooped up or... I don't know, *crazy*, being stuck here? Especially after living in the city for as long as you both did."

Lizzie glanced at Jared, who nodded at her to go ahead and reply. "I love it here. I love everything about it, from the natural beauty of the island, to the work we're doing at the Chesterfield and now with the health care facility, to the people. I've made some of the best friends I've ever had here. Does it get quiet? Sometimes, but I've found the quiet allows me time to breathe in a way that I never could in the city. Life there was always frantic and fast-paced. It's a slower life here, to be sure, but no less satisfying."

"I agree," Jared said. "It's a totally different life than we had in the city, but that's a good thing. I don't know how much longer I could've kept up that pace and not had some sort of breakdown."

Lizzie was surprised to hear him admit that.

"We're still working almost as hard as we used to," Jared continued, "but our downtime is more relaxed here. It works for us." Smiling, he took Lizzie's hand and gave it a squeeze.

"And being hot and heavy newlyweds has nothing to do with the contentment?" Quinn asked with a sardonic grin.

"Of course it does," Jared said. "That's the best part. But it's not the only thing we love about being here."

"There's something special about this island and the people who live here," Lizzie said. "I've never felt so instantly at home anywhere else I've lived since I left my parents' home."

"I can see why," Quinn said. "I really liked your friends and how easily they accepted me into the group."

"And that's only one small fraction of our island tribe," Jared said. "Wait until you meet the McCarthy family and the rest of our friends."

"I'll admit to being tempted to take you up on your generous offer," Quinn said.

Lizzie held her breath, waiting to hear what else he would say.

"I do have a few stipulations."

"Name them," Jared said, speaking for both of them.

"*If* I take the job, the business end would be all yours, but the medical part would be all mine. I hire, I fire, I set policy and oversee everything having to do with patient care."

"Done," Jared and Lizzie said at the same time.

"That was easy," Quinn said, laughing.

"We need you to do all of that because we haven't the first clue," Lizzie said.

"The offer appeals to me because someone else would deal with the insurance companies, the licensing, the state—all the crap that doctors hate—and I'd get to be part of it from the beginning. I like that."

"We're currently recruiting for an administrator," Lizzie said.

"And when you hire that person, you'd tell him or her that I'm in charge of the medical end?"

"Absolutely," she said. "We'd make that crystal clear."

"The one thing we haven't talked about is your salary," Jared said. "I hope you know you can name your price. My wife has her heart set on having you on the team, and I like to make her happy."

"That's very generous," Quinn said. "Thank you both for the vote of confidence. If nothing else, your interest in me for this has been good for my ego."

After a long pause, during which Lizzie had to hold her tongue to keep from trying to hard-sell him, he said, "Brutus and I could use a change of pace. We'll give it a whirl."

"Yes!" Lizzie cried, loud enough to wake the sleeping puppy, who came to barking and growling.

"Easy, boy," Quinn said, patting his head. "Auntie Lizzie gets a little excited."

"She loves nothing more than when one of her plans comes together," Jared said, sending her a warm smile.

Lizzie could tell he was every bit as thrilled as she was that Quinn would be coming to the island. "You can stay with us for as long as you need to," she said. "We've got plenty of room."

"You guys don't need me underfoot. I'll find my own place."

"You can stay in the caretaker's suite at the Chesterfield," Jared said of the estate they owned and operated as a wedding venue. "That'd be perfect."

"How soon do you want me here?"

"Um, last week?" Lizzie said.

"I'll need a week or two to get my shit together, but it won't take long. And then I'm all yours."

Lizzie rubbed her hands together gleefully.

"Why do I feel like I've made a deal with the devil?" Quinn asked, amused by her reaction.

"You have no idea, bro," Jared said with a long-suffering sigh even as he looked at her with love and affection. "No idea at all."

A MADHOUSE GREETED SLIM AND ERIN WHEN THEY ARRIVED AT THE

McCarthy home, which was filled with family members and friends. Thomas McCarthy and his cousin Ashleigh Sturgil chased each other through the house, their faces flushed with Christmas excitement. The house smelled of evergreen and spices, and a fire cast a warm glow over the big room full of people.

"Welcome to Bedlam," Evan said as he took their coats and offered them drinks.

Slim asked for a beer, and Erin said she was good for now.

"Sorry about the insanity," Evan said, handing the cold bottle to Slim. "This family gets bigger every year."

"From the looks of things, it's been a good day," Slim said.

"It's been fun. So did Jenny burn dinner?"

"Not even close," Erin said.

"Alex said she's had a few challenges with the new stove."

"Did he tell you that he has, too?" Erin asked.

Evan laughed. "Somehow he left that part out."

"I can't wait to tell her that."

"You didn't hear it from me."

They were welcomed into the boisterous group with hugs and kisses from Big Mac and Linda, and were drawn into a conversation about Adam and Abby's New Year's Eve wedding. Plans were being made for impromptu bachelor and bachelorette parties three days before the wedding.

"Gentlemen," Mac said in a grave tone, "this is our chance for revenge."

"What're you spouting off about now, Mac?" Janey asked her brother as she patted the back of baby PJ, who was asleep in her arms.

"The *prank*," Mac said. "The time for revenge is upon us. It may not happen this week or even before Evan's wedding, but you ladies need to be on guard against the power of our revenge."

"Does he believe half the crap that comes out of his own mouth?" Tiffany asked her sister.

"The sad part is, I think he does," Maddie replied wearily, drawing laughs from Mac's family.

"I'm with Mac," Tiffany's husband, Blaine, said. "You all need to be punished for leading us to believe you'd hired male strippers for Jenny's bachelorette party."

"I agree," Grant McCarthy said.

"Me, too," Evan and Adam said together.

"Boys, boys, *boys*," Big Mac said to his sons. "The first rule of combat is you don't *tell* the enemy you're coming. Haven't I taught you *anything?*"

"My brother is right," Frank McCarthy said from his perch on the floor in front of a huge Christmas tree. His girlfriend, Betsy, was seated next to him. "Why're you tipping your hand, Mac?"

"Well," Mac said, "we do love them *most of the time*, except when they're lying to our faces about strippers. We wouldn't want them to be unprepared for our revenge."

"I don't know about the rest of you ladies, but I'm not particularly scared of this so-called revenge," Laura said.

"Me either," Janey said as the others nodded in agreement.

"Do your worst," Grace said, smiling at Evan.

"And don't you dare do anything to ruin my wedding," Abby said, "or I will have to kill you."

"I'd help you," Maddie said.

Laughing, Mac held up his hands to fend them off. "I hear ya."

"Nothing is going to ruin our wedding, babe," Adam assured her. "Not even my brother and his thirst for revenge."

"Has love made you soft, Adam?" Mac asked. "You don't think they deserve a taste of their own medicine?"

"No, I definitely think they do, but *not* at my wedding."

"And not at mine," Evan said.

"We'll have a captive audience for *days* in Anguilla," Mac said to Blaine and Joe, who nodded in agreement.

"You boys are heading for trouble," Linda said, leaning against Big Mac. "Mark my words."

"They never have known when to quit while they're ahead," Janey said, earning snorts of outrage from her brothers.

"I'm just watching and learning," Finn said.

"That's your first mistake," Linda said.

Enjoying their banter, Slim put an arm around Erin and gave her shoulder a squeeze. She smiled at him, and he was happy to see her enjoying herself.

"Joe," Big Mac said, "how're your mom and Seamus holding up today?"

"They're exhausted," Joe said of his mother and her husband, who'd recently taken in two young boys after their mother's tragic death. "We were there for dinner, and the boys were so excited, running around screaming, playing with their new toys and having the best time. Mom and Seamus went all-out to make sure it was a great holiday for them, but she said to give you their regrets. They were turning in early tonight."

"I'm so glad to hear the boys got through the holiday and had a good time," Linda said.

"They're doing great," Janey said. "A few rough moments here and there, but overall, they're coping as well as can be expected."

A shriek from the stairs preceded Thomas and Ashleigh running through the crowd, butt naked.

"What the heck are you doing?" Mac asked his son.

"We playing naked boy-naked girl, Dada."

While everyone else howled with laughter, a horrified Maddie grabbed her son while Tiffany corralled Ashleigh.

"I'm not getting to play naked boy-naked girl," Mac grumbled. "Why should they get to?"

"Shut *up*, Mac," Maddie said, blushing as she took Thomas upstairs to find his clothes.

"That's officially my new pickup line," Grant said to Stephanie. "Hey, baby, wanna play naked boy-naked girl?"

"Is that just for me, or will any girl do?"

"Only you, my love," he said, smiling as he leaned in to kiss his wife.

"This is Mallory's first Christmas with us," Linda said. "We're going to scare her off."

"Not a chance," Mallory said, wiping laughter tears from her eyes. "That was the funniest thing I've ever seen."

"I'm *mortified*," Maddie said when she returned with Thomas, who was now dressed in pajamas.

Mac reached for his son and took him from Maddie. "That won't be the first time a woman leads you astray, son."

"*Hey*," Blaine said. "There's *no way* that was Ashleigh's idea."

"I'm afraid it was," Tiffany said, chagrinned as she returned with her daughter.

"God, she's more like her mother than I feared," Blaine said, earning himself a smack upside the head from his wife while the rest of the room lost it laughing again.

"Ashleigh doesn't have a pee-pee, Dada," Thomas said.

"*Oh my God!*" Maddie took Thomas from Mac and headed for the front door while everyone else screamed with laughter. "Time to go home!"

"Yay, cuz I wanna play naked boy-naked girl," Mac said, flashing a giddy grin.

"Does anyone have a muzzle I could borrow?" Maddie called from the foyer.

"If we had one," Janey said, "we never would've taken it off him."

"Have your laughs, citizens," Mac said, taking the sleeping Hailey from his mother, "but when I get home, I'm having mine. I've been cock-blocked for *days* thanks to sick kids, who are apparently feeling *just fine* now."

"Did he just say cock-blocked in front of Mom?" Grant asked.

"Yep," Adam said, "and now you have, too."

"Where did you guys find Mac anyway?" Frank asked Big Mac and Linda after Mac and his family had departed.

"At a baby flea market," Linda said. "We've been trying to make him civilized ever since."

Big Mac's best friend Ned Saunders laughed at that. "Still got a long way ta go." He and his wife, Francine, were holding hands like the newlyweds they were.

"I'm never having kids," Riley said.

"You say that now, son," Kevin said, "but it'll happen to you."

Riley grimaced at the thought. "Not any time soon, please."

"I think it's time to get our little temptress home to bed," Tiffany said, standing to leave.

"I'm locking her up until she's thirty," Blaine muttered to more laughter.

"Thank you for a lovely day, Mac and Linda," Tiffany said, kissing them on the way out.

"Thank you for the best laugh I've had all year," Big Mac said.

"I'm *dying*," Tiffany groaned on the way out. "If this is three, what will eighteen look like?"

"I need to start drinking more," Blaine said.

"I haven't laughed that hard in years," Erin said to Slim when things quieted down again. "That was awesome."

"I don't know what was the best part—the reaction of their parents, or Thomas saying Ashleigh doesn't have a pee-pee."

"Don't even," Erin said, laughing again. "I can't take anymore."

"This is what Tiffany gets for opening a store called Naughty & Nice," Slim said.

"A store the men in this town *love*, by all accounts."

"I heard Tiffany say she had the biggest month since her opening ahead of Christmas."

"Good for her. I love that store."

Speaking close to her ear, he said, "Is that right?"

"Uh-huh."

"I'm going to need you to model some of your Christmas presents for me."

"That could be arranged."

The promise he heard in her softly spoken words traveled right to his cock, making him instantly hard. "Let's go. Right now."

"Relax, stallion. It'll keep until later."

"I won't survive that long in this condition you've put me in."

She glanced over at his lap, which was all it took to make his situation even worse.

"Knock it off," he said in a low growl.

She smiled at him, and the most incredible sense of rightness overcame him, leaving him staggered by the realization that he wanted much more than this week with her. He wanted everything with her, and he'd never wanted that with anyone else.

"What?" she asked, her brows knitting with concern.

He forced himself to rally. "Nothing. Just looking forward to having you all to myself again later."

Erin leaned her head on his shoulder and linked her fingers with his, deepening the feeling of rightness.

Before this, before her, he might've tried to disengage from something that smacked of seriousness. But with her, the last thing he wanted was to disengage. He wanted more, much, much more of her.

Talk turned to Evan and Grace's upcoming wedding in Anguilla, travel plans and excitement to escape winter on the island for a week.

"Speaking of our wedding," Evan said, glancing at Grace, who smiled at him. "Gracie and I have a little news about what's going to happen after the wedding." Taking hold of her hand, he said, "Buddy has talked me into riding the hit record for a while longer, and Grace is coming with me on the road. Her friend Fiona from school has agreed to come over to manage the pharmacy, and Josh will cover me at the studio."

After a moment of stunned silence, everyone spoke at once, congratulating them on their news and firing off questions about where they were going.

"We're joining the second half of Buddy's current North American tour that starts up again in February, and then we'll see what happens after that."

"I'm happy for you, son," Big Mac said. "As much as we'll miss you both here, I'd hate for you to have regrets later about what might've been."

"Thank you, Dad. That's what my very wise future wife said, too."

"I suppose I should mention that after Anguilla, Steph and I are heading to LA for a couple of months," Grant said.

"Was it something we said?" Linda asked her husband.

"Ha-ha, Mom," Grant said. "I've got some work to do with the company that's producing the film about Charlie and Stephanie's story, and it's easier for me to be there for a while. Since the restaurant is shut down for the rest of the winter after this week, Steph's coming with me."

"Dan and Kara are going to be out there, too, aren't they?" Joe asked.

"They are, and we're looking forward to hanging out with them."

"You'll be back for the summer, though, right?" Adam asked.

"Wouldn't miss summer on Gansett for anything," Grant said, "and my lovely wife has a booming business to tend to."

"That's right," Laura said. "I need you to feed my hotel guests."

"I'm on it," Steph said, "don't worry. I'm just sorry we won't be here when the twins are born."

"We'll send pictures," Owen assured her. "I can't wait to meet these two little people."

"I can't believe you guys aren't finding out what you're having," Laura's brother, Shane, said. "I'd be out of my mind with curiosity. Hell, I'm out of my mind with curiosity about *your* babies, let alone my own."

"We can't wait to know either," Owen said, gazing at Laura, "but we want it to be a surprise."

"Who knows what's going on with Syd?" Abby asked. "They've been sticking close to home this week."

"I heard she had a little scare with the baby," Linda said, "but all is well."

"Thank God," Janey said to agreement from everyone else. "While we're sharing news, I probably ought to let the rest of you know that Joseph has knocked me up again."

Her announcement was met with dead silence.

"I know what you're all thinking, and believe me, we're thinking the same thing. We've got an appointment with a specialist in Providence after the holidays, and we're going to do everything we can to make sure baby number two's arrival is far less dramatic than his or her brother's was."

"Janey," Grant said, his expression agonized, "are you sure about this?"

"No," Joe said, answering for both of them, "we're not sure of anything other than we're going to hope for the very best and thoroughly prepare for every possible scenario. I'm going to see to it personally, Grant. You have my word on that."

The brothers who so loved to razz their sister had gone silent at the thought of the kind of danger she'd faced when PJ was born.

"If I may," Mallory said, and all eyes turned to her. "What happened to Janey when she had PJ is extremely rare. There's no reason to believe she can't have a perfectly normal pregnancy and delivery this time."

"That's very reassuring, Mallory," Big Mac said to his daughter. "Thank you."

"She's right," Katie Lawry said. Shane's fiancée was also a nurse. "But you're going to need to be very careful about doing anything too strenuous or lifting PJ in the last trimester."

"If I have my way," Joe said, "she'll be on full bed rest by then."

Janey's expression told them what she thought of that.

"We're going to be overrun with babies around here before long," Frank said.

Abby got up and went into the kitchen. Adam went after her.

"Is she okay?" Kevin asked.

With her gaze fixed on the kitchen door through which Adam and Abby had disappeared, Linda said, "They got some news before the anniversary party. They're both fine, but they're facing a difficult challenge."

Everyone pounced on Linda for more information, but she held them off with her hands in the air. "It's not my news to tell. You'll hear it from them when they're ready."

The boisterous group fell silent when Adam and Abby returned, holding hands as they came into the room.

"Abby," Laura said. "Are you all right?"

Abby glanced at Adam, who nodded in encouragement. "Not as all right as I'd like to be," Abby said, her eyes glistening with unshed tears. "We recently learned that I have polycystic ovarian syndrome or PCOS, which comes with a variety of health complications, including fertility issues."

"We're going to fight it, though," Adam said. "There's a lot we can do, and we're going to do all of it. If we can't have a baby on our own, we'll adopt. But we *will* have a family."

Stephanie left her perch on Grant's lap to hug Abby. "I'm so sorry to hear this, but if anyone is tough enough to fight it, you are."

"I don't know about that," Abby said. "I've been a basket case ever since we got the news."

"Stay off the Internet," Mallory said. "Every situation is unique, and you don't want to scare yourself with too much information."

Adam nodded in agreement. "That's what I said, too."

"The one thing I want to say," Abby said, seeming to marshal her defenses, "is I don't want any of you to feel you can't be excited about your babies in front of me. I can't wait to meet all of them and to love them and spoil them. Please... Don't let our challenges take away from your joy. Adam and I would hate that."

Janey stood to hug Abby. "Love you. That's all I want to say."

"Love you, too."

Erin leaned in to speak to Slim. "We ought to go. This is kind of a private family thing."

"Sure, sweetheart. We've got important private business of our own to see to anyway."

She rolled her eyes at him, but her face lit up with the blush he loved so much. He couldn't wait to see more of that blush when he got her back to the lighthouse.

CHAPTER 15

"Why do you have to announce to our entire family that you're cock-blocked?" Maddie asked when she came into the bedroom after getting Thomas down for the night.

Hailey had gone much easier, which was why Mac beat her to bed.

"Because I am, in fact, cock-blocked by kids lately."

"They've been *sick*, Mac."

"They're not sick now," he said, waggling his brows suggestively.

"All I want is eight straight hours of sleep."

"You're kidding me, right?"

"No, I'm not kidding you. This has been a hellacious week between sickness and Christmas preparations, I could sleep for a week. In fact, I might sleep all day tomorrow and let you handle things around here."

"I'd do that for you."

Her gorgeous caramel eyes lit up with surprise. "You would?"

"Of course I would. If…"

Hands on hips, she gave him a challenging look. "If what?"

"If you help me out with this tiny little issue I seem to have."

"What tiny little issue do you have?"

"A hard-on that won't quit."

"Are pigs flying in hell? Are you actually referring to your precious manhood as *tiny* and *little*?"

"Don't be ridiculous. Of course I'm not. My problem is little and tiny. As we both know, my manhood is massive. Now will you please get in this bed and give me the only present I really want for Christmas?"

"So I can send back that new power tool you were so excited about?"

"Absolutely not. You can come and tend to the power tool that gets *you* excited."

"Honestly, Mac," she said with a huff of laughter. "You get more outrageous with every passing day."

"You love me."

"You're very lucky that I do."

"Yes, I am. Now get over here and let me show you how lucky I am to be loved by you."

"I need to change and get the food out of my hair that Hailey put there during dinner."

"You don't need to do a damned thing besides get naked."

"Five minutes, Mac. Give me *five* minutes."

She went into the bathroom, and he dropped to the pillows, resigned to having to wait five more interminable minutes. A crackle of life from the baby monitor in Hailey's room had him holding his breath. *Please, no... Not tonight, sweet girl. Give Mommy and Daddy a break. Please...*

Thankfully, there were no more noises from the monitor, and Mac began to relax. Then Maddie emerged from the bathroom wearing one of the new sexy nightgowns he'd bought her for Christmas at Tiffany's shop. Her hair had been brushed into shiny submission and fell to below her shoulders.

Game on. Hello, sexy wife.

"Wait," he said, sitting up on his knees for a better look at the pale pink gown with the black lace accents that did spectacular things for her spectacular breasts.

"What am I waiting for? I thought you were in a huge rush."

"I am, but I want to memorize the way you look right now so I never forget it."

"Just when I think I've actually married a teenage boy, you surprise me."

He held out a hand to bring her onto the bed with him.

She met him on her knees in front of him, her hands on his shoulders.

"I may joke around a little—"

"*A little?*"

"Okay, a lot, but one thing I'd never joke about is how stunningly beautiful you are. You take my breath away, Madeline, and I love you more than I can ever tell you."

"Sometimes, especially on days like today, I can't believe that this is my life now. You and our kids and this house and your family and mine, all together. It's like a dream."

"Even the naked boy-naked girl part?"

Groaning, she dropped her head to his shoulder. "We'll still be talking about that when they're in college."

"We'll be talking about that forever. And PS, it's like a dream for me, too. I never imagined anything for myself like what we've found together, and that we get to share our lives with the people we love the most... We're truly blessed."

"Yes, we are," she said, rubbing shamelessly against him.

He rested his hand on the small curve of her belly over the baby no one else knew they were expecting. "If you're too tired tonight, I'll understand."

She glanced up at him, seeming relieved. "You will?"

Mac wanted to shoot himself for saying that. "Of course I will. If you don't want to, we don't have to."

"Oh thank God. I'm exhausted." She withdrew from him and sacked out on her side after positioning her pillow where she wanted it.

With his cock hard enough to pound nails, he suppressed a groan and got under the covers, shutting off the light. He lay there trying not to think about the throbbing coming from his lap when he realized the bed was shaking. What the hell?

He turned the light back on to realize the shaking was coming from his wife, who was laughing her ass off. *"What are you laughing at?"*

"I can't believe you fell for that so easily. You're losing your touch, Mac."

"Are you fucking kidding me? You *faked* being tired?"

"I am tired, but not *that* tired."

"That was so mean! I'm hard as a rock, and you leave me hanging." She laughed so hard, tears fell from her eyes.

"You're really racking up the demerits lately, Mrs. McCarthy. First the evil prank you perpetrated against me and my boys, and now this."

"I'm very sorry," she said, wiping the tears from her face. "Let me make it up to you."

"I don't know if I want you to."

She wrapped her hand around his erection and gave it a squeeze that made him see stars. "Really?"

"Okay, I want you to."

"Thought so." She left a trail of kisses from his chest to his belly as she continued to stroke him.

Mac ran his fingers through her hair, watching her and loving her, even when she was mean to him.

Maddie swirled her tongue around the tip of his cock. "Am I forgiven?"

"I haven't decided yet. All depends on how things go in the next few minutes."

Smiling, she drew him into the heat of her mouth and nearly finished him off with the perfect combination of tongue and suction.

"Getting closer to forgiveness," he said through gritted teeth. His hips surged off the mattress, and she took him deeper, until he nudged against the back of her throat and still she didn't back off. "Maddie... Fuck... *Baby*." God, he was going to come in her mouth if she didn't stop right now.

A sharp cry from the next room made them freeze.

"Mama." Thomas. And he was crying. *No. Just no.*

Maddie's lips slid over his shaft as she withdrew, leaving him with a look of sincere regret. The sight of her silk-covered ass as she left the room did nothing to ease the ache.

"*Fuck*," he muttered to an empty room.

THIS HAD BEEN, ERIN DECIDED, THE NICEST CHRISTMAS SHE'D HAD IN years. Other than the emotional blip at Jenny's house, she'd gotten through a day that had been difficult for her in other years. Much of the day's success was due to the man who was now driving her home.

He'd been quiet since they left the McCarthys', and Erin wanted to know what he was thinking. But she didn't ask. She wanted to thank him again for being such a rock for her when she was spinning earlier. She wanted to tell him how, in the past, an episode like that could've ruined her for days, but because of him, that wouldn't happen this time.

There were so many things she'd like to tell him, but she wasn't sure he was ready to hear them. They were in the odd position of having been close friends for months but romantic partners for only a few days. It would be easy—too easy—to press the accelerator on the new romantic portion of their relationship in light of the many hours they'd already spent together, talking, laughing, flirting, sharing confidences.

When the silence became weighty, she decided to ask what he was thinking about.

"Naked boy-naked girl," he said with a sly grin.

"How funny was that?"

"Funniest thing I've ever seen, but I wasn't thinking about the kids. I was thinking about you. And me."

Was it warm in here, or was it her? "How many McCarthy men do you suppose are using that line on their women tonight?"

"I suspect all of them. It's an instant classic. Have I mentioned how incredibly hot you look in that skirt?"

"Um, no, I don't think you have." It was definitely getting warmer in the small cab of his truck.

"Major oversight on my part. All day today, I've been wondering what you've got on under there."

"Will you be disappointed to find plain old white cotton?"

"Absolutely not. Nothing about you has disappointed me."

Would he be disappointed to learn that she would never want to fly with him? That thought threatened to ruin the nice warm buzz she had building thanks to his shameless flirting, so she pushed it aside for another time.

He reached over to run his hand up her leg, under her skirt, stopping at the top of her thigh, which he gave a gentle squeeze that ignited her desire. That he could make her feel so much by barely touching her was remarkable and unprecedented. For a long time after she and Mitch broke up, she'd wondered if she'd made a terrible mistake by letting that relationship go. In just a few days, Slim had shown her what'd been missing with Mitch.

By the time he pulled into the driveway at the lighthouse, he had her on the verge of explosion, and he still hadn't done anything more than touch her leg. When he got out to deal with the gate, she shivered from the cold as much as the loss of his warm palm on her thigh.

He drove the truck through the gate and then got out again to close and lock it.

She was practically vibrating in her seat as they pulled up to the door. He cut the engine and the lights, casting them into inky darkness that would last until the motion-sensitive lights came on.

"Stay put," he said gruffly.

Erin's heart beat so fast with anticipation and excitement that she couldn't seem to draw air into her lungs. The door opened, and he reached across her to unbuckle the seat belt she'd been too flummoxed to do herself. His arm brushed against her nipple, and she gasped.

She expected him to back away and let her out of the truck, but instead, he lifted her right into his arms. Her legs encircled his waist and her arms wrapped around his neck as his lips found hers in a hungry, desperate kiss. While she was lost in the hottest kiss of her life, he somehow got them inside. He kicked the door closed and pressed her against the mudroom wall, his cock rigid against her core as the kiss went from desperate to wild.

Erin buried her fingers in his hair, keeping him anchored to her. Then he surprised her by softening the kiss before breaking it to turn his attention to her neck. His hands were everywhere, under her coat, cupping and squeezing her breasts, then under her skirt, his fingers finding her clit.

She cried out from the pleasure that shot through her system like a shock wave. "Upstairs," she somehow managed to say.

"Here. Right here." He put her down only long enough to toss both their coats to the floor, pull her tights and underwear down her legs and free himself from his pants and roll on a condom. "Now." His desperation seemed to match hers as he lifted her again, bringing her down slowly onto his rigid length. "*Yes*," he whispered fiercely.

As her body stretched to accommodate him, she held on tight, half afraid he would drop her but knowing in her heart of hearts that he never would. She was safe with him. That much she knew for certain.

"God," he said, his lips close to her ear. "You're so hot and tight. You make me crazy."

She wanted to tell him he made her just as crazy, but the words were lost in a deep thrust that triggered her orgasm.

His fingers dug into the dense flesh of her ass as he hammered into her, riding the wave of her climax into his own.

"Christ," he uttered between deep breaths. His forehead dropped to lean against hers, the heat of his skin warming her from the inside. "What just happened?"

Erin laughed at his befuddled tone. "I think we had mudroom sex."

"Hottest mudroom sex I've ever had."

"Me, too." She stroked the sweaty hair off his forehead. "How about we take this somewhere more comfortable?"

"Mmm, as soon as I'm sure my legs still work, we'll do that."

Smiling, Erin stroked his hair while he continued to breathe like he'd just run a marathon. A feeling of profound contentment and peace came over her, making her wish for things she'd thought weren't going to happen for her. Now she wasn't so sure. She wasn't sure of anything other than how he cut through the numbness that had been so much a part of her and made her *feel*.

He took a deep breath and released it before withdrawing from her and setting her gently on her feet, holding her until she got her bearings. Tugging her tights and underwear over her knees, she followed him up two flights of stairs to her bedroom. Only then did he drop his hold on her hand so she could sit on the bed to remove her boots.

Her body continued to quake and tingle with aftershocks from the hottest sex of her life.

After ducking into the bathroom to deal with the condom and removing his sweater, Slim sat next to her on the bed, putting his arm around her. "I was rough with you. Are you okay?"

"You really have to ask?"

"Yeah, I do. I don't know what came over me—"

She rested her finger on his lips. "Please don't apologize. It was incredible. I've never done anything even remotely like that, and if you apologize, you'll ruin it."

His lips curved into a smile, and he nibbled on her finger. "We can't have that, now can we?"

Erin shook her head and withdrew her finger, her eyes closing as he kissed her so softly, so tenderly that her body trembled anew. That he gave her both wild passion and abiding tenderness within the scope of ten minutes was almost too much to process. Laying her hand flat against his cheek, she pulled back from the kiss. "Give me one minute."

"Take all the time you need."

Her legs were wobbly when she walked into the bathroom, closing the door behind her and leaning against it to catch her breath. Images from the mudroom played through her mind like an erotic movie. She already knew that no matter what happened next, she'd never forget it.

Erin cleaned up and changed into one of the sexy nightgowns he'd bought her at Tiffany's. She brushed her hair and teeth, examining her reflection in the mirror, noting the razor burn on her neck and jaw that were stark reminders of what they'd done. Erin's shiver had nothing to do with the cold and everything to do with him.

Emerging from the bathroom, she found him wearing only his boxers, sitting on the edge of the bed, checking his phone. He looked up at her, his gaze heating at the sight of her in the nightgown. Standing, he tossed the phone on the bed and came to her, his hands warm upon her shoulders, his expression hungry despite the intense sex they'd already had.

"I'll be quick," he said, stepping around her to go into the bathroom.

Erin released a deep breath and got into bed, turning to look at the picture of her brother on the bedside table and trying to remember the last time she'd felt as elated as she did now.

A memory came to her, sharp and vivid, as if it had happened yesterday rather than almost fifteen years ago. She recalled a warm summer weekend at the beach in East Hampton about a month before Toby died. She and Mitch and Toby and Jenny had pooled their resources to rent a small two-bedroom house for a weekend that had been full of love and laughter and promises of a happily ever after that hadn't materialized for either couple.

They'd been so excited for Jenny and Toby's wedding in two short months, and even though it had ended with a disagreement between her and her brother, that weekend was the last time she remembered feeling the way she did right now—happy and hopeful, with every possibility still open to her. Everything had changed a few weeks later, and her life had never been the same. She'd been spinning, as if caught up in a riptide that she'd been fighting ever since. Only recently had the spinning stopped, and Slim was the reason.

He came out of the bathroom looking sexier than any man had a right to at nearly forty. His chest and abs were ripped with muscles and covered in a light dusting of dark hair, his jaw chiseled with just the right amount of scruff and his eyes... He looked at her with such affection and desire. A man who looked at a woman that way could convince her to change her life for him.

After he got in bed, the heat of his body drew her to him, and he wrapped her up in his arms.

"Thank you for an amazing Christmas," he said. "And for the painting of the lighthouse. I'll find a very special place for that in my Florida house."

"I thought you might like a memento of your stay here."

"I'll never forget staying here or being with you this Christmas."

"I love my new necklace, too." She touched the sterling silver sand dollar to make sure it was still there.

"Glad you like it. Looks as good on you as does that nightgown."

She looked up at his handsome face. "Tell me something about you that I don't know."

CHAPTER 16

$\mathcal{E}$rin wasn't sure where the inquiry had come from. All she knew was that she wanted more of him—and not just sex, although more of that would be fine with her, too.

"Like a deep, dark secret?"

"Do you *have* a deep, dark secret?"

After a long pause, he said, "There is one thing that no one knows, not even my family."

"You don't have to tell me if it's too personal."

"It's very personal, and I've honestly never told anyone. But I want to tell you."

Intrigued and insanely curious, she propped her chin on his chest so she could see his face.

"My high school girlfriend got pregnant."

His grim expression made Erin sorry she'd asked.

"We were juniors. She was my first, and I was hers. We were crazy about each other until she realized she was pregnant. It all went to shit after that, to put it mildly."

"Did she blame you?"

"She never actually said that, but I blamed myself enough for both of us. We did it once without protection, and I thought I'd pulled out in time… I've never had unprotected sex again." He sighed. "It's hard to talk about even all these years later."

"You don't have to. I'm sorry. I never meant—"

He cupped her cheek and stroked her face with his thumb. "It's okay, Erin. I wouldn't have told you if I didn't want to."

"What did you do about the baby?"

"I left it completely up to her. I told her I'd support any decision she made, including keeping the baby. After a torturous month, she decided to end the pregnancy."

"How did you feel about that?"

"If I'm being totally honest, I was relieved. We were so young, and the thought of a baby was… It was the most overwhelming thing I could imagine at that time. I gave her the money I'd saved from cutting grass the summer before, and I went with her to the clinic. It was horrible and heartbreaking. I thought she was never going to stop crying."

Erin's eyes filled with tears. "I'm so sorry you went through such a traumatic thing when you were so young. Your parents really didn't know?"

He shook his head. "We went to tremendous lengths to make sure no one would ever know. I didn't want her to be the talk of our school, so I insisted we tell no one. Somehow we managed to get through it without anyone knowing. Afterward, we tried to get back to normal, but our normal had been permanently altered. We broke up a couple of months later, which was a second round of heartbreak." Even as he stroked her hair, he seemed a million miles away. "I think about the baby and who he or she might've been. It's hard to believe he or she would be twenty-four now, a fully grown adult, maybe a college graduate."

Hoping to hide her emotional response to his heartfelt words, she closed her eyes and kissed his chest.

"You know what's funny? When you're sixteen, you think you'll grow up and get married and have kids and everything will unfold in a certain expected order. But then life happens and nothing goes as planned, and you wake up at nearly forty and realize you never again came close to being a father."

"It's not too late, especially for guys. Look at Tony Randall, who became a dad at seventy something."

Slim grunted out a laugh. "Yeah, no thanks on that."

"Still, it could happen."

Smiling, he let her hair slide through his fingers. "I told you mine," he said with a teasing glint in his eye that let her know he was okay after sharing his secret pain with her. "Now tell me yours."

Erin knew she was under no obligation to tell him her deepest secret, but after what he'd told her, she didn't feel right giving him anything less. "Mine is also something that no one else knows."

He tilted his head, giving her his undivided attention.

"After Toby died, I… There's just no way I can adequately describe the despair. And the worst part? We had to share our agony with three thousand other families and an entire nation that was changed forever by what happened that day. But for us, for me, it was so intensely personal."

"I didn't know anyone who died that day, but as a pilot and an American, it was one of the most gut-wrenching things I've ever lived through. I can't even begin to know what it was like for people who lost loved ones."

"It was a very dark time. A couple of months later, after the initial shock wore off and the insanity settled somewhat, I began to wonder how I'd ever find my way out of the darkness. Part of me didn't think I had the right to feel that way because look at what my parents had lost and Jenny and all of Toby's friends who saw him far more often the last few years than I did. But as his sister, his twin, his only sibling, I simply didn't know how to *live* without him. I'd never had to."

"Baby," he said softly, wiping away her tears with his thumb.

"I began to make plans to stop the pain."

"Erin… God."

The distress she heard in his voice made her feel safe to continue. "I wasn't thinking clearly. I know that now. But at the time, I couldn't see any other way out. I wanted it to stop. I wrote letters to my parents and Jenny and even one to Toby in which I told him that I couldn't wait to be with him again. I even set the date. For the first time since it happened, I had something to look forward to."

"Come up here." He tugged gently on her arms and arranged her so she was on top of him, his arms wrapped tightly around her. "What stopped you?"

"My parents did, and they don't even know it. They stopped by on their way to brunch, which was something they did every Sunday before. It was their first time going back to the place they always went, and they wanted me to come. They said it would make it easier for them if I went, too. I think they came over rather than calling me the way they normally would so I wouldn't be able to refuse. I found out later they were worried about how withdrawn I'd become. They didn't know that I was dealing with the onset of what became severe obsessive compulsive disorder. I was plagued by worries about my safety and theirs. I would get up thirty or forty times in the course of a night to check to make sure the locks were on, that the windows were closed, that the nightlights were on. I was exhausted from the need to perform these rituals over and over and over again, like a hamster on a wheel. I was afraid *not* to do them, that something else awful would happen if I didn't. It took years of therapy to get me to the point where I only do some of the weird stuff you've probably noticed.

"On that day, only because they asked me to, I took a shower, did my hair, put on some makeup for the first time since the funeral, and I went with them. We saw a lot of people we knew, people who cared so much about us and how we were doing. I remember thinking if my parents could endure this unbearable tragedy, maybe I could, too. And seeing them and the courageous way they were facing their loss made it impossible for me to compound it. By the time I got home, my plan had lost its allure. I've had a lot of really low moments over the years, and I continue to struggle with the OCD at times, but I've never again been that low."

To his credit, he didn't say anything. He only held her and rubbed her back in tiny circles and made her feel loved and protected. Maybe he didn't love her, but his quiet support made her wonder if he did.

Listening to the strong beat of his heart comforted her and made her feel less alone with the grief that had never gone away, even if it had become more manageable.

After a long period of silence, she raised her head off his chest to look at him. "I really know how to ruin a mood, don't I?"

"You didn't ruin anything. You only made me admire you more than I already did."

"I'm not proud of my lack of courage."

His eyes went wide. "Are you *kidding* me? Your courage was—and is—astonishing. It would've been so much easier for you to follow through with your plan. Instead, you thought of what it would do to your parents, and you put them ahead of yourself. You chose to live with nearly unbearable pain. If that's not courage, I don't know what is."

Moved by his emphatic words, she said, "I realized that day the grief is always going to be with me, that my life was permanently changed, and I had to find a way to live with it or it would destroy me."

"I'm so glad you found a way." Holding her face in his hands, he kissed her. "I'm so very glad."

"I am, too. I would've hated to miss out on knowing you."

Kissing her again, he slayed her with the tender way he held her and touched her, as if she was the most precious thing in the world to him. Wouldn't that be something if she were?

"I have other less probing questions," she said, looking to lighten things up again.

"Hit me."

"What's your Chinese order?"

"Kung pao chicken extra spicy. You?"

"Broccoli chicken with fried rice. Your Girl Scout cookie of choice?"

"Are there any others besides Thin Mints?"

"Very good answer. I buy extras and freeze them so I have them all year long."

"I'm incredibly turned on right now."

Erin's laugh became a moan when he gripped her bottom and pressed his erection into her belly to show he meant it. "So Girl Scouts turn you on. Good to know."

"Your year supply of *Thin Mints* turns me on. Get it right."

She giggled at his outrage.

"What else you got?" he asked.

"What do you like on a pizza?"

"Meat. Lots of it. You?"

"I knew you were too good to be true," she said, sighing dramatically. "I'm a veggie girl all the way."

He crinkled up his nose. "I can't work with that. Get off me, and let me out of this bed."

"I can't take care of *that*," she said, moving subtly over his cock, "if I let you out of bed."

"Good point. Please continue."

Laughing, she said, "What's your favorite word?"

"Clean or dirty?"

"Give me one of each."

"Let me think… For clean, I'd say it's *delectable*."

Erin wondered if there was double meaning in his choice. "That's a good one."

"My favorite dirty word is, understandably, pussy."

Erin groaned as she laughed. "Why am I not surprised, and PS, female body parts are not *dirty* words."

"Would you be embarrassed if I used that word in front of your parents? For example, Erin's pussy is delectable."

Shrieking, she covered his mouth with her hand. "Don't you dare do that."

"Wasn't gonna, don't worry," he said, laughing, his words muffled by her hand. "What're your words?" he asked when she removed her hand.

"Moist—clean or dirty—I hate it."

"*Erin's moist pussy is delectable*. See? We were meant to be. Even our words go together."

Her face burned with embarrassment. "I *cannot believe* you just said that." Though she loved hearing he thought they were meant to be.

"Yes, you can," he said, laughing.

"Least favorite punctuation?"

He raised his brows. "You have a favorite and least favorite punctuation?"

"Doesn't everyone? This is a very serious question, so think carefully before you answer."

"I've never been so stressed out." He paused before he said, "My least favorite would have to be the semicolon."

"Oh thank God," she said with a dramatic sigh of relief. "Any other answer would've been flat-out wrong."

He blew out a deep breath with equally dramatic flair. "My relief is overwhelming. And just for the record, what's your favorite?"

"The exclamation point. Isn't that everyone's favorite?"

"Of course it is. Why did I even ask?"

Smiling at his reply, she said, "Cats or dogs?"

"Dogs. Cats creep me out."

"Oh my God! Me, too! Worst job you ever had."

"EMT. Loved the job, hated the suffering we encountered every day. How about you?"

"My foray into hairdressing was very unfortunate for everyone involved."

Laughing, he asked, "What about your best job?"

"The one I have now."

"Being a lighthouse keeper is very cool."

"It is, but that's not the job I'm talking about."

"You have another one?"

"Uh-huh. I write a nationally syndicated advice column called Ask Erin."

His eyes nearly bugged out of his head. "That's *you*? Ask Erin is *you*?"

"Why? Have you seen it?"

"I read it every day. I'm a huge fan."

"Come on. No way."

"I'm not kidding. I love the practical advice and the way you're nice to even the stupid people who deserve their problems because they're too dumb to know that their own behavior is their biggest issue."

Erin stared at him, agape. "You really *do* read the column!"

"Yes," he said with a laugh. "How have you never told me this? I can't believe that's you. I'm sleeping with *Ask Erin*."

"You say that like I'm Judge Judy or something."

"I have a secret crush on her, too. I love smart, sexy women."

His use of the word *love* did crazy things to her insides, resurrecting the lighthearted, giddy feeling she'd experienced earlier. She returned her head to his chest, and he resumed playing with her hair.

"Hey, Slim?"

"Hmm?"

"For a very long time my life has been spinning out of control. When I'm with you, the spinning stops. I thought you should know that."

"That might be the nicest thing anyone has ever said to me."

CHAPTER 17

*P*rofoundly moved by her confession, Slim tightened his arms around her and turned them so he was on top, gazing down at her lovely face. Something had changed in the last hour, and what had been simmering began to boil. He was falling in love with her. Hell, he was probably already done falling.

"What're you thinking?" she asked, looking up at him.

He realized he'd been staring at her while he tried to reconcile his feelings. "I'm thinking about how hard I'm falling for you."

"Oh. You are?"

Nodding, he said, "Is that a bad thing?"

"No, it's good. Very good."

"Am I the only one falling?"

Looking madly vulnerable, she shook her head.

He wanted to take away her pain and sorrow and fill her life with joy. He wanted to always feel the way he did when he was with her, but he had no idea if she felt the same way. They didn't have to decide that now, but the more time he spent with her, the more unbearable the thought of leaving her became.

After the insanity of their earlier coupling, now he wanted to make love to her. He wanted to show her how he felt about her, how essential she was becoming to him. Beginning with soft, openmouthed kisses to her neck and throat, he had her arching into him before he'd even gotten to the really good parts. He loved the way she responded to him and how his heart beat faster every time he got to touch her this way.

Slim tugged on the sexy nightgown, raising a brow to ask if he could remove it.

She nodded, and as if he were opening the best of all Christmas gifts, he unveiled her long limbs and creamy white skin until she was bare before his hungry gaze.

Taking his time, he cupped her breasts and spent long minutes tending to one nipple and then the other, drawing the tight beads into his mouth and using his tongue and teeth to make her moan. God, he loved the sound that seemed to come from the deepest part of her. He could easily become addicted to her moan. Though he wanted to spend hours tending to her gorgeous breasts—and he would do that sometime very soon—he moved down, kissing the quivering skin of her belly, nibbling on her hip bones and squeezing her ass cheeks.

By the time he was positioned between her legs, she was so wet he could see and smell how ready she was for him. The scent of her arousal sent his yearning for her even further into the red zone. He was about to burst from the need to plunge into her, to possess her, to make her his in every way. But he held off, wanting to see to her before he took what he wanted.

With his hands flat against her inner thighs, he could feel the deep trembling in her muscles as he spread her legs farther apart.

He zeroed in on her hands, which were gripping tight handfuls of the comforter, holding on in anticipation of what was to come.

Bending over her, he propped her legs on his shoulders, resulting in yet another of those incredible moans. And when he traced the outline of her outer lips with his tongue, she nearly levitated off the bed. "So wet, so sweet, so hot," he whispered. "Do you want to come, Erin?"

"*Yes*," she whispered, the single word erupting from her in a choppy, nearly incoherent sound.

"Tell me." He glanced up in time to see the panic that crossed her expressive face when she realized he was going to make her say it. "Tell me what you want."

"I-I want to come."

He blew a light stream of air over her sensitive flesh, and the keening sound that came from her made his dick even harder than it already was. "How?" he asked. "How do you want it?" Touching his finger lightly to her clit, he said, "Do you want my finger or my tongue?"

"Can I have both?"

"So greedy," he said with a low chuckle. "I like that. Since you've been a very good girl, Santa will let you have both." She was like a live wire about to snap by the time he touched his tongue to her clit and drove two fingers deep into her. She was fully primed, and he felt the telltale signs of her impending climax so he backed off.

"W-what... *why?*"

"That would've been too easy. What do you say we make this interesting?"

Panting, she said, "What do you say you let me come, and I let you live?"

His bark of laughter earned him a scowl from her. "My lovely lady has some claws under all that sweetness. I had no idea."

"And I'm more than happy to use them if need be," she said with a smug smile. "Now get back to it. I'm getting rather bored."

"Ha-ha, very funny. I'll show you bored." He bit the inside of her thigh, just hard enough to leave a mark and pull a sharp gasp of surprise from her saucy mouth. "Do I have your full attention?"

"Mmm." With her fingers in his hair, she directed him to focus on her core, which he was happy to do.

He sucked hard on her clit, and she came with a screaming cry that was almost enough to finish him off, too.

Somehow he managed to find enough control to roll on another condom, grasp his cock, align it with her liquid center and thrust into her heat. So good. *So fucking good*. His balls were tight and his spine tingled from imminent release. Looking to make it last, he rolled them

MARIE FORCE

over so she was on top of him, her hair covering her face until she gathered it up in a move that put her luscious breasts on display.

Slim reached up to tease her nipples, pinching just tight enough to make her dark eyes go wide with surprise and desire. Not to mention what happened when her internal muscles clamped down on his cock. "Ride me, baby. Make me come."

"Maybe I ought to torture you the way you tortured me."

"Do whatever you want." Slim dropped his hands to the pillow. "I'm all yours." As he said the words, he realized it was absolutely true. He was hers. Watching her move above him, her hair long and wild, her lips swollen from their kisses and her breasts swaying with every movement of her hips, brought him quickly to the edge of release. He tried to hold back, but then she came again, and he couldn't stop the inevitable.

With his hands on her hips to anchor her, he surged into her, their eyes meeting in a moment of perfect unity that he'd never forget.

Exhausted, she fell forward onto his chest, and he wrapped his arms around her, their hearts beating together in an erratic, choppy rhythm that matched their uneven breathing. She pulsed around him, aftershocks rippling through her body and into his.

"I want to be tortured by you more often," he said, drawing a laugh from her.

"I went easy on you."

"I like your brand of easy." He kissed her forehead. "In fact, I like everything about you."

"Everything?"

"Every damned thing."

"Wow, that's a whole lotta like."

"It sure is." After a pause, he said, "I'm still hoping I might convince you to come back to Florida with me on New Year's Day."

"I'd like to. I hope you know that."

"Why do I sense a 'but'?"

"The 'but' has nothing to do with you and everything to do with me."

"What do you mean?"

"I'm starting to feel settled here. I've got friends and a life and responsibilities to the town. Even if they're minor, they're still mine. I've been sort of drifting for a long time, and I finally feel anchored again. I'm not sure I'm ready to give that up yet, even for something as wonderful as what I have with you."

His stomach sank with disappointment, even if he understood what she was saying. "So you're really going to make me wait months to see you again? I can't even convince you to come for a long weekend?"

"I... Sure. Maybe."

"That doesn't sound too convincing, sweetheart."

"I'll definitely try. Is that better?"

"Yeah, sure." He kissed her shoulder and gave her a gentle nudge. "I need to hit the bathroom."

She moved to the side, taking her heat with her and leaving him chilled in more ways than one.

ERIN WATCHED HIS SPECTACULAR NAKED ASS AS HE WENT INTO THE bathroom and shut the door. Sighing, she rolled onto her side and hugged a pillow to her chest. Her refusal to commit to more time together after this week had hurt him, which was the last thing she wanted to do. But how could she tell a man whose passion was flying that she couldn't bear to get on an airplane, even for him?

Maybe it was time to seek professional help about her unreasonable fear of flying. Though all the things she'd told him were true, the flying issue was the primary reason she couldn't commit to a visit—or more. Sure, she could drive to Florida, but the idea of driving more than a thousand miles by herself wasn't all that appealing.

And how would she explain that choice to him when flying would be so much simpler?

You could just tell him you don't fly anymore. He would understand. Yes, he would, and he'd probably be great about it. However, she didn't tell people about her phobia. Only her parents and Jenny knew that she hadn't flown since 9/11, and though all of them had urged her to seek counseling to manage the fear, she hadn't done it, and that made her feel cowardly.

Prior to Toby's death, she'd never been a coward. Afterward was a whole other story. Everything scared her—loud noises, cars backfiring, crowds, silence, howling wind, darkness. Any time she ventured into a public place, such as a concert venue, a movie theater or a mall, she wondered if that would be the site of the next attack. She obsessively looked for exits, a way out, just in case. All this on top of her other obsessive compulsive attributes were her burdens to manage.

How did she tell Slim how deeply her wounds went? How did she burden *him* with her fears and worries when he was such an easygoing, happy kind of guy? How long would it take for her darkness to cast a shadow over his lightness?

Before she'd resolved anything, he came out of the bathroom and got back into bed with her, snuggling up to her, his arm around her waist. Kissing her shoulder, he said, "I didn't mean to push you for more than you're ready for."

Touched, Erin covered his hand with hers. "It's not that. And it's not you. It's me. It's…"

"Shhh. Not tonight. Today's been a fantastic day. Let's leave the hard stuff for tomorrow, okay?"

Relieved to have a reprieve, she expelled a deep breath. "Okay."

He let her go long enough to kill the light and snuggled up to her again.

She would tell him tomorrow that she was afraid to fly and that was why she didn't want to go back to Florida with him, even if the other things she'd told him were true, too. The life she was building on the island was important to her, but it wasn't like she couldn't come back for the summer and pick up where she left off with Jenny and her new friends.

Thinking about the possibility of months with him in Florida made her feel giddy and excited. If only the dark cloud of terror would go away and leave her alone, everything would be perfect—or as close to perfect as it had been for her in a very long time.

Erin took visions of sunshine and palm trees—and the sexy man in her bed—to sleep with her, dreaming of him as she slept. She awoke to his voice.

"Erin, your phone is ringing."

"What?"

"Your phone."

"Oh." Erin pushed her hair back from her face and reached for the phone that was charging on her bedside table where the clock read four thirty. The sight of MOM on the screen sparked panic. Why would her mother be calling before dawn? "Mom?"

"Oh thank goodness you answered."

Undone by her mother's panicked tone, Erin sat up in bed. "What's wrong?"

"It's Daddy." Her mother's voice broke, and Erin's anxiety spiked. "He woke up with a bad headache right before he collapsed. I called 9-1-1, and they got him to the hospital very quickly. They did an MRI and found an aneurism in his brain. They just took him to surgery, and… They said it's a very grave situation, honey."

"Oh my God," Erin whispered as tears slid down her cheeks and her heart beat so hard she feared she would hyperventilate.

Slim sat up to put an arm around her, and she leaned into him, thankful for his presence and support.

"I'm so sorry to do this to you, especially when you can't get here, but I thought you'd want to know."

"I do, of course I do. Is he… Did they say…"

"They said to hope for the best but prepare for the worst."

"No," Erin said, whimpering. "*No.*"

Her mother's sobs echoed through the phone line.

Erin forced herself to focus on her mother when she wanted to wail with despair. "Who's with you, Mom?"

"No one right now. I'll call Aunt Sue later," she said of her sister.

"Call her now. She'd want to be there with you."

"Okay, I will, and I'll let you know if I hear anything more. They said the surgery will take a few hours."

"I don't know what to do. What do I do?"

"Say a prayer, sweetheart. That's all we can do right now. I'll call you the second I know more."

"I'll see about getting the car on the ferry, and I'll get there as soon as I can. Will you text me the info about where you are?"

"I will."

"Love you."

"Love you, too."

Erin ended the call and dropped her head into her hands, sobs shaking her body.

"I'm so sorry, honey," Slim said as he rubbed her back.

"Did you hear all that?"

"Enough to put the pieces together. Sweetheart, look at me."

Erin raised her head to meet his gaze.

"I could get you there pretty quickly. They live in Philly, right?"

"Just outside," she said, her throat closing with panic and anxiety at the thought of flying. She would've thought nothing could trump that fear, but the fear of losing her dad, of never seeing him again, was greater than her flying phobia.

"That's just over an hour by air."

"I... I should tell you..."

Gazing down at her, he caressed her bare shoulder. "What, honey?"

She forced herself to look at him when she said, "I haven't flown since before 9/11."

After a long pause, he said, "Oh. Okay."

"I'm not entirely sure that I can."

"How about we try and see how it goes?"

"What if I freak out in the air?"

"I'd get you down as fast as I could."

"Then what would we do?"

"Hire a car to drive us to Philly?"

"You'd do that?"

"I'd do anything I could for you."

With just one sentence, he managed to convey a world of meaning that had her sobbing all over again, this time from the emotional overload that came from realizing, right in that already fraught moment, that she was falling hard for him.

Leaving that discovery to deal with at a later date, she said, "How long will it take to get there?"

"About an hour and twenty. I have a twin-engine plane, so it won't take long."

"Good to know there's a backup if one engine quits."

"The engines won't quit. You don't need to worry about that. Come here." He gathered her into his arms. "I promise you'll be completely safe with me. I'd never take any chances with your safety—or my own." As he spoke, he continued to rub her back in soothing circles. "It'll be a really quick flight."

"I'm afraid of so many things that never used to scare me," she whispered. "I'm afraid of everything."

"Then you need to stick with me, because in addition to my former careers as an EMT and circus performer, I'm an outstanding dragon slayer. Never met one yet that could defeat me. I gotcha covered, sweetheart."

There was nothing, absolutely *nothing*, he could've said that would've meant more to her. To know he wasn't judging her or finding her lacking because of her fears was a huge relief. And that he didn't push or try to coerce her into a decision but instead gave her quiet time for contemplation made it easier for her to accept his offer.

"Okay," she said tentatively. "Let's try it."

"Do you have anything for the anxiety? Something to take the edge off?"

"I have Xanax for when I can't sleep, but I don't take it very often anymore." In the early years after Toby died, she'd taken it every night. But it had been a long time since she'd depended upon it.

"That'd work." He tucked a strand of her hair behind her ear. "So we're doing this?"

Erin summoned the courage she needed from deep inside, where the person she used to be still resided, and nodded. "We're doing it." Now if only she could get through it without losing her mind.

CHAPTER 18

*S*lim took the first shower while she packed a bag. She was all thumbs as she tried to figure out what to take while wiping away tears that continued to fall. She wasn't ready to fly, and she certainly wasn't prepared to lose her dad, let alone possibly both in the same day.

Was it only last night that she'd been thinking it was time to tell Slim about her fear of flying? That seemed like a long time ago now that the phone call from her mother had changed everything. This wasn't the first time her life had been changed forever by a phone call. She'd been in a law school class at UPenn on a Tuesday morning in September when her phone lit up with calls and messages from her parents.

Erin vividly remembered, with the surreal detachment that comes from recalling a seminal moment, that she'd gotten up and left the crowded lecture to call them back. She vividly remembered the hysteria in her mother's voice as she tried to convey to Erin what was happening in New York. Erin had made her say the words twice before she ran from the building, looking for a television, which she found in the student union. She'd pushed through the crowd, and when she'd gotten her first look at a building on fire, she'd passed out.

Her fellow students and the EMTs they called to tend to her had been kind. She remembered that, but not much else about that first day. She was given a sedative that calmed her for a few hours, long enough to miss seeing the buildings collapse in real time, long enough for Jenny to tell them she'd actually spoken with Toby, that he'd been above the point of impact, that he'd had no chance of escaping.

Sitting on the bed, Erin broke down into deep, wrenching sobs as she relived the worst day of her life. The emotional firestorm wasn't unexpected. Whenever something triggered her anxiety, she went right back to her own personal ground zero, the day that had changed everything forever.

Slim came out of the bathroom, sat next to her on the bed and put his arm around her, offering comfort and strength. "Shh, it's going to be okay. We'll get you home, and by then, maybe your mom will have some good news about your dad."

"I'm sorry," she said, wiping away tears.

"There's no need to apologize. I totally get it."

"You have no idea what a mess I am."

"You're not a mess, Erin. You got bad news, and it upset you."

"It's so much more than that."

Rather than ask what she meant, he tightened his hold on her and kissed her temple. "I'm sort of glad you told me you're afraid to fly. I was starting to wonder if you aren't as into me as I'd hoped you were."

Pained by his confession, she looked up at him. "I'm very into you. Extremely into you."

His smile made his eyes twinkle. "That's exceptionally good news. Let's get going. Your mom needs you." He kissed her forehead. "Take the Xanax now so it'll kick in by the time you need it."

Erin took the pill and a quick shower and sent Jenny a text to let her know what was going on before they left the lighthouse to drive through predawn darkness to the airport. Rather than think about where they were going—or why—she closed her eyes and put her head back against the seat, trying to calm herself while praying for the pill to do its magic. He held her hand, which went a long way toward calming her.

"We got lucky with the weather," Slim said, breaking a long silence. "It's forty degrees, so no need to deice. That saves us some time."

"Oh," Erin said, surprised to realize she'd never thought about ice or deicing. Thank goodness he was thinking for both of them. "That's good."

He pulled into a parking space at the island's tiny airport, which was dark and deserted.

"Are we allowed to do this?" Erin asked.

He grinned at her. "No worries. I've got keys. They know me well here. I'm allowed to do what I want. Because they're closed, I'll file a flight plan with the airport in Providence, and we'll be all set."

"I was sort of hoping you'd say we're definitely *not* allowed to so we can go home and pretend like I never agreed to this."

"Is that what you want to do?"

Her eyes filled with tears. "I want to get to my parents as fast as I can. This is the fastest way. And I trust you."

He brought her hand to his lips. "You can trust me with this and all things. I have to be honest, though. It'll be a little bumpy leaving the island because it always is. There's nothing at all to be afraid of, but you might not like it."

"Maybe the Xanax will knock me out before we take off."

"Either way, I'll hold your hand the whole time."

"No, you won't! You need your hands to fly the plane."

Laughing, he said, "I could fly the plane wearing a blindfold with one hand tied behind my back."

"None of which will be happening on this flight."

"Yes, ma'am," he said, grinning at her saucy comeback. "Let's get going." He used a key on his ring to open the gates to the airfield, and after ushering Erin through, he closed and relocked the gate. Shouldering his backpack and her bag, he took her hand and led her to a white plane. In the murky darkness, she couldn't make out the details, and that was probably for the best because she also couldn't obsess about how small the plane was.

He opened the passenger-side door for her and helped her into the cockpit. "Get comfortable while I do a preflight check. I'm going to close the door so you won't get cold, okay?"

Comfortable… Sure. Like that was going to happen. "Um, sure, that's fine."

The door closed, sealing her off from the cold and from him. Her gaze darted around the small cockpit, taking in the vast array of knobs and buttons and two sets of U-shaped controls. Was she really going to do this? Was she really going to sit here passively while he took them hurtling down a darkened runway and lifted off into the pitch-black sky?

As much as she wanted to get to her parents, she was no longer sure that flying was the best idea. She was about to open the door and say as much to Slim when he got in the left-side door and got busy continuing his preflight check, systematically going through a checklist that she could see after he turned on the interior lights.

He donned a headset and began talking to someone in a language she could barely understand, except for the words *Gansett Island* and *Philadelphia*. Things began to happen quickly after that. The engines fired up, more checks and rechecks were done, switches were flipped, knobs were turned, and Erin watched it all, feeling detached and removed from the scene that was unfolding right in front of her.

If she tried hard enough, she might convince herself to believe that she was watching this happen on TV rather than living through it personally.

Slim glanced over at her, found her watching him and offered a small smile. "Ready?"

"Not even kind of."

"I've got this. I promise. There's nothing to worry about."

Between his assurances and the soothing effects of the medication, Erin was able to remain still while he belted her in and taxied the plane to the end of the runway.

"I need both hands for takeoff, but after that, one of them is all yours. And remember—there'll be a few bumps on the climb, but it'll smooth out as soon as we get above the clouds. Okay?"

She nodded because that was all she was capable of at the moment.

As he revved the engine for takeoff, her hands curled into fists and her eyes closed, but not tightly enough to contain the tears that rolled down her cheeks. They lurched forward and hurtled down the runway before lifting off. A small squeak of surprise crept through her clenched jaw as she felt the plane gain altitude.

"We've got this. It's all good."

His assurances went a long way toward calming her nerves. If she kept her eyes closed, she could almost convince herself she was home in bed, dreaming that her mother had called about her dad and Slim had offered to fly her to Philly. She could pretend that nothing had ever happened to ruin her love of travel and adventure.

As he'd predicted, the plane rocked and rolled on the way through the clouds, but the warmth of his hand surrounding hers and the sound of his voice as he continued to reassure her worked to soothe her frayed nerves.

"Should get better now," he said after about ten minutes.

That was the last thing she heard before he squeezed her hand, jarring her out of a deep sleep.

"There you are," he said, smiling when she looked over at him, blinking his handsome face into focus. "We're going to land in fifteen minutes."

Outside the window, the sky was pink and purple and orange, the colors of sunrise. "Did I really sleep the whole way?"

"You really did. But that's for the best, don't you think?"

"I did it," she said softly. "I got on an airplane."

"You didn't just get on a plane. You flew for more than an hour."

"Does it count that I was in a medically induced coma for most of that time?" she asked, groggy and fuzzy from the medication.

"What counts is you overcame your fears, you didn't freak out, and you got through it. Who cares how you did that? What counts is that you did it. I'm so proud of you."

"I'm rather proud of myself right now." She withdrew her phone from her coat pocket to see if there was any word from her mother since she'd sent the hospital name and address. There'd been no calls or texts while she was asleep. Was that a good sign or a bad one?

"She would've called if it went bad," Slim said, reading her mind.

"Would I receive the call up here?"

"Yeah, we're within cell range."

"Oh good," she said, expelling a sigh of relief. "Thank God."

"Hang in there. Won't be long now."

"Thank you," she said, looking over at him. "I appreciate this so much."

"I'm just glad I could do something for you."

"You've done so much. You have no idea how much."

"Every minute with you is a pleasure, Erin. From the minute I picked you up on the side of the road—"

"Stop saying it like that! You make me sound like a hooker!"

Chuckling, he said, "You hooked me, all right. With your determination, your sweetness, your resilience, your humor. I've been hooked on you ever since that night, if you must know the truth."

"That long?"

"Uh-huh."

After that, there was no more conversation for a while as Slim focused on landing at Philadelphia International Airport and Erin wallowed in the thrill of hearing he was hooked on her. As the wheels touched down, the tightness in Erin's chest loosened somewhat. She'd managed to survive the flying portion of the program, which was a huge accomplishment. But she couldn't celebrate that until she knew her father was going to be okay.

They taxied to an area of the tarmac where private planes were kept. Slim secured the plane, talked to a guy about when they'd be back and had them heading for the cab stand—all in less than ten minutes.

"Have you flown in here before?" she asked while they waited in a short line for a cab.

"Twice."

"So that's how you knew where to go."

"Yep."

In the cab, Erin asked the driver to take them to the UPenn hospital on Spruce Street. During the fifteen-minute drive, Slim held her hand between both of his, continuing to prop her up as he had since she received the upsetting call from her mother. At the hospital, they were directed to the surgical waiting area, where Erin found her mother, Mary Beth, and Aunt Sue huddled together. Her mother burst into tears when Erin and Slim walked in. She rushed over to hug Erin and then Slim.

"How is he?" Erin asked.

"We've only heard that the surgery is going well, but that was more than an hour ago. What're you doing here? I didn't think you could get off the island."

Erin glanced at Slim. "I have this friend who's a pilot, you see."

"Oh, Erin. Oh God, *you got on an airplane?*"

"I did."

"And she did great," Slim added.

"Thanks to the best pilot ever and medicinal intervention," Erin said, offering him a small smile. She hugged her aunt and introduced her to Slim.

"Wait until Daddy hears you got on a plane," Mary Beth said. "He won't believe it."

Her mother's certainty that her dad would recover helped to reassure Erin. If her mom believed it, surely it must be true, right?

CHAPTER 19

*T*hey waited for hours. Slim went to get coffee for all of them, and the jolt of caffeine helped to offset the lingering effects of the Xanax, although the medication was probably the only thing keeping her from climbing the walls.

She took advantage of the opportunity to call Big Mac McCarthy, her contact with the town of Gansett, to let him know the lighthouse would be unattended for the time being—and why.

"I'm so sorry to hear about your dad, honey," he said. "Don't worry about a thing here. I can take care of filing the daily report with the Coast Guard while you're gone."

"Are you sure you don't mind?"

"I don't mind at all. I'll take a run out there every couple of days to check on things. It'll get me out of the house and out of my wife's hair for half an hour. She'll appreciate that."

Erin wouldn't have thought it possible to laugh, but Mr. McCarthy always managed to charm her. "Thank you so much."

"No problem. You give your folks our best and tell your dad to make a speedy recovery."

"I will, and I'll let you know when I'll be back."

"We'll look forward to seeing you."

With that taken care of, she had one less thing to worry about.

Finally, the surgeon came into the room, still wearing operating room scrubs. A strand of her red hair had escaped from her surgical cap, and a mask hung around her neck. The color of her hair reminded Erin of Sydney.

"Mrs. Barton?"

"Yes, I'm Mrs. Barton, and this is my daughter, Erin. How is he?"

"He came through the surgery very well. We were able to clip the bleed and repair the vessel."

"So he's going to be all right?" Mary Beth asked.

"We'll know more when he wakes up, but I'm cautiously optimistic."

Erin and her mother both broke down with relief at the good news. While Sue hugged Mary Beth, Slim took care of Erin.

"You might want to go home and get some rest," the doctor said. "He's going to be in recovery for hours yet."

"I can't leave him," Mary Beth said. "I need to be here, but the rest of you should go. I'll be fine."

"I'll stay with you," Sue said.

"We'll let you know as soon as you can see him," the doctor said before she left them.

Mary Beth convinced everyone else to go home for the time being, promising to call as soon as Tom was awake—and promising she would get something to eat at some point.

"I don't feel right leaving you," Erin said.

"I'm going to curl up on the sofa and try to sleep." Mary Beth gestured to the small sofa in the waiting room. "You go on home, and I'll call you the second I hear any news."

"If you're sure," Erin said.

"I'm very sure. You guys must be tired. Let's sleep while we can." She handed her keys to Erin and told her where to find the car. "I had to drive because there wasn't room for me in the rescue wagon."

Erin's heart ached at the thought of her mom's lonely drive to the hospital, not knowing what was happening to her husband on the way.

Slim kept his arm around Erin as they walked out of the hospital into the cold morning air. It took a few minutes to find the car in the crowded parking lot. Erin handed him the keys. "You'd better drive. I'm still groggy from the Xanax."

"No problem."

Erin directed him out of the city to I-76 West to Bryn Mawr.

"Am I going to get to see where you grew up?"

"In all its glory."

"Why have I heard of that town before?"

"There's a very prestigious women's college there. Lots of famous graduates."

"Ahhh, that's it."

After a thirty-minute drive, they arrived at Erin's childhood home, a two-story white colonial with black shutters, a big front porch and a white picket fence that was tricked out with greens for the holiday season. She punched in the code to the cypher lock—her and Toby's birthday—on the back door and led Slim into the house where the scent of Christmas pine and spices greeted them.

Erin hung their coats in the foyer and led Slim into the kitchen, which had wide knotty-pine floors, white cabinets and stainless appliances that her parents had bought last summer when they renovated the kitchen.

"What a nice house," Slim said, taking it all in.

"It was a wreck when they bought it. They've restored every inch of it over the last thirty-five years."

"It's beautiful."

"What do you want most? Food or sleep?"

"I could eat something, but we can go out, if you want. You don't have to entertain me."

"Sure, I do. You're still my guest, even if we've switched locations."

He came over to her, put his hands on her shoulders and kissed her. "All bets are off. If you're still feeling groggy, you don't have to cook or anything."

"All bets are off? Really?"

"Well, not *all* bets," he said, flashing that sexy grin that made her melt, "but the part about you feeling like you have to feed me—that's off."

With her hand around his neck, she drew him in for another kiss. "I don't mind feeding you. I actually kind of like it."

"In that case, feel free to feed me, cuz I love to eat."

Raiding her mom's fridge, Erin whipped up omelets with cheddar, green peppers and tomatoes. She made coffee and toast to go with them.

Slim polished off all of his and half of hers. Worrying about her dad had put a damper on her appetite.

"You're an amazing cook. You should open a B&B. It'd be a huge hit."

"I'd love to do something like that someday. I've always enjoyed taking care of people."

"You should do it. Talk the town into turning the lighthouse into a B&B. You'd make a killing."

"The town might not want that, but it sure would be fun."

"Can't hurt to ask."

"But then where would I live?"

"My place?"

"With Big Bertha, the stubborn furnace?"

"She's cranky, but she gets the job done."

It was fun to imagine the sort of possibilities he suggested, but Erin didn't want to get ahead of herself—or him. "What do you say we grab some sleep while we can?"

"I'd be all for that, as long as I get to sleep with you."

"Not in my mother's house. I swear she still has cameras in every room from when we were teenagers."

"Your mom loves me. She'd want me to watch over you while you sleep."

Rolling her eyes, Erin said, "You're so full of it." When she got up to tend to the dishes, he surprised her by tugging on her arm, which knocked her off-balance and straight into his arms. "Very smooth."

"It's the circus training." He nuzzled her neck and made her shiver.

"I'm full of it, all right, and it's all your fault." To make his point, he pressed his erection against her belly.

"My fault? What did I do?"

"You cooked for me and you were so brave about flying and you're so very, very nice to look at. Oh, and you're super sexy, too, especially when you blush like you are right now." He kissed both of her cheeks. "I really like that."

Erin sank into his embrace, thrilled by him and the things he said to her and how he'd helped her conquer her greatest fear. Not that she thought she was suddenly over her flying phobia, but he'd made her feel safe enough to take the first big step toward putting it behind her.

He helped her with the dishes, and then they went upstairs, taking turns in the bathroom before ending up in her childhood room, which had been repurposed into a guest room since she moved out. In one corner, her mom had kept the desk Erin had used to do her homework along with some of the trophies she'd earned in gymnastics and dance.

Slim examined every one of them while she watched him from the bed. "I never knew you were so limber."

"That was twenty years ago. I'm not that limber anymore."

"I bet your inner gymnast can still do a mean backbend."

"I'd prefer to not have to prove that."

Smiling, he pulled his shirt over his head and dropped his jeans into a pile on the floor. He crawled into bed and reached for her, snuggling her in close to him.

"I should go check to make sure I locked the door."

"I did that."

It took all the fortitude she could muster to deny the powerful need to see for herself. "I said we can't sleep together here."

"I can't hear you."

Smiling at his predictable reply, she said, "I'm getting awfully used to using your chest for a pillow. What'll I do when you go back to Florida?"

"Come with me?"

"What would I do there while you're working?"

"Sit by the pool and work on your column or go get a mani-pedi or a massage or go shopping or hit the beach or go to lunch with the amazing group of women I'll introduce you to."

"Your harem?" she asked with a touch of annoyance in her tone.

His bark of laughter only added to her annoyance. "Hardly. They're my friends' wives and girlfriends, so you can sheath your claws, wildcat."

"I don't have *claws*."

"It's okay, sweetheart. I like it when you're possessive."

"I'm not being possessive."

"Yes, you are, and I like being possessed by you."

"I don't have a jealous bone in my body."

"So does that mean you wouldn't mind if that group of women *had* been my harem?" She thought about that just long enough for him to pounce. "Ah-*ha*. I knew it. You are a jealous little she-cat."

"You're going to be a neutered *he*-cat if you don't shut up."

His low chuckle made his chest rumble under her ear. "So is that a *yes* to coming to Florida?"

"After all that she-cat business, I don't want to go anywhere with you."

"I'm very sorry I called you a jealous little she-cat. Will you come home with me now?"

"That apology wasn't even kind of sincere."

He surprised her when he rolled them over so he was on top of her, looking down at her with amusement and affection and desire. "You want sincerity? I can show you sincerity."

"Are we still talking about jealousy?"

"So you admit you were jealous?"

She poked him in the side with her index finger, drawing a grunt of laughter.

"We're talking about you and me and making a go of this."

"Oh. We are?"

Nodding, he smiled as he brought his lips down on hers, kissing her with the sweet tenderness she was coming to expect from him. "Aren't we?" he asked after several kisses.

"Is that what you want?"

"Yes, Erin. That's what I want."

"I thought you liked your freedom."

"Are you planning to shackle me to your bed? Not that I would object."

She felt her face go hot at the thought of such things. "You know what I mean."

He kissed the blush that flamed each cheek. "I do know, and I've had a lot of years of freedom. I might be ready to try something else."

"What if you decide you don't like it?"

"What wouldn't I like about flying and hanging out with you the rest of the time?"

"I don't know. What if we don't get along when we're together every day?"

"I'm not worried about getting along with you." He pressed his hard cock against her core. "We get along just fine."

"Because it's new and fun and exciting. What happens when it gets boring and routine?"

"*Boring and routine?* What do you take me for? I'd never let that happen."

"Be serious. We both know what happens when the blush wears off the rose."

"Sweetheart, if I got to hold you and kiss you and make love to you every day, my life would never again be boring or routine. And the blush will never wear off our rose."

"I worry that you're not being realistic. We're not idealistic twentysomethings doing this for the first time, expecting everything to be good times and smooth sailing. We both know better."

"For what it's worth, I *would* be doing *this* for the first time. And do you want to know why that is?"

Erin nodded.

"Because until I found you, I hadn't met anyone I could imagine spending every day with. And after only a few months with you and the amazing time together this week, I can't imagine my life without you in it. I've waited a long time to take this kind of leap with a woman, Erin, and it's not something I do lightly. It's something I'm willing to do because it's *you* I'd be leaping with. Does that make sense?"

Overwhelmed by his words as much as the emotion behind them, Erin blinked rapidly but was unable to stop a stray tear from escaping.

He kissed it away. "Are these good tears?"

"These are holy-cow-you-blow-me-away tears."

"You do the same for me."

After that, there were no more words and no more tears as he kissed her and caressed her and made love to her. The thought of being with him every day was almost too good to be true.

He hooked his arms under her legs, opening her to deep, intense thrusts that had her screaming from the nearly unbearable pleasure that overtook her.

"Ah, God, *Erin...*" He was right behind her, surging into her as he came with a groan.

As they settled after the incredible high, Erin wrapped her arms around him to keep him close for a little while longer. She wanted to bottle the way he made her feel so she could keep it forever. "I can't believe I just had sex in this room."

He grunted out a laugh. "If your mom has it bugged, she's getting a great view of my bare ass."

Erin pulled the covers over his spectacular ass. "I told you we weren't going to do what we just did in this sacred room."

"What can I say? You're powerless against my charms."

"Apparently, I am."

"That's okay," he said, flashing a cocky grin before he kissed her. "I like you that way."

Erin was finding she liked being powerless to resist him. She liked it a whole lot.

"You know," she said tentatively, "if we're going to make a go of this, as you say, we might be able to skip the condoms. I'm on long-term birth control, and I'm healthy."

"I'm kind of skittish about that after what happened way back when."

"I totally understand. I was only tossing it out there as an FYI. Think about it."

He pressed his reawakened cock against her hip, making her groan. "Not sure how I'll think about anything else."

ERIN AND SLIM RETURNED TO THE HOSPITAL EARLY IN THE AFTERNOON to find Jenny and Alex sitting with her mother in the waiting room.

"What're you guys doing here?" Erin asked, shocked to see them.

"We're on our way to Las Vegas to meet Paul and Hope," Jenny said. "But I couldn't go anywhere until I knew that Tom was okay, so we flew through Philly."

"I can't believe you're here," Erin said tearfully as she hugged them both.

"The second she got your text, she was online changing our flights," Alex said.

"It means so much that you came," Mary Beth said to Jenny.

"What's the latest?" Erin asked her mom.

"He's still in recovery, but stable and holding his own at last check. They said he should be awake within an hour or two, and we'll know more then."

They took Mary Beth to get something to eat in the cafeteria and returned to the waiting room, hoping to be able to see her dad soon. The doctor came in a short time later and said they were moving him to a room in the ICU and that they could visit him two at a time.

"How's he doing?" Erin asked.

"Better than expected at this point," the doctor said. "He's responding to stimuli and squeezing our hands, which are good signs. He has a long road ahead, but I'm feeling optimistic."

An audible sigh of relief went through the room. The doctor gave them directions to the ICU and said Tom would be there in about thirty minutes.

Erin hugged her mom while Slim rubbed both their backs.

"I'm so relieved," Mary Beth said, wiping away tears as she hugged Jenny.

They moved as a group to the ICU waiting room, where Mary Beth and Erin were allowed in to see him first. Erin was overwhelmed by the sheer number of machines attached to him as well as the pasty gray color of his complexion. But when he opened his eyes and looked at them, she could see that the dad she loved was still in there.

"Hey, Dad," Erin said. "We're all here, and you're doing great." She leaned over to kiss his forehead, working to contain her emotions so he wouldn't see that she was upset.

On the other side of the bed, Mary Beth held his hand and stared at him intently.

Erin decided to give them a minute alone and left the room to find Slim waiting for her. She stepped into his outstretched arms.

"How is he?"

"He opened his eyes and saw us there."

"That's good news."

"I'm going to give Jenny a turn to see him so they can get going." Erin left his warm embrace long enough to get Jenny, and then she returned to him, appreciative of his support during another challenging time. It wasn't lost on her that she was becoming dependent on the tender support he offered so willingly any time she needed him.

CHAPTER 20

*P*aul Martinez had planned every detail of their Las Vegas wedding down to the cake so that Hope could enjoy the day without having to obsess about the details. She'd been working three days a week as a private-duty nurse on the mainland, commuting back and forth on the ferry. The arrangement had been working out well, but noticing how tired she'd been, he'd seen to the wedding details so the only thing she had to do was buy a dress and pack for her and Ethan, who was out of his mind with excitement about the trip.

Paul had shown him pictures of the Hoover Dam online, and he couldn't wait to see it for himself. One of the many things he loved about Ethan was his endless enthusiasm for anything that interested Paul. A man could get hooked on that kind of adoration coming from a boy who'd had more than his share of upheaval in his life.

He'd love to adopt Ethan if that option became possible. That would depend on what happened when his father was released from prison, which was hopefully years in the future. They'd cross that bridge when they got to it, but in his mind, Ethan was already his son in every way that mattered. The two of them were inseparable, to the point that Hope worried endlessly that Ethan was annoying him. He repeatedly assured her that he loved every minute he got to spend with the boy who would soon be his stepson, and he was more than happy to take care of him when Hope was working on the mainland.

Paul couldn't imagine anything better than the way things had worked out for the three of them, though he wished his mother could still be at home and that Hope could still work as her nurse rather than having to commute for a job that was critical to her need to support herself. Selfishly, he wanted her at home with him. However, he respected her need to pay down the debt her ex-husband had left her with and to ensure that she was never again in the position she'd been in after her ex was charged with having sex with the girls he'd coached at their local high school.

Standing now in their suite that looked out over the Vegas Strip, Paul adjusted the cufflinks on his shirt and donned the gray suit coat he would wear to get married.

Married.

For a long time, he'd thought this day would never happen for him, but then Hope came to the island to work for them, and everything had changed. He'd made the mistake of fighting his growing feelings for her because she was their employee, and he'd worried his late father would've disapproved. But the more time he spent with Hope, the more it didn't matter what anyone thought. He was completely in love with her and couldn't wait to marry her, and Ethan, too.

Wearing a navy blue suit and a tie that he tugged at as if it were a noose, Alex came out of the adjoining room that he and Jenny were sharing. Paul was thrilled that his brother and sister-in-law had wanted to join them and that they'd be their witnesses, too. After their stop in Philadelphia to see Erin's dad, they'd arrived late that afternoon, in plenty of time for the seven o'clock ceremony.

"You clean up pretty well," Paul said to his brother.

"Likewise. You even managed to shave without cutting yourself."

"Fuck off," Paul said, laughing. The two of them had been needling each other their entire lives. Why should his wedding day be any different? "Even though you're a consistent pain in my ass, I'm glad you're here."

"So am I. Cost me a freaking fortune to book it last minute, so I'll be sending you the bill."

"Please do. I'll happily pay it."

"I'm just kidding. Money well spent."

"I should've thought to ask you sooner. Sorry that I didn't. I was so focused on making everything nice for Hope that I didn't think of it."

"No worries. We were fine with inviting ourselves." Alex made a big production out of straightening Paul's tie. "You ready for this?"

"You know it. Can't wait."

"She's awesome, and so is Ethan. You got it right, brother."

"I'm glad you approve."

"I do, and Mom and Dad would've loved her, too."

"I agree."

The bedroom door opened, and Hope came out wearing a sexy, form-fitting off-white dress that landed just above her knee and three-inch heels that did wondrous things for her already-exceptional legs. She'd spent the afternoon at the spa downstairs, and her hair had been done in an elaborate updo that left her future husband dazzled by the sight of her.

Paul couldn't seem to do anything but stare at the gorgeous woman who would become his wife in just over an hour.

She ran her hands over the skirt of her dress in a move he recognized as nerves.

Alex nudged him out of the stupor and nodded toward Hope, telling him to go to her, to acknowledge her with more than just a greedy stare. He didn't need to be told twice. Crossing the room, circling the sofa and the seating area, he went over to her, taking her hands and stepping back for an up-close look.

"Is this okay?" she asked.

"*Okay?*" he asked with a laugh. "It's incredible. *You* are incredible."

The smile that stretched across her face indicated her relief at his approval.

"Do I really get to marry this sexy, beautiful woman?"

"If you still want to."

It pained him to think that she'd question his commitment at this late date, but he understood. Life had conditioned her to be wary, and he was determined to change those expectations until all she knew was happiness and joy. Because he couldn't wait, he took a taste of her sweet lips and had to remind himself that not only did they have somewhere to be, but they also had an audience.

There'd be plenty of time for more kissing later. For now, they had a wedding to get to.

The jovial group of five headed to the wedding venue Paul had chosen from the hundreds of options. It had been the classiest one he could find, and he'd opted for an outdoor ceremony in a gazebo. Despite the general cheesiness of Vegas, Hope loved everything about the place, from the music he'd chosen for them to the bouquet of white roses to the boutonnieres for the three "men."

Ethan wore an adorable little suit and was bursting with excitement as Paul pinned the flower on his lapel. He looked up at Paul with adoration Paul would never grow tired of. "Thanks for bringing me."

"Where else would you be when your mom and I get married?"

Ethan shrugged. "Sometimes kids get left at home for stuff like this."

"Not my kids."

"I'm not really your—"

"Yes, you are." Paul squatted down to Ethan's level and put his hands on the boy's shoulders. "As of today, you're my son."

Ethan hurled himself into Paul's arms, probably crushing the white rose, but who cared about such things at a time like this. "Thank you."

"Aww, buddy, thank *you*. You and your mom are the best thing to ever happen to me." He held Ethan for another minute. "What do you say we go get married?"

Ethan nodded and pulled back from Paul, subtly wiping his eyes with his sleeve and nearly reducing Paul to tears in the process.

Alex did double duty, giving Hope away and serving with Ethan as Paul's best men while Jenny was Hope's matron of honor. They recited traditional vows, exchanged the rings they'd bought earlier in the day and shared a long, and according to Ethan, totally gross kiss. And then they were husband and wife, and Paul wanted to shout from the rooftops of the craziest place he'd ever been that this beautiful woman and her adorable son were now his family.

Life didn't get much better than this.

JUST BEFORE MIDNIGHT BACK AT HOME ON GANSETT, MAC LOCKED UP after another fun gathering with family and friends. He loved the time they'd spent with their island clan during the holidays, but he was ready for some alone time with his lovely wife after a frustrating few days. With that in mind, he shut off the lights and headed upstairs.

Tonight was the night to finish what they'd started multiple times. Both kids were back to full health, and he'd made sure Maddie had a three-hour nap that afternoon so she would be ready to have friends over, among other things.

He looked in on both kids and saw they were sound asleep, Thomas snuggled up to his favorite bear and Hailey with her thumb in her mouth. Perfect. *All systems go.* In their room, he saw no sign of Maddie so he went into the adjoining bathroom through the open door.

Her silk-covered back was to him and her hair swept up in a messy bun, leaving her elegant neck exposed. He approached her, placed his hands on her hips and had started kissing that lovely stretch of skin when he noticed the thermometer in her mouth.

Groaning, he dropped his forehead to her shoulder, wishing he could get the message to his hard cock that it was game off—again. The poor guy had been through hell this week. "What's wrong?" She'd been fine all night, laughing and talking with their friends while serving as the ultimate hostess, as always.

The thermometer beeped, and she removed it from her mouth, giving it a passing glance. "I'm not sure. I started to feel woozy while I was getting changed. Hope I don't have what the kids had."

He wanted to moan, but this was no time to be selfish—or so he told his cock. "What's your temperature?"

She took another look at the thermometer. "Hmm, perfectly normal. That's odd."

Something about the way she said that had Mac taking a closer look at her. "Are you fucking with me?"

An inelegant snort of laughter spewed from her, and then she bent in half, crippled with laughter.

"Oh, this is *war*, Madeline. *This is freaking war!*" Mindful of her pregnancy, he was careful but insistent when he picked her up and carried her into the bedroom, putting her on the bed.

He looked down at her smiling face and the beautiful eyes that danced with mischief. "You think you're so funny, don't you?"

"Come on. You have to admit that was funny."

"I'll admit no such thing." It took everything he had to maintain a scowl when a smile was trying to bust out. "Your behavior lately has been terrible. If I didn't know better, I'd think you were trying to get me to spank you again."

"You wouldn't dare."

"Oh, yes, I would."

A flush of heat moved from her chest to her face, and he went harder than stone at knowing the thought of being spanked turned her on. "I'm very sorry for messing with you, Mac. It'll never happen again."

He laughed out loud at that. "Yes, it will. You should take your punishment like a big girl."

"No, Mac, *please don't.*"

"Is this one of those cases where no means yes? Feel free to nod in the affirmative."

The little vixen bit her lip and nodded. And in case he wasn't already so turned on he was about to explode, she raised her hips so he could feel the heat of her arousal against his cock. Fucking hell. She was going to be the absolute death of him. But oh what a way to go.

"Turn over, naughty girl, and take your punishment."

"I'm scared."

Though he knew her comment was part of the role-playing game, he couldn't bear the thought of her being afraid of him, even in jest. "You know I'd never hurt you, baby. Tell me you know that."

"I do, I know."

"Then turn over and take what's coming to you." He smiled and winked at her as he helped her into the position he wanted her in. God, yes, just like that, propped up on her elbows, her silk-covered, delicious ass raised for his pleasure and her golden eyes watching him warily over her shoulder. Could she be any hotter?

Mac made a slow production of raising her nightgown, letting his fingertips slide over the backs of her legs, making them quiver. He loved the way she reacted to his touch. He loved playing these games with her, and the way she teased him, even if he'd never admit that to her.

There were times, such as now, when he still couldn't believe that *this* was his life—that *she* was his life. How had he ever gotten so lucky as to find his perfect match?

He nearly lost his shit when he saw that she was bare under the nightgown, further proof that she'd planned to have her wicked way with him. "Mmm," he said as he peppered her ass with kisses that had her squirming and panting.

"Mac…"

"Shhh, let me have my fun." After days of frustration, he ought to be in an all-fired rush to *have* her, but now that she was laid out before him, he wanted to take his time, to savor her, to drive her as crazy as she made him.

"Come on."

He delivered a light spank to her left cheek, drawing a surprised gasp from her that nearly finished him right off. *Christ have mercy.* Biting his lip to give himself something to focus on other than his needy cock, he gave the right side the same treatment. He kept up a steady pattern, moving from left to right, rubbing each spot afterward to ramp up the effect for her.

Judging by the sounds she made, the scent of her arousal and the way her legs moved farther apart with every spank, his efforts were having the desired effect.

"Mac, *please*… I've learned my lesson. I'll never torment you again."

That earned her another set of spanks. "Now you're lying to me, too? This is not good, Madeline. Not good at all."

She made a noise that was equal parts frustration, laughter and desire.

"Tell me what you want."

"You *know* what I want."

"You have to say it." One of his favorite things was getting her to talk dirty, which she wouldn't do without his encouragement.

"Mac! I want you to make love to me."

"You'll have to be more specific." He dragged two fingers down her backbone and into the crevice between her cheeks, where he found the abundant evidence of how much she loved their game.

She dropped her head to her forearms. "I want you to make me come."

Mac could almost picture the bright red blush that would be flooding her cheeks and decided he wanted to see that. "Turn over." He helped her onto her back, and sure enough, the blush was every bit as spectacular as he'd expected. "How do you want me to make you come?" Pressing against her clit, he said, "With my fingers or my tongue or my cock?"

"Your choice."

"No, baby, it's lady's choice."

"Your cock."

"I didn't hear you."

"Mac! You did, too!"

Had he ever had more fun in his life than he did with her? No. Never. "Look me in the eye and tell me exactly what you want."

His adorable, sweet, sexy wife looked at him and said, "I want you to fuck me. Right now."

"Well, why didn't you just say so?"

She grabbed a handful of his hair and pulled hard enough to hurt. "Hurry up."

Amused by her desperation, he took himself in hand and pressed against her, teasing her for as long as he could stand it.

"I'm going to remember this, Mac."

"That's the whole idea."

She pressed against him, all but begging him to take her. "I'm not going to remember it in a good way. I'm going to remember it in a revenge-is-a-bitch-and-so-am-I way."

That made him laugh—hard. How could he not laugh? She was so damned cute. "You could never be a bitch, sweet Maddie."

"You don't think so? Keep it up, and you're going to see a whole other side of me."

"I love when you need me."

"Mac, honestly," she said with a deep sigh. "I always need you, and I always will."

His heart skipped a beat at the blatant honesty he saw in her expression and heard in her words. Pressing into her, he gave her what they both needed, the connection they lived for.

"*Yes*," she said on a long sigh. "Like that. Just like that."

All games were forgotten as the sublime pleasure took over. Everything faded away when he was with her like this—sick kids and holiday madness and pressure at work faded to nothingness, eclipsed entirely by his love for her.

Reaching beneath her, he cupped her ass, which was still warm from the spanking. She gasped in reaction, her inner muscles tightening as her fingers dug into the muscles of his back, all signs that she was close.

"Let me feel you, baby," he whispered gruffly in her ear, picking up the pace to take them both to the finish line.

Ahhh, fucking finally, he thought as they both came with cries that he muffled by kissing her with deep thrusts of his tongue. God forbid they should wake the kids. He softened the kiss to light touches of his lips on hers before dropping his forehead to hers as he tried to catch his breath.

"Oh my God, Mac. Just when I think we can't get any crazier…"

He huffed out a laugh. "It's you. You make me that way."

Her hands smoothed over his back, gliding through the dampness that had come from exertion. "*I make you* that way. Whatever you say."

"It's true. I've never been like this with anyone else."

"I hate to think of you doing this with anyone else."

He raised his head to look into her eyes. "I have never done *anything* like *this* with anyone but you. I've told you before—my whole life started the day you tried to run me over with your bike."

She smacked his shoulder. "You're rewriting history."

"Best day of my life," he said, kissing her. "But every day since then, even when you're mean to me, has been ever better."

"Even days when you're cock-blocked by sick kids?"

Laughing, he said, "Even then. I love those kids and their mother with all my heart."

"We love you, too."

He gathered her into his arms and rolled to his side, bringing her with him. "I was kinda rough with you. You're okay?"

"You really have to ask?"

"Yeah, I really do."

"I'm fantastic. You may not believe it, but I get as frustrated as you do when we can't have this time alone together."

He tucked her head in under his chin and wrapped his leg around her hips. "Sleep right here with me. Just like this."

"There's nowhere else I'd rather be."

CHAPTER 21

Over the next several days, Slim and Erin took turns with her mother, making sure someone was always at the hospital. They grabbed meals and sleep when they could, between short visits with her dad, who was a little better every day.

Eventually, they moved him from ICU to a regular room, which was a big milestone. Erin and her mom worked the phones, looking for a rehab facility close to home where he could complete his recovery after he was released from the hospital.

Hearing that the rehab could take weeks, Erin made the decision to stay in Pennsylvania to support her parents until her dad was finally home.

"I have to go back to the island today," Slim said over breakfast in her mother's kitchen on the morning of New Year's Eve. "My close friend is getting married," he said of Adam McCarthy. "I need to be there."

"I understand," Erin said, though she was bereft at the thought of even a day without him after all the time they'd spent together.

"I wish you could come with me."

"So do I."

"That's progress on all fronts. One, that you want to be with me, and two, that you'd have to fly with me to get there."

"I definitely want to be with you. The flying? Still not high on my to-do list, but getting the first time out of the way was huge. I... I've been thinking I might see about an appointment with Dr. McCarthy when I get back to the island to work on my long list of issues."

"Your list isn't that long."

"It's longer than you think. Have you noticed that I need everything just so, that I'm constantly arranging and rearranging? Or that I have to touch things with my left hand or something awful will happen to someone I love? My OCD is about having control over things—or the perception of control, anyway."

He reached for her hand and linked their fingers. "People don't get to our age without baggage, Erin. We've all got stuff. Yours doesn't make you any less attractive to me, in case you were wondering."

"That's nice to hear," she said, smiling at him. How would she live without that gorgeous face to look at all day every day? "What am I supposed to do for fun without you around?"

"Call me? FaceTime? Text?"

She made a pout face. "Hard to go back to that after the last eleven days."

"I want you to think about coming to Evan's wedding and to Florida after. Talk to Mr. McCarthy. He'll help you find a way to be gone from the lighthouse for a couple of months."

"That'll be asking a lot after leaving the way I did to come here."

"It won't hurt to ask. I'll even put in a good word for you."

"You're sweet to want to help and to want me underfoot in Florida."

He kissed her hand and nibbled on her knuckles, which set off fireworks inside her. That was all he had to do to get her motor running. "I want you more than underfoot. I want you under me in bed, on top of me, next to me. I want *you*, Erin Barton."

Moved and aroused by his passionate words, she said, "I want you, too."

"We're going to figure this out. I promise."

"You're awfully certain."

"I'm certain that I've waited a long time to feel this way about someone, and there's no way I'm going to let you slip through my fingers."

Keeping her hand linked with his, Erin got up to go around the countertop to where he was sitting. She stepped between his legs and let go of his hand to put her arms around him. "I'm going to miss you like crazy."

"Same goes, sweetheart."

"I'm not ready for our time together to be over."

"It's not over. It's just getting started." He drew back from her, framed her face in his hands and kissed her.

Erin wanted so badly to believe him that this was the beginning and not the end, but she was programmed to expect the worst. Her heart was heavy with dread and worry for his safety when she drove him to the airport later that morning in her dad's prized Audi. She pulled up to the curb and got out to see him off.

He put his backpack on the sidewalk and wrapped her up in a tight hug. "I'll see you soon, okay?"

"Okay." The air was so cold, their warm breath made clouds around them.

"You believe me?"

"I want to."

"Have some faith." He kissed her one last time, mindless of where they were and who might be watching as he left her with no doubt whatsoever that he wanted her more than ever. When he pulled back from her, they were both breathless and aroused and, at least in her case, despondent.

"Let me know that you get there okay."

"I will. And I'll check on you later, too. You'll hear from me so much, you'll get sick of me."

"Not possible."

"We'll see about that," he said, flashing the rakish grin that she adored. He gave her another quick kiss and lifted his backpack onto his shoulder. Walking backward, he made his way to the terminal where he'd told her he could cut through to the area where his plane was housed. Smiling at her, he waved before he turned to go inside.

Erin got back in the car and wiped away tears that she told herself were from the cold, but her heart knew better. It already ached without him by her side to make her laugh and smile and to tell her everything would be all right. It had taken just over a week for him to become essential to her, and now he was leaving for who knew how long. He had to be back in Florida tomorrow night for a scheduled trip to the Bahamas the next day.

The next break in his schedule was for Evan's wedding on the eighteenth of January, which was almost three weeks away.

Erin used the time it took to drive to the hospital to indulge in the emotional wallop of Slim's departure. She pulled into the parking lot and tried to rally her spirits so she could be supportive of her parents, but her spirits were low today, and there was no hiding that from her mother when they connected outside her dad's room.

"So he's left?" Mary Beth asked.

"Yes, just now. How's Dad?"

"He had a good night. They've taken him for a few tests. Now back to your Slim. He's a lovely, lovely guy, but I don't suppose I have to tell you that."

As her eyes filled once again, Erin shook her head. "No, you don't."

Mary Beth hugged her. "What're you going to do about him?"

"I don't know yet."

"Has he said he wants to see you again?"

"You could say that," Erin said, laughing. "The first day he was home on Gansett, he asked me to come back to Florida with him for the rest of the winter."

"Are you going?"

"I don't know yet. I'd love to spend more time with him, but I made a commitment to the town and the lighthouse. I'm building a new life on Gansett, and I love it there."

"I'm so glad you've found a place you love, Erin, but Gansett will still be there if you take some time away."

"I know. I'm thinking about it."

"Do you love him?"

Leave it to Mom to ask the hard questions. "I think I might, but it's been so long since I've loved a guy that I don't remember how to do it."

"Sure, you do. I've spent the last week with you two. If you're not in love with him—and vice versa—then I know nothing about love. I've never seen any man look at you the way he does, as if you personally hung the moon."

"He's very special."

"I hope you'll give him an honest, genuine chance to make you happy. I haven't seen you smile or laugh as much as you do with him in a very long time. Last night, Dad said you light up around him. I completely agree, and I've thought so since I first saw you with him last fall. I told Dad then that this guy was going to be something special to you."

From the first night she met him, she'd had the same feeling.

"You know what the most beautiful thing is about being an adult?" Mary Beth asked.

"What's that?"

"You can do *anything* you want—or not do anything you want. It's entirely up to you."

"That's sort of the problem. I'm paralyzed with indecision. It would be different, I think, if he lived where I do and we could date like normal people, but for most of the year, he's elsewhere. Being with him would require me to change my whole life, and I'm not sure I'm prepared to do that again. I've already done it too many times."

Mary Beth leaned back against the wall. "That's true, you have, and I can see why the thought of doing it again doesn't appeal, especially when you've found a place that makes you so happy and have started to put down roots. But think of it this way—you've never had a better reason to turn your life upside down."

Her mother made a good point.

They were interrupted by the hospital employee who was working with Mary Beth to get Tom a spot in a rehabilitation facility close to their home.

Erin listened to what they were saying and participated in the conversation, but she kept thinking about what her mother had said. She was thinking about it when Slim texted to let her know he was safely back on Gansett and already missing her. She thought about it during the afternoon she spent with her dad while her mom went home to shower and change. She thought about it on the ride back to her parents' home later and when she took her own shower.

She was still thinking about it when she got into bed in the final minutes of the year, desperately wishing she was at the wedding with Slim and could kiss him at midnight.

And when her phone rang exactly at midnight, a smile stretched across her face because she knew it had to be him.

SLIM HAD LEFT THE REVELRY OF ADAM'S WEDDING TO FIND A QUIET corner at midnight. It hadn't even been twelve hours since he'd last seen her, and he was already dying for her. If he'd needed proof of how bad he had it for her, today had been an excellent wake-up call.

"Happy New Year," she said when she answered.

The sound of her voice quieted the agitation he'd been carrying around since he left her. "Happy New Year, beautiful."

"How was the wedding?"

"Amazing. They're so perfect for each other, which is kind of funny when you consider the fact that she dated his brother for ten years."

"Abby dated one of Adam's brothers? Which one?"

"Grant. They lived together in LA for the last five years they were together, but that's been over for a long time."

"I had no idea! I can't imagine Grant with anyone but Stephanie or Abby with anyone but Adam."

"I keep forgetting you're new to these parts. I have to do a better job of keeping you up to speed on island gossip."

"Yes, you do."

"How's your dad?"

"He had a good day. They're talking about trying to get him up tomorrow. Lots of tests of his functionality, but they seem very optimistic he'll make a full recovery. It just won't happen overnight."

"Optimistic is good news."

"Yes, we're very thankful."

"I wish you were here."

"I was just thinking that very same thing."

"Were you now?"

"Uh-huh."

"I also wish I didn't have to go back to Florida tomorrow. This has been the nicest vacation I've had in years."

"Me, too. Eleven days never went by so fast."

"I know you've got a lot going on there with your dad, but the invite to Evan's wedding and Florida after still stands."

"Thank you. We'll see how the next few weeks go."

"You're making me feel cautiously optimistic about more than just your dad's recovery."

The sound of her laughter made him happier than he'd been since he left her. "You're always a charmer. I'll give you that."

"I don't want to charm anyone but you, Erin. I hope you know that."

"You're doing a pretty good job so far."

"Only *pretty good*? Now I know what my New Year's resolution will be."

"Just call me once in a while, and I'll be happy."

"That I can do." That—and so much more. Eleven days with her had been nowhere near enough. He wanted every day with her, and was determined to make sure she knew that. "Did you do anything special for New Year's Eve?"

"My mom and I went out to dinner and came home to watch the goings-on in New York City, which is a mob scene, as usual."

"I heard people wear adult diapers because there're no bathrooms in Times Square."

"That is the grossest thing I've ever heard!"

"Really? I've heard grosser stuff than that."

193

"Like what?"

"Like you want an example?"

"I want an example."

"I'm going to think about that and get back to you."

"Just remember, you have to do better than peeing yourself in frigid temperatures and then walking around with a stinking twenty-pound diaper *in your pants* in a crowd of a million or more people."

"It's a tall order. I'll give you that, but I'm up to the task."

"I'll await your example."

Smiling like a giddy fool from the entertaining conversation, he said, "I should probably get back to the wedding."

"Yes, you should. Enjoy the time with your friends, and thanks for calling. You made my day—and my New Year."

"That's nice to hear. I'll talk to you tomorrow, okay?"

"Okay."

"Erin, I..." What he wanted to say couldn't and shouldn't be said for the first time over the phone. "I really miss you."

"I miss you, too. Good night."

"Night, sweetheart."

With his face flushed from dancing and a smile stretching from one side of his face to the other, Adam McCarthy came into the lobby, stopping when he saw Slim sitting in one of the chairs. "Everything okay?"

"Yeah, sure, just had to make a phone call."

"Right at midnight?" Adam asked, brows raised. "Must've been Erin."

"If you must know, yes, it was her."

"How's her dad doing?"

"Better every day."

"That's a relief."

"Sure is. She and her family have been through enough. They were due a break."

"You like this one, huh?" Adam asked.

"Says the happy newlywed who wants everyone to be as happy as he is tonight?"

"Guilty," Adam said with a laugh. "But you didn't answer the question."

"I like her."

"This is big news."

"Could I ask you something?"

Adam sat in the chair next to Slim's. "Anything."

"How'd you know Abby was the one for you?"

Adam thought about that for a minute before he began to speak. "We'd been hanging out for a while when I got called back to New York to deal with my business. I was stuck there seeing to the details for a couple of weeks, and the whole time, I was *dying* to get back to her. That was all I could think about when I wasn't working. Her. Just her. I need her like I need oxygen, you know?"

Slim nodded because he was beginning to understand all too well. Leaving Erin had been excruciating.

"So is she it for you?" Adam asked.

"I'm starting to think she might be."

"Oh damn! Never thought I'd see the day!"

"Do me a favor? Don't tell anyone? We're a long way from being ready to make declarations."

"I gotcha. It's cool, and I won't say anything, except I'm happy for you."

Slim shook his friend's outstretched hand. "Thanks and likewise. What a great night this has been."

"Indeed it has. I gotta hit the head and get back to my wife before she gets a better offer."

"She's never going to get a better offer, and she's smart enough to know that."

Adam smiled. "I got really lucky. I hope you do, too." He took off toward the men's room, leaving Slim alone to think about his next move.

CHAPTER 22

Owen had brought Laura home from Adam's wedding at ten o'clock. She'd wanted to stick it out until midnight, but he could see that she was exhausted and had talked her into coming home to bed.

While she slept in his arms, their busy babies played a soccer game in her belly.

Owen smiled in the dark each time a little foot or elbow connected with his body and wondered how she could be sleeping through the party they were having. She'd been incredibly tired as the third trimester got under way, which was why they'd been arguing over the Christmas gift she'd given him—tickets to Anguilla for Evan and Grace's wedding.

Laura had cleared the travel with Victoria and David, and insisted they had to be there when his best friend and her cousin got married.

Owen disagreed, preferring to stay home where they'd be close to her doctor and midwife in the event of any problem.

They were at a standoff, with Laura insisting they were going and he insisting they weren't. The rare disagreement was working on his already frazzled nerves as he waited to see if his father would call again. It had been more than ten days since the last call, and Owen wondered if he'd missed the opportunity by ignoring the first two calls.

They'd spent a lot of time with his mom and Charlie over the holidays, and seeing how happy they were together made Owen determined to do what he could to win her freedom from her nightmare of a marriage.

But the bastard had yet to call again. Why didn't he call? It wasn't like Owen could call him in prison. No, he was forced to wait for Mark to make the next move, which only added to his anxiety.

Between the ongoing argument with Laura and the stress of waiting to see if his father would call, Owen knew there was no chance he'd sleep tonight. He disentangled from Laura, who'd reached for him in her sleep out of habit, and settled her on the pillow next to his. Sweeping her hair back from her face, he kissed her cheek and stared down at her for a long moment, wishing he could make her see his side of their debate.

After what'd happened to Maddie when she had Hailey and then Janey with PJ, he was terrified of something going wrong for Laura and the babies. The last place they ought to be eight weeks before her due date was in the Caribbean for a wedding, but she was determined to go, to have a last hurrah before the babies came and upended their peaceful existence.

Owen retrieved his cell phone from Laura's bedside table, took his guitar and went downstairs to the sitting room off the lobby where he wouldn't bother anyone by playing at two in the morning. Closing the door behind him, he lit a fire and settled into the armless chair that was his favorite place to practice.

Thank God for the music that had always been there for him, transporting him to another world where troubles didn't exist. He'd taught himself to play at twelve on a flea market guitar with bad strings. That guitar had opened up a whole new world to him, one that he still ran to whenever life got to be too much for him.

He was lost in the music when Laura slid her arms around him from behind. Owen wasn't surprised to realize he'd been there for ninety minutes by then.

"I woke up and you weren't there," she said. "I was worried."

"Sorry. Couldn't sleep and didn't want to bother you."

She kissed the back of his neck. "What's keeping you awake?"

"Lots of stuff."

"The trip?"

"For one thing."

"Can I say something about that?"

"Something you haven't already said?"

Smiling, she came around to sit on the footstool in front of him, which was when he noticed the baby monitor she held in her hand so they could hear Holden if he woke up. "We've had such a crazy year, O, between Holden's birth, renovating the hotel, your dad's trial, the wedding and the twins on the way. I want us to have a wonderful time away from it all before the babies come. Your mom and Charlie are thrilled to have Holden for a week, and we know he'll be in very good hands with them. Please. I just want out of here for a week, and I really want to go to my cousin's wedding—and I want you to be there, too. Evan is your best friend. He can't get married without you. And," she added, waggling her brows, "a whole week alone in Anguilla."

"Alone with your whole family and all our friends."

"With our own room to flee to any time we want."

"I'm worried something will happen while we're away."

"If it does, we'll deal with it. I'm not being frivolous with my safety or that of the babies, Owen. I have clearance from my doctor and midwife. We are still within the range where it's safe to travel. I really, really want to go, but not if it's going to keep you awake at night with anxiety."

He put down the guitar and reached for her, bringing her onto his lap. "That's not the only thing keeping me awake."

"Your father and that freaking phone call, too."

"Yeah."

"I hate him for doing this to you."

"I hate him for a lot of reasons, and then I feel guilty for hating my own father."

"He's given you plenty of reasons to feel that way."

"Still..."

"I know."

"So a whole week alone in the Caribbean, huh?" Owen asked, desperate to talk about anything other than his father.

"That's what I'm offering."

"It would take a stronger man than I am to turn down an offer like that from you."

"Yes?" she asked, her face alight with giddy excitement that made him smile. If she was happy, he was, too.

"We can go, but you'd better not let anything happen to you or our babies."

"I won't. I promise." She kissed his lips and then his neck again. "Come upstairs. I've got another offer you won't be able to refuse."

Owen laughed as his body reacted to her blatant come-on. "I don't know what I ever did without you, Laura Lawry. I was in a funk when I came down here, and then you showed up and made everything better."

"I seem to recall you doing the same for me once upon a time." She got up and held out her hand to him.

Owen took her hand and brought his guitar with him when he followed her upstairs to their apartment. They looked in on Holden, who was sleeping with his arms thrown over his head and his covers kicked off as usual. Laura covered him while Owen stashed his guitar on the stand in the corner of the living room.

They met in the bedroom, where Laura treated him to the pleasure of watching her remove her nightgown, revealing a rounded belly and breasts made large by pregnancy. He thought she was, quite simply, the most beautiful woman he'd ever laid eyes on.

"Don't look too close," she said, suddenly shy after revealing herself to him.

Owen pulled off his T-shirt and went to her, running his hands over her abundant curves. "Don't ever tell me not to look at what's mine. And there will never be a time when I don't think you're perfect."

"You're blinded by love."

"Maybe so," he said, resting his hand over the babies, "but I hope you know I mean it. I look at you, and I just see everything."

"Me, too," she whispered, drawing him down to her for a kiss.

Owen wrapped his arms around her and fell into the kiss, drowning in the sweet comfort he always found with her. He was so fully engaged with her that he almost missed the sound of his phone ringing in the pocket of his pajama pants. Withdrawing from the kiss, Owen kept one arm around her as he retrieved the phone. A quick glance showed a Virginia number on the screen.

"Give me the phone, Owen. I've got this."

"Thank you, honey, but I'll do it." Her love had given him the strength to face anything, even his monster of a father.

He took the call and accepted the collect charges. Owen sat on the bed, and Laura put her nightgown back on and sat next to him. He held the phone so she could hear, too.

"Finally," Mark Lawry said in a low growl that immediately put Owen on guard. Nothing good had ever followed that particular tone of voice.

"What do you want?" Owen asked.

"I wanted you to pick up the goddamned phone when I called you."

"Why would you think I have anything at all to say to you?"

"Maybe it's time you did some listening rather than talking. There are things you don't know."

"If you're going to tell me some sob story that you think will change how I feel about you, then you're wasting my time—and yours."

"It's not a story. It's the truth. I... I was knocked around by my old man. I never knew anything else. They've got me going to court-ordered counseling here, and the guy got me to tell him that. He said I needed to tell my kids so they'd understand why I am the way I am."

Stunned by the confession from a man who'd never once admitted to weakness of any kind, Owen tried to wrap his brain around what he was hearing.

"I told the shrink that you kids would think I'm making excuses, and he said you can think whatever you want as long as I tell you the truth. I swear on my life I'm telling you the truth, and it's something I'd never told anyone until I told him—even your mother has never heard any of this. She only knew that there was no love lost between me and my father. You were lucky you never knew him. The sadistic bastard died before you were born. One of the best days of my life was when he was hit by a car crossing the street. As far as I was concerned, he'd gotten exactly what was coming to him, but his rage... It was like he left it all to me. The first time I hit your mother was the day he died. I was wrong to do that. I knew it then. I know it now, but... It was like something would come over me, and I'd lose control of myself. The shrink... He's helping me see how it's all connected—what was done to me and what I did to all of you. I'm not making excuses. I swear that's not what this is. I just... I wanted a chance to say I-I'm sorry for what I did, Owen, to you and the others. You all deserved better than me, and I won't bother you anymore after this. I just... I wanted you to know. I'm sorry. Will you tell the others? Will you tell your mother?"

Owen couldn't breathe, let alone speak. Tears flooded his eyes, blinding him. He'd never heard his father say so many words at one time, unless they were angry words.

"Owen, are you there?"

Clearing the huge lump from his throat, he said, "I'm here."

"Will you tell them?"

"Yeah, I will."

"Two other things I want to say, and then I'll let you go. The first is that if you're ever so angry with your wife or your kids that you feel you could harm them, get help. Get help right away. If I'd done that, my life would've turned out so different. Tell your brothers I said that, okay? Tell them to get help if it happens to them."

Owen took deep breaths as the tears continued to flow. "What's the second thing?"

"No matter how it might've seemed, I loved you all. I loved you very much."

Owen had absolutely nothing to say to that.

"Thank you for taking my call. I'll sign the papers for your mother right away and get them back to the lawyer."

"Dad..."

"Yes?"

"Thank you for telling me."

"Least I could do. You'll tell your mother I said... Tell her I said to be happy. She's certainly earned the right."

Owen wiped away more tears. "I'll tell her."

"Take care, son." And then he was gone, having dropped an emotional bomb into Owen's lap, changing everything he knew to be true in one ten-minute conversation.

He ended the call and took a deep breath, trying to regain control of his emotions. "Sure as shit wasn't expecting that."

"Oh my God, Owen."

That was when he realized Laura was crying, too. He reached for her, and they held each other as they tried to comprehend what his father had told him.

"What're you thinking and feeling?" she asked after a long silence. "I can't even begin to know." She raised a hand to his face to wipe away his tears.

"I... I don't know either. All I've ever done is hate him. I don't know how to think of him as anything other than a monster. But hearing that..."

"You believe him?"

"I do, and you want to know why? Because General Mark Lawry would never, *ever* admit to anything that smacked of weakness, even to further his own agenda. There's no way he would've told me something like that if it wasn't true."

"Come lie down with me."

They crawled into bed and came together in the middle, arms and legs intertwined, her head on his chest.

"Now I have to tell everyone else about this. How do I do that?"

"The same way he told you. He came to you with this because he knew you'd be strong enough to handle it the same way you've handled everything else for your family all these years."

"I guess."

"It's true, Owen. He chose you, despite your differences, because he has faith in you to take care of the others."

"Will you take care of me while I take care of them?"

"Always." She pushed herself up on one elbow so she could kiss him.

Needing her desperately, Owen grasped handfuls of her long hair and held her close to him, losing himself in the sweetness and heat of a kiss that became desperate and needy in no time at all. Whenever he was drowning, she was there to save him, to anchor him, and he loved her more with every passing day.

Without her, the bomb his father had just dropped in his lap would've blown the lid off his life. With her, it was shocking but manageable. They'd figure out the way forward together, and knowing that made it possible for him to cope.

"Let me," she whispered against his lips, rising to straddle him. Her baby belly made this the most comfortable position for her, which was fine with him. She groaned as she took him in.

"Don't say it."

"Why not? Did you or did you not get more than your share?"

Owen wouldn't have thought it possible to laugh or smile, but she showed him otherwise as she came down on him, taking him in until he was fully seated in her tight heat. Making love with her was as close as he'd ever come to heaven, and he couldn't get enough.

She shuddered on top of him, proving that while he might've gotten more than his share, she loved every bit of what he had to give. Rocking in a slow, sensual rhythm, she drove him mad as he tried to remain still, to let her set the pace. He was always so afraid of hurting her, so he kept his hands on her hips and tried not to lose his mind as she rode him.

With her head thrown back and the faint glow of the lights from outside illuminating her pale skin, she looked like a goddess come to life. She was his goddess, the love of his life, his reason for being and the only one who could make him forget his painful past, even if only for a while.

"Owen," she whispered.

"I'm here, baby. What do you need?"

"You. Just you."

He sat up, wrapped his arms around her and held her as she came, taking him with her into bliss. There was no other word for what they found together. "Love you, Laura. I'd be losing my mind if I didn't have you to hold me together."

"I love you, too, and I'll always be here to hold you together if you do the same for me."

"Nothing else I'd rather do."

CHAPTER 23

*a*dam danced with Abby to "Stay With Me" by Sam Smith, singing the lyrics in her ear as she giggled from the champagne they'd consumed over the course of the unforgettable evening. The wedding they'd thrown together in just over a week's time had come together perfectly, with everyone they loved best in attendance, the winter wind howling outside while a huge fire burned in the fireplace in the dining room of the McCarthys' Gansett Island Inn, which had been transformed by the hotel staff for the wedding.

"So how'd we do?" Adam asked Abby. "On a scale of one to ten, ten being the best."

"I'd give this night a one thousand."

"I was thinking more like one in a million."

"One in a billion."

He smiled down at her. "Are you happy?"

"You can't tell?"

"Just making sure, since your happiness is my sole reason for being."

Sighing, she rested her head on his shoulder. "Sometimes I still think I dreamt this whole thing—from that first day on the ferry and every day since then. There's no way this can possibly be real."

"Oh, it's real, sweetheart. It's as real as it gets."

"After what happened two weeks ago, with the doctor and the diagnosis and everything, I wanted to give up, but you wouldn't let me. Thank you for that and a million other things."

"Thank *you* for marrying me and giving me a whole lifetime to share with you."

"I apologize in advance for the hard parts."

"No apology needed. We'll figure it out as we go. As long as I have you and you have me, the rest is easy."

"You really think it'll be that simple?" she asked, looking up at him with gorgeous brown eyes gone liquid with emotion.

"Probably not, but I really believe there's nothing we can't handle as long as we do it together." He kissed the top of her head and breathed in the bewitching scent of his love, feeling the silk of her hair against his face. No matter what came their way, he would do whatever it took to protect her from hurt or disappointment. She'd already had enough of both in her life. Now was the time for happily ever after.

They were surrounded tonight and in life by the people they loved best—his parents and siblings as well as their partners, his cousins, their friends, Abby's family and their larger island family. That community would celebrate with them during the good times and prop them up through the tough times. Adam truly believed they would successfully weather the storm of her illness, and they would find a path to parenthood, too. Maybe it wouldn't be the conventional path, but it would be their path.

Next to them, Dan danced with Kara, Evan with Grace, Grant with Stephanie, Mac with Maddie, Joe with Janey, Shane with Katie, Tiffany with Blaine, Seamus with Carolina, Adam's dad with his mom, his Uncle Frank with Betsy, his Uncle Kevin with Chelsea, and Luke with Sydney. Others had come and gone throughout the evening, but the core group remained and would be there for them through it all.

"What do you say we get out of here, Mrs. McCarthy?"

"Ready whenever you are."

His reply was a not-so-subtle tug on her hand, leading her in the direction of the lobby.

"Shouldn't we say good night to everyone?"

Adam took a look around to find all the happy couples engrossed in each other. "Nah. They'll figure out for themselves that we split."

"That's kind of rude."

"I'm kind of horny for my wife."

"Honestly, Adam. Did I marry a man or a teenage boy?"

"I'm all man, baby. Let's go upstairs, and I'll show you."

She was still giggling when he steered her through the lobby and up the stairs. His mother had assigned them the hotel's top-floor honeymoon suite, and their bags had been delivered earlier. It'd been years since Adam had been up here, and he couldn't remember what the room looked like. However, with his mother managing the hotel, he knew the room would be first class.

Adam used the key card she had given him to open the door. "Wait a second," he said to Abby when she would've gone in ahead of him. He could tell he surprised her when he swept her off her feet to carry her across the threshold, making her giggle some more.

He loved that champagne made her giggle, and he loved the light-hearted sound of her laughter, especially in light of the trauma of her diagnosis. He'd worried for a while that she might never laugh again, but his resilient Abby had bounced back after a few rough days, determined to battle her illness and fight for the life they both desperately wanted.

Adam swung her around in a big circle before setting her down in the middle of the sitting area, in front of another fireplace that had been lit for them. When he was certain she was steady on her feet, he went to open the glass doors to let the heat and scent of the fire into the candlelit room.

Someone had gone to a lot of trouble to ensure a romantic setting for the newlyweds. Adam fervently hoped it was Daisy and not his mother. It was Daisy. That was his story, and he was sticking to it. Then he looked down at Abby, saw tears in her eyes and was instantly on alert. "What's wrong?"

"Nothing is wrong. Everything is absolutely perfect. This is beautiful." Her gaze took in the fire, the candles, the four-poster bed with the crisp white linens that had been turned down for them, the red rose petals scattered over the bed and the champagne chilling in a bucket next to the bed.

"So are you," he said, running his fingers through her dark silky hair. He'd been so glad she left it down the way he liked it best. It might be safe to say he was obsessed with her hair, constantly touching it, burying his face in it, breathing in the scent he'd know anywhere as hers. "How do you like being married so far?"

"Best thing ever, but only because I married you."

"That's a good answer."

"What about you?"

"I'm actually relieved."

Her brows knitted adorably. "How come?"

"I was afraid you might run away from me before we could make it official."

"I thought about it."

"I know you did. Why do you think I've spent every waking minute with you for the last two weeks?"

"It wasn't because of the holidays?"

Adam shook his head. "I was afraid to give you too much time to yourself to think about how much better off I'd be without you when that couldn't be further from the truth."

"I still feel guilty about marrying you, knowing I might not be able to—"

He silenced her with a deep, passionate kiss that he hoped removed all doubt from her mind that he'd gotten exactly what—and who—he wanted most tonight. "No more of that. No more guilt or thoughts of running away or anything other than happily ever after. You hear me?"

She slipped her arms around his neck and went up on tiptoes to kiss him. "I hear you."

"Do you really? Do you know I mean every word I said to you tonight? That I love you no matter what happens? That I love you even if we can never have children the old-fashioned way? Even if you gain weight or lose some of your gorgeous hair?"

Her big eyes were shiny with unshed tears. "I believe you, Adam. And I'm so very thankful that you feel that way about me. It makes me feel like the luckiest girl in the world."

"We're both lucky to have been on that ferry together last summer. That was fate bringing us together at our lowest point and showing us a whole new path forward together. I honestly believe that." He kissed her neck and nibbled on her earlobe. "I don't want you to spend one more second worrying about what *might* happen. I want you to stay completely focused on right here and right now." He cupped her breasts and ran his thumbs over her nipples, which tightened into hard points under her dress. "Can you do that?"

"Mmm, if you keep that up, I certainly won't be thinking about anything else but you."

"I plan to keep this up forever," he said, lightly pinching her nipples to make his point.

She gasped and leaned into him, pressing her body against his erection.

Adam reached around to her back, found the zipper and lowered it slowly, dragging his fingers over her heated skin as he went. Her face was flushed with excitement, her eyes bright with desire and her lips swollen from their kisses.

"Why are you staring at me?"

"Because I've never seen anyone look more beautiful than you do right now."

"You don't look too bad yourself, Mr. McCarthy, but then again, I've always thought you were hot, even when I was dating your brother."

"We've agreed to never speak of that."

"With him," she said, giggling again. "What he doesn't know won't hurt him. Besides, he's not too shabby to look at either."

Adam scowled playfully as he helped her out of the dress, his eyes boggling at the sight of the sexy getup he found underneath. "Don't remind me that you used to sleep with my brother."

"That was a lifetime ago. It has no bearing on us."

"I know, baby. I feel like my whole life began all over again that day I found you on the ferry when you were swearing off men, and I was prepared to never have sex again if it meant I had to get involved with another woman."

"That vow didn't last long," she said, flashing the saucy smile he adored.

"Let's talk about what you're wearing."

She took a step back from him so he could get the full impact. "This old thing?"

It was almost too much for his brain to process—a bustier that showcased her full breasts, trim waist and curvy hips, a garter belt, sheer thigh-high stockings and three-inch heels. She was a sexy vision in virginal white, and she was all his for the rest of his life. "Someone pinch me, please. I can't possibly be married to the sexiest woman to ever draw a breath."

"Stop," she said, her chest and face flushing in embarrassment.

"Never." He closed the small space between them and ran his hands down her back to cup her cheeks, which had been left bare by a thong. "Do I have Tiffany Taylor to thank for this heart-stopping moment?"

"Perhaps," she said with a coy smile.

"She's very, very good at what she does. So good, in fact, that all my plans for a slow, sexy seduction of my wife have gone right out the window in favor of a quick, hard, urgent fuck."

"Yes, please."

"Mmmm, such lovely manners from a woman wearing a getup intended to make her husband insane."

She removed his tie and unbuttoned his shirt, pushing it off his shoulders. "Are you insane?"

"Absolutely, positively, out of my mind crazy about you."

"We can go slow the next time," she said, going to work on his belt and the button to his pants, which dropped into a pile at his feet. Her hands inside the back of his boxers, squeezing his ass, was nearly the end of him.

Adam helped her along by removing the shorts himself and walking her backward to the bed. "What's about to happen here is all your fault, Mrs. McCarthy."

"I can live with that."

He came down on top of her, devouring her mouth with deep, passionate kisses.

She wrapped her arms and legs around him, pressing her heat against his cock and making him crazy with need.

Adam moved her thong to the side and thrust into her, groaning at the tight fit, the heat and the squeeze of her internal muscles. Nothing in his life could compare to the singular experience of being inside her, wrapped up in her, in love with her.

Abby made it even more intense when she clutched his ass and pulled him deeper into her.

He looked down at her, his eyes meeting hers in a moment of perfect unity. "Love you forever, Mrs. McCarthy."

"Love you, too, Mr. McCarthy."

Smiling, he hammered into her until they were coming—loudly —together.

"Holy wow," she whispered, running her fingers through the sweaty strands of his hair.

"Holy loud sex."

She laughed. "At least our families will know this marriage has been well and truly consummated."

"Indeed." He raised his head to kiss her softly. "No escaping now."

"You're stuck with me."

"Good, because you're all I need."

CHAPTER 24

*A*lone in his room on the third floor, Slim was unbearably lonely for Erin, especially after hearing signs of marital bliss from the room down the hall. He who had slept alone for most of his life was suddenly tossing and turning without her to hold on to.

He wondered if she was feeling the same way, so he texted her, hoping she was still awake.

Favorite ice cream?

The message immediately showed as read, and he could see that she was replying. That was all it took to make him feel less lonely and breathless with anticipation as he waited to see what she had to say.

Depends on the season. Sherbet in the summer, and cookie dough the rest of the year. What about you?

Rocky road all year long, baby.

What're you doing awake?

Missing you. How did you ruin a successful career of sleeping alone for me in just one week?

The same way you ruined it for me. Does that mean you didn't pick up a single girl to take home from the wedding?

Slim knew she was joking, but the idea of her thinking he would do that had him calling her. "None of the single girls at the wedding were you," he said when she answered. "So no pickups for me."

"That's nice to hear." Her voice sounded sexy and husky and way too far away.

"I hope you know I mean that. We've started something here, and I'm not going to run out and get laid the second you're somewhere else."

"Also good to know."

"What about you? Do I need to be worried?"

"Seeing as how I hadn't gotten *laid*, as you put it, in two years before last week, I think you're safe with me."

"*Two years?* That's a federal crime. A woman as hot and sexy as you needs regular care and servicing."

"*Servicing?* Is that what they're calling it these days?"

"I miss you."

"So you said."

"I mean I *really* miss you."

"I really miss you, too."

"I can't wait months to see you again. You have to come with me to Evan's wedding."

"I hope you know I'd love to go. It's just going to depend on how my dad is doing."

"Of course. I don't mean to pressure you."

"Yes, you do," she said, laughing.

"Maybe just a little. Can't blame a guy for trying." After a long pause, he said, "Tonight was incredible. I've never seen Adam so happy."

"They're a great couple."

"So are we."

"Are we a couple?"

"Why must you tease me? Didn't we just say we aren't planning to be with anyone else?"

"I think we did."

"So doesn't that make us a couple?"

"I suppose maybe it does."

"Are you screwing with me, Erin?"

"Would I do that to you?"

"Yes, I believe you would," he said, amused by her even if she was most definitely screwing with him.

"Who's your favorite president?" she asked.

Though he realized she was steering the conversation away from serious stuff, he was okay with that. There'd be time to figure it all out later. "Ohh, that's a tough one." He took a long moment to consider his answer. "I'm going with Millard Fillmore."

"Seriously?"

"Very seriously."

"Why him?"

"I feel kind of bad for the guy. He was a lifelong public servant and the last of the Whigs to be president, but he never makes anyone's top-ten presidents list."

"So he's your favorite because you feel sorry for him? That's not a good reason."

"Is he like the semicolons of presidents?"

Sputtering with laughter, she said, "Something like that."

"Who's your favorite?"

"Reagan."

"So you're a Reagan Republican, then?"

"Not really. I vote for people rather than parties, and I always thought he seemed like a nice guy. He was crazy about his wife, too. He wrote her the most amazing love letters."

Note to self—look up the letters Reagan wrote to his wife. "They say she wore the pants in the White House."

"I love that! Imagine all the West Wing suits back in the '80s afraid of a ninety-pound woman. That's the way it ought to be."

So his girl was a card-carrying feminist, too. He liked that.

"Is Millard Fillmore really your favorite president?"

"Nah," he said with a low chuckle. "I always liked to read about Kennedy."

"I liked to read about his family. Imagine having *nine* kids!"

"Um, no, thank you very much."

They talked for another hour about nothing in particular, but that was okay. He loved the sound of her voice and was interested in everything she had to say.

"You should get some sleep," she said as the clock edged closer to two. "You've got a long day in the air tomorrow."

"You're right. I should get some Z's, and so should you."

"I'm glad you called."

"I'm glad I called, too, but I still miss you."

"Me, too."

"Does this mean you'll be my girlfriend?"

"Is that what you want?"

"I believe it is."

"Okay."

"*Yes?*"

"Okay generally means yes," she said, laughing.

"And I'm your boyfriend?"

"Aren't we kind of old for these titles?"

"Not at all. My eighty-six-year-old grandfather had 'girlfriends' until the day he died."

"Something tells me you're going to be just like him."

"My gramps was a bit of a hound dog with the ladies at his nursing home, whereas I'm more of a one-girl-at-a-time kind of guy."

"That's good to know."

"So that's a *yes* on the boyfriend thing?"

"I haven't had a boyfriend in a long, long time. I might need a refresher course on what's involved."

"You're in luck. I'm a certified instructor."

"Certified in *what* exactly?"

"Well, technically pilot training, but a lot of the skills are transferable to this situation."

She laughed so hard, she couldn't talk, which put a huge smile on his face.

"I'll be calling my new girlfriend tomorrow. Will she take my call?"

"Yes, Slim," she said with a sigh of what sounded like pleasure. God, he hoped so. "She'll take your call."

~

THE NEXT AFTERNOON, ERIN ROLLED HER DAD IN HIS WHEELCHAIR TO physical therapy, giving her mother a much-needed break from the hospital. They'd insisted she keep an annual New Year's lunch date with friends and enjoy the time away. As they went, she was careful to step on each new floor tile with her left foot first. God only knew what would happen if she didn't do that, and she certainly didn't want to find out.

"Sorry to drag you away from your island," Tom said, his speech halting but improving every day. In an ironic twist of OCD fate, his left side had been impaired by the aneurism, but the physical and occupational therapists had assured them he'd regain functionality eventually.

"Where else would I be when you're in here? It's no bother at all."

"When will you see your pilot friend again?"

"I'm not sure yet. Maybe in a couple of weeks." She wanted to go to the wedding in Anguilla more than she'd wanted anything in a very long time. The thought of a week in paradise with Slim was almost enough to make her drool.

"You should go be with him. I'm fine. The doctors said so."

"I know, Dad, but I'm not going anywhere just yet."

"I like him."

Erin smiled. "I'm glad you do."

"I like the way he looks at you."

"I do, too."

"You might want to think about keeping this one, Er Bear."

The childhood nickname, which he hadn't used in years, brought tears to her eyes. "You think so?" she asked, her voice hushed.

"Yeah." When they arrived at the physical therapy department, Tom raised his right arm slowly, waggling his fingers in her direction.

Curious, Erin stepped around to the front of the chair and squatted down so she could see him, noting the slight sag on the left side of his mouth.

"Don't do what you do with this guy."

"What do I do?" Erin asked, genuinely baffled.

"Sabotage." He held out his hand to her. "Remember that nice guy Dave? We liked him. You liked him. He liked you—a lot. But what did you do when it started getting serious? Took a job two hours away, which put a damper on the relationship. Then there was Miles. He was a good guy, too, until he invited you to meet his family. Remember what happened then?"

Astounded by his recall and the point he was trying to make, Erin nodded. She remembered all too well. For a guy who was recovering from brain surgery, he was awfully sharp.

"You broke up with him because you weren't looking for anything serious—and meeting his family smacked of serious. Don't do that this time, Er Bear. Mom and I aren't going to live forever. I don't want you to be alone in this world when we're gone."

"Don't say that. You're not going anywhere."

"Not any time soon, but eventually we are. You've got a wonderful guy who's crazy about you. Take a chance. Your brother wouldn't want you hiding out in fear of losing someone else. He'd want you to live as fully as you possibly can."

"I'm not doing that. I'm not hiding out."

He raised a brow. "No? Sure seems that way to me sometimes."

"How long have you been wanting to say these things?"

"Long time. Something about having your head nearly explode puts things into perspective. No time like the present to see my little girl happy. No one deserves it more than she does."

Erin laughed and wiped away tears. "I'm so glad you didn't die, Dad."

"Me, too. I still want to walk my daughter down the aisle someday. It's on my bucket list."

She stood to hug him, holding on tight to one of her anchors. They'd been through the hell of losing Toby together and had survived, somehow.

The door to PT swung open. "Mr. Barton? We're ready whenever you are."

"Two hours of torture," Tom whispered to Erin.

"Do what they tell you so we can get you out of here." He was making such great progress that they were now thinking he'd be able to go right home rather than to rehab, which had been huge news earlier in the day.

"Don't wait around," Tom said. "Go take a walk or have something to eat. They'll get me back to my room, and I'll need a nap after they wear me out."

"Okay. I'll check on you later." She kissed his cheek and watched the therapist roll him through the double doors. For a long time after he went in, she stood outside the doors, watching through the windows as the therapist transferred him from the chair to a table, where she put him through a series of exercises, focusing on his left side.

Erin thought about what he'd said, and couldn't hide from the truth he'd exposed. Though it hadn't been intentional, she was guilty of running away from relationships that got too serious for her to handle. Life was easier on the surface. No one got hurt. No one's existence was shattered if they lost the one they loved.

While avoidance had kept her safe from hurt, it had also made for a rather lonely existence. It had taken Slim Jackson less than a week to show her how much more fun it would be to have him around, rather than spending every day by herself.

CHAPTER 25

*E*rin carried that thought with her as she rode the elevator to the lobby, intending to take a walk while her dad was in PT. Her mom wouldn't be back for a couple of hours yet. Erin was walking through the main doors when she nearly collided with someone coming in.

The familiar scent of leather and the unmistakable cologne had her gasping and looking up at Slim's face as he grasped her arms to keep her from tripping over him.

"W-what—"

He kissed her right there in the middle of the busy doorway, generating a few catcalls and laughs as people went by them. "There you are."

"What're you *doing* here?" She'd thought he'd be halfway to Florida by now.

He took her by the arm to move them out of the stream of foot traffic. "My client moved his flight to the Bahamas from tomorrow to the day after, so I figured I'd stop by on my way south. Hope that's okay?"

Erin threw herself into his arms, hugging him so tight that he gasped and then laughed.

"I take it that's a yes?"

She nodded. "I'm so happy to see you."

"Likewise. I was going crazy missing you after one night away, and when my client texted early this morning, I ran for the airport."

"I'm so glad your client texted you." She kissed him again, not caring in the least that they were drawing the attention of everyone who walked by.

"How's your dad?"

"He's doing great. He's at PT for the next couple of hours."

"And your mom?"

"Is at lunch with her friends."

"So you're free and clear?"

"For the moment. Why?"

He took her by the hand and began walking—quickly—so quickly she had to scramble to keep up with his long-legged stride.

"Where're we going? Slim!"

"You'll see." He led her around the corner and two blocks over to a hotel, walking into the lobby like he belonged there. At the registration counter, he said, "Could we get a room for the night, please?"

Erin's entire body went hot with desire and longing and embarrassment when she realized what he was doing.

The clerk eyed them suspiciously—or so it seemed to her—and said, "Let me see what we have available." He clicked around on the computer until he found an available room. "Our check-in time isn't until three."

"We have a family member in the hospital," Slim said, producing his credit card. "They encouraged us to get some sleep while we can. I'm sure you understand."

"Of course."

Erin didn't dare look at him, out of fear she might spontaneously combust from the yearning, not to mention trying not to laugh at his shamelessness.

The clerk returned Slim's credit card along with two key cards and gave them directions to the elevator. "I'll pray for your loved one," he said.

"Thank you so much," Slim said gravely. "That means the world to us." Taking hold of Erin's hand, he half walked, half dragged her to the elevator. The moment the doors closed to the lobby, they lost it laughing.

"*Oh my God*," she said when she could talk again. "You used my father so *shamelessly*." And after their talk earlier, she knew her dad would've loved it. Well, maybe not the part about what was sure to be a wild booty call, but that she was off having fun with a man he admired. That part he would like.

"I know," he said, wincing. "I feel kind of guilty about that, but I have a feeling I'll get over it."

On the seventh floor, the elevator dinged to announce their arrival. He tugged her along behind him as he found their room, dropping her hand only to get the door open and usher her inside ahead of him. The second the door clicked shut behind them, he pounced, devouring her mouth and touching her everywhere he could get to under her coat, which quickly fell to the floor along with her sweater, jeans and bra.

"*Hurry*," he said, as he worked the buttons on his shirt while she took care of his jeans.

His urgency fanned the fire burning inside her, which only intensified when his cock fell hard and hot into her hand.

She stroked him, drawing a hiss from him that had her dropping to her knees to take him into her mouth.

"Holy shit," he whispered. "Erin, *fuck*... God, don't stop." He buried his fingers in her hair, holding on tightly as she took him as deep as she could, until the head was snug against her throat. "*Babe...*" Tugging on her hair, he tried to warn her before he came in her mouth, his big body shuddering as wave after wave overtook him, leaving him gasping when it was over.

Erin looked up at him, feeling shy in the wake of the storm.

He reached for her, helping her up and into his arms for another wild kiss. By the time they came up for air, he was already hard again and lifting her right off her feet to press her against the wall.

"Slim, wait..."

"I don't want to wait." Forgoing the condom, he thrust into her in one smooth movement that had her head falling back against the wall in complete surrender. "Ahhh, there," he said, his lips close to her ear. "That's it. So hot and so tight and all mine."

His possessiveness was as much of a turn-on as the deep thrusts of his cock and the tight squeeze of his hands on her ass while he took them on a wild ride. She'd never wanted to be possessed by a man, but now...

He bent his head to draw her nipple into his mouth, sucking and biting just hard enough to trigger an explosive orgasm.

"Ah, *fuck*," he muttered, dropping his head to her shoulder and taking his own pleasure.

For a long time afterward, the only sounds in the room were that of them breathing hard as they recovered.

When he finally raised his head to look at her, he looked as poleaxed as she felt. "Holy moly."

"Mmm." She was so blissed out, she couldn't form coherent thoughts. "No condom."

"Noticed that, huh?"

"Uh-huh. How was it?"

"Spectacular. But then again, it always is with you."

Erin caressed his face and stared into his eyes, lost in the sea of emotion she found there.

"Hold on to me." That was the only warning Erin got before he lifted her and carried her to the bed while maintaining their intimate connection. He came down on top of her, his chest hair rubbing against her nipples, which reawakened her recently well-satisfied libido.

Propped up on his elbows, he gazed down at her and brushed the hair back from her face. "In case it's not obvious, I probably ought to tell you..."

"What?" she asked, immediately on alert for bad news.

"I seem to have fallen completely and absolutely in love with you at some point in the last four months."

"Oh," Erin said, stunned by his blunt confession. "You have?"

Nodding, he kept his gaze fixed on her face as he kissed her softly, tenderly, slaying her with sweetness.

Overwhelmed by the powerful emotions he stirred in her, she raised her hands to his face and opened her mouth to his tongue, allowing him to sweep her up in another wave of powerful desire. She loved him, too. Of course she did. But if she told him so, if she said the words, it would change everything.

Was she ready to change everything? To take a huge leap with a man she'd known only four months? Her father's words from earlier echoed through her mind as Slim began to move again, thrusting slowly this time, leaving no doubt in her mind that while the first time might've been wild sex, this time was all about lovemaking.

He never looked away, he never stopped touching her or kissing her or letting her know with everything he did that he meant what he'd said.

Erin felt like a coward when she closed her eyes against the intensity that was suddenly too much for her—and not enough at the same time. Yes, she was that much of a mess on the inside as she tried to make sense of the powerful feelings he evoked in her.

"Mmm, so good," he whispered in her ear. "It's never been so good."

Erin tightened her arms around him, determined to enjoy every second of this unexpected time together. There'd be time for life decisions later.

He told himself it didn't matter that she didn't say it back, because it didn't. At least, not yet it didn't. If this went on for much longer, it would start to matter, but for now, he was thankful to be with her, to be naked in a bed with her in the middle of the day, to have her soft skin brushing up against him and the sweet fragrance of her hair invading his senses.

It was enough.

"When do you have to be back to the hospital?" he asked, nuzzling her neck. After three explosive orgasms, he should've been completely spent, but the soft ass cheeks cradling his cock had him hard and ready to go again. He would never forget the way she'd dropped to her knees to take him into her mouth. Just thinking about it made him even harder than he already was.

"Not until later." She covered the hand he had on her belly with hers, linking their fingers. "I should text my mom at some point and tell her I left to do some errands or something."

"Is that what we're doing?" he asked on a low chuckle. "Errands?"

"That can be our code word."

He could hear the amusement in the words that gave him hope there might be a future for them, because suddenly that was the one thing he wanted the most—more of her.

"Slim…"

"Hmm?"

"What you said before…"

"I said that because I wanted you to know, not because I'm trying to pressure you."

"I want you to know… I feel so much for you, and I'm trying to process it all and to figure out what to do about it."

"That's more than enough for me. Take all the time you need. I'm not going anywhere."

"Except Florida."

"And you're welcome to visit any time you want, or better yet, move there to live with me for the rest of the winter." He nudged her ass with his erection. "Then we could do *this* any time we wanted." Cupping her breast, he punctuated his point by lightly pinching her nipple.

She pushed back against him, which he took as a green light for more.

Slim released her hand and began kissing his way down her back, intending to kiss every soft inch of her. He'd do whatever it took to make her see that they were meant to be.

ERIN WAS COMPLETELY SEX DRUNK BY THE TIME THEY WALKED HAND IN hand back to the hospital later that afternoon. She'd done what she could with the small amount of makeup she carried in her purse to hide the razor burn on her chin and on her neck. The swollen lips, however, were impossible to hide.

"I bet I look like a well-used floozy," she muttered under her breath as they waited for the elevator.

He tugged her in closer to him with his arm tight around her shoulder. "You look beautiful."

"Said the man who had sex four times in three hours."

"Shhh, don't tell everyone."

Since there was no one around to hear them, she elbowed his ribs, making him grunt with laughter.

"And PS, that was *all* because of you. I've never done anything like what we just did with anyone else."

"Neither have I," she said, looking up at him and noticing his lips were rather swollen, too. "I've never once, in my entire life, checked into a hotel without luggage."

"What do you think of it?"

"I think it's something everyone should do at least once."

"Or at least four times."

Erin was still laughing when the elevator deposited them on her dad's floor.

Slim gave her a light tap on the ass. "Get yourself together before we have to face your parents."

She managed to find some composure but was still wearing a happy, dopey grin when they walked into the room where her dad was napping and her mom was knitting. Mary Beth's eyes lit up with pleasure at the sight of Slim. She put down her knitting needles and got up to hug him.

"What a nice surprise! I didn't think we'd see you again for a while."

"I didn't think so either, but a very accommodating client changed his plans and made it possible for me to stop by on my way to Florida."

"I'm sure Erin was happy to see you."

He looked down at her, a stupid grin on his handsome face. "I think she was."

"Did you get all your errands done, honey?"

Erin began to choke, coughing as Slim patted her back and her mother poured water from the pitcher on her dad's bedside table.

The racket woke Tom, who also brightened when he saw Slim there. Apparently, Erin wasn't the only one falling in love with him. "You're back," Tom said.

"Just for the night," Slim said.

"Good to see you."

"You, too. I hear you're doing great."

"That's right and ready to get out of here."

"Couple more days, Dad," Erin said when she'd recovered from the coughing fit.

They stayed until the end of visiting hours, when Tom encouraged them all to go get a good night's sleep. "I'm fine, and you'll be no good to me if you get sick from exhaustion," he said to Mary Beth, who wanted to stay.

He talked her into going home, and Erin and Slim walked her to the car.

"I'm going to stay in town tonight," Erin said, feeling her face and ears go hot as she basically confessed to her mother that she'd be spending the night with Slim.

"I figured as much. Can I grab you a change of clothes?"

"That'd be great, thanks."

Mary Beth hugged both of them before getting into the car.

"Okay, that was *mortifying*," Erin said after her mother had driven off.

"What was?" Slim put his arm around her as they walked to the hotel.

"Telling my mom that I was staying with you tonight."

"You're thirty-eight, Erin."

"So what? To her, I'm still sixteen and about to sleep with my boyfriend."

"Did you sleep with your boyfriend at sixteen?"

She elbowed his ribs and realized he gave her cause to do that about once an hour. "You know what I mean. She's still my mom."

"I bet she knows we slept together at her house, too." Since they'd traded off shifts at the hospital, Mary Beth hadn't been home at the same time they were. "As only one bed was used."

"You're enjoying this, aren't you?"

"Every minute. Every single second of it."

Erin had been referring to her discomfort over her mom knowing they were sleeping together. She suspected he meant something else altogether, and his comment brought back the giddy, breathless feeling she had experienced so often with him.

"I need to buy a toothbrush," she said when they reached the hotel lobby. They went into the store, where she got a toothbrush, a hairbrush and a couple of bottles of water.

Being in the elevator with him at her side took her right back to the urgency of their earlier encounter, making her tingle with anticipation for an entire night with him. She was trying not to think about him leaving again in the morning. That was hours from now, and she'd deal with that when she had to.

As they walked, she was careful to step properly around the art-deco design on the hotel rug that made it difficult to keep to her rituals.

"I was thinking about something on the way here earlier that I wanted to run by you," he said when they were in their room.

"What's that?"

"You were saying how your OCD and fear of flying are about feeling anxious when you don't have control of a situation. What if I taught you how to fly? Then maybe you wouldn't feel out of control when you're on a plane."

Erin removed her coat, hung it over the back of the desk chair and turned to him. "You want to teach *me* how to *fly*?"

"If you'd like to learn. I was joking about being an instructor last night, but I really am a qualified flight instructor, and I'd love to teach you, if you think it would help."

"I've never considered that possibility."

"Well, think about it, and let me know." He slid his arms around her waist and looked down at her, a sexy grin making his eyes glow with mischief. "I've got some more errands to do. You want to help me out with that?"

She smiled up at him. "I'd love to."

CHAPTER 26

*E*rin cried the next morning when it came time for him to leave. She wasn't proud of the waterworks, but she couldn't seem to help it.

"You're killing me," he whispered as he held her close to him. He was fully dressed and smelled delicious after a shower and a shave. She was still naked in bed, disheveled and distressed after a night she wouldn't ever forget.

"I'm worried about you flying. You didn't get much sleep."

"I'll be fine. Don't worry about me."

"That's like asking me not to breathe."

Cupping her face, he kissed her. "I'll see you soon."

He said what she needed to hear, but they both knew it would be a while before they saw each other again. His schedule would be hectic when he went back to work, and there'd be no more sweet, sexy stolen nights for quite some time.

"Let me know when you get home?"

"You'll be the first to know." He wrapped her up in his strong arms and held her for a long moment.

Erin clung to him, breathing in the subtle scent of his cologne, committing it to memory.

"We're going to figure this out. I promise you that."

"I'm not usually such a crybaby."

"It's okay," he said, kissing away a tear. "It makes me feel hopeful that you might like me as much as I like you."

"I do."

Smiling, he kissed her again before he released her, leaving her bereft without the heat of his body pressed up against hers. He was headed for the door when he turned back to kiss her one more time, lingering long enough to draw more tears. "This time, I've really got to go."

"This time, I've really got to let you."

"Something this great? It has to work out. Don't worry, okay?"

"I'll try not to."

When the door clicked shut behind him, Erin fell back against the pillows and gave in to a good cry. This was crazy! She was a mature woman crying over a *man*! But he wasn't just any man, and he'd swung into town unexpectedly and rocked her world in more ways than one.

"I seem to have fallen completely and absolutely in love with you at some point in the last four months."

Why didn't I tell him that I've fallen, too? I should've told him. Erin covered her face with her hands, desperately trying to regain her equilibrium. After a long pity party, she got up, showered and left the room where they'd created so many precious memories.

Her heart ached that day and every day that followed as she went through the motions of supporting her parents and writing her column whenever she could steal a quiet moment.

Despite frequent texts, calls and FaceTime chats with Slim, she couldn't seem to shake the malaise that began that morning in the hotel room and stayed with her over the next week, prompting her mom to ask more than once what was wrong.

She couldn't say, exactly. But for some reason, she felt like she was fighting against a rip current, trying to figure out where she belonged now that her life had been irreparably altered by a handsome, sexy, wonderful man who wanted everything from her.

Could she do it? Could she hand over her heart to him and hope that nothing would ever happen to crush her again the way she'd been crushed once before? In a middle-of-the-night moment of clarity more than a week after she'd last seen him, Erin finally understood why she couldn't shake the disquiet.

It was because she was on the verge of possibly taking the biggest risk she'd taken since losing her brother, and the fear of the many ways it could go wrong had her paralyzed with indecision. She didn't have the slightest doubt that Slim was sincere in his feelings and his intentions. He was a good and honorable man who would treat her like a queen. He wasn't the problem. She was.

Could she turn over control of her heart, her life, her love to someone who had the power to devastate her? What if something happened to him, too? How would she ever endure that kind of loss a second time? Wouldn't it be easier—and safer—to stay single and unencumbered, to never risk more than she could afford to lose?

These were the questions that kept her awake at night as she tried to find the courage she would need to take the enormous step he was asking her to make. The woman she'd once been, before life and tragedy changed her, would've been all in. She would've run to Slim with her arms and heart wide open to the possibilities. She would've embraced the joy and given no thought whatsoever to the fear of what *might* happen.

Post-9/11 Erin had learned to be wary, cautious and obsessive about the safety of those she loved. Would her obsessiveness smother a man like Slim, who was used to doing his own thing without anyone to answer to?

She went through her days and nights exhausted and over-whelmed by the debate that raged within her as she supported her parents, talked to Slim and texted with her Gansett friends, who checked in regularly as she tried to figure out her next move.

Her dad had been released from the hospital three days after Slim's visit and was receiving at-home physical and occupational therapy as he continued to recover quickly.

"There's really no need for you to stick around here if you've got

better things to do," Tom said to her over breakfast on a Friday morning, ten days after Slim went home to Florida.

"I don't mind staying awhile longer to keep you guys company."

"Or you could get on a plane tonight and go see the guy you're
thinking about constantly."

Erin stared at her dad, her mouth agape from his unusually blunt
statement.

"Are you denying that you're thinking constantly about him?"

She tried not to squirm under his intense stare. "No."

Tom struggled to butter his own toast, but Erin knew he wanted to
do it himself, so she refrained from helping him. "You ought to do
something about that."

"I agree, honey," Mary Beth said. "You haven't been yourself since
he left, and we just want you to be happy. He makes you happy."

Yes, he certainly did. He made her happier than she'd ever
dreamed of being, and she wanted nothing more than to grab on to
that feeling with both hands and never let it go. But what if… *No. No.
No.* She simply couldn't bear the merry-go-round of thoughts her
brain was torturing her with any longer. She was about to snap from
the unending debate.

The doorbell rang, giving her a temporary reprieve. "I'll get it." She
opened the front door to a FedEx delivery guy who handed over a
letter-size package and asked her to sign for it.

"Have a good day," he said.

"Thanks, you, too." Her heart took a happy leap when she saw
Slim's name on the return address portion of the label and his address
in West Palm Beach. It was the first time she'd seen his masculine
handwriting. She tore into the envelope that had a big lump in the
middle of it that turned out to be a CD case. The envelope also
contained a white sheet of paper and a second sealed envelope.

The note said: *Dear Erin, listen to the song on the CD and then open the
other envelope. Love, Slim.*

"Who was at the door, honey?" Mary Beth called from the kitchen.

"FedEx for me. I'll be right back." She ran into her dad's study and
fumbled her way through putting the CD into the drive on his

computer. Erin recognized the song immediately—it was the hit single "Please" by the young winner of *The Voice*, Sawyer Fredericks. She'd loved watching him perform on the show and adored the song that had all new meaning to her in light of the man who'd asked her to listen to it, especially because he knew she loved it.

She wept as she listened to the song that perfectly summed up their current situation and her yearning for him. And then she opened the second envelope.

You did it once; you can do it again; and no one is ever afraid to fly in first class; it's a rule. There's nothing I'd love more; than to have you in Anguilla with me; for my buddy's wedding; PLEASE come; and make me the happiest guy; who ever lived.

Erin laughed and cried as she read his sweet note and found a first-class ticket from Philadelphia to Anguilla for next Thursday in the envelope. The words, the song, the semicolons, the ticket, the plea... All of it added up to make the decision she'd been wrestling with seem rather foolish in light of what she felt for him.

When her phone chimed with a text, she pulled it from her pocket, not surprised to see it was from him. Of course he'd been tracking the package and knew exactly when it had been delivered.

Well...

You ruined it with the semicolons. ;-)

The semicolon is for unfinished thoughts; we are unfinished; I thought it fitting in this one instance; I promise to never insult you with a ; again if you come finish what we started...

You're amazing. Thank you for this.

You know the part where Sawyer says he's down on his knees? That's me right now. Oh, and where he says he was born to kiss your mouth? That's me, too.

You've got me in tears. Was that your goal?

Is that a yes?!?!!!! Note enthusiastic use of exclamation marks!!!

Laughing, she held her phone in her hand, staring down at the screen, hovering on the verge of putting her fears behind her and grabbing on to what she wanted more than she'd wanted anything in fifteen long, torturous years.

She texted one word: *Yes*. And just that simply, the cloud of disquiet lifted, and the giddy, breathless anticipation came rushing back. How would she *survive* until Thursday?

~

OWEN INVITED HIS MOM, CHARLIE, KATIE AND SHANE TO THEIR PLACE for a dinner he and Laura prepared together. He'd taken a couple of days to process what his father had told him, and was ready now to share it with his mom and Katie to begin with and then his other siblings.

While Laura changed Holden into pajamas, he stirred the marinara they'd made from scratch. The activity had helped to keep him busy and focused on the meal rather than what he had to tell his guests.

Laura held Holden's hand as he toddled from his bedroom to the kitchen.

"Look at my big boy walking like a grown man," Owen said, scooping him up to place kisses on his neck that resulted in the belly laugh they loved so much.

"Dadadada."

Owen closed his eyes and breathed in the sweet baby scent of the boy he adored, determined to take this last step to put the past behind him so he could focus entirely on the family he and Laura were creating together.

"I need to get him down before they arrive, or he'll never go to bed," Laura said.

Holden had spent the afternoon with Uncle Shane and Aunt Katie and was rubbing at his eyes with tight little fists.

"I'll take him in." Any day now, she would have to stop picking up Holden until after the babies were born. Owen settled him in the crib with his blanket, which Holden immediately kicked off. Laughing, Owen covered him again, and Holden kicked it off. "Mommy, someone is misbehaving."

"Holden, is Daddy being naughty?"

"Gagagaga Dadada."

"I knew it." Laura resettled him, turned on the mobile that took his attention off the blanket and swept her fingers through the baby's downy hair one more time before leaving him to sleep.

"Mommy is good at that," Owen whispered outside the bedroom door.

"Daddy is good at winding him up at bedtime, which won't be quite so funny when there're three of them."

Owen waggled his brows at her. "Daddy loves when Mommy chastises him."

Smiling up at him, Laura cupped his cheek and caressed him with her thumb. "You seem good."

"I feel good, ready to get this over with and start packing for the trip."

"I'll be right there with you if it gets hard."

"That's the only thing that's gotten me through this latest crisis." He dropped his forehead to rest against hers. "You've got to be so tired of my family issues by now."

"Not at all. It's a small price to pay to get to be married to you."

"Thank you, baby."

A soft knock on the door indicated their guests had arrived.

"Ready?" she asked.

"Let's do it." He went to admit his mom, Charlie, Katie and Shane, who spoke in whispers because they knew Holden had just gone to bed and would put up a fuss if he heard them. They stayed quiet through dinner, after which Laura checked on Holden and said it was safe to speak normally.

"Thank you for the lovely dinner," Sarah said, refilling her wineglass. She had a serenity about her these days that was hard to miss, and Owen couldn't wait to let her know that she'd soon be free to marry the man she loved.

"You're welcome." He glanced at Laura, who reached for his hand and gave it a subtle squeeze under the table, fortifying him to take the next step. "So there was a reason other than dinner that I wanted to get together tonight."

"Well," Katie said, "we know you're not going to tell us you're pregnant."

Their laughter diffused the last of Owen's nerves. "Very funny. Actually, I wanted to tell you I heard from Dad."

Stunned silence greeted his statement. Owen went on to tell them about the remarkable conversation he'd had with Mark. As he spoke, Sarah raised her hand to her heart, and Charlie put his arm around her. Katie stared bleakly at the far wall while Shane moved his chair closer to hers. Such was the Mark Lawry effect on his family members.

"He's full of shit," Katie said fiercely. "He realized he's all alone in the world, and this is what he's doing about it."

"I don't think so, sis," Owen said, knowing his opinion would matter to her and the others. "I think it's the truth. If you could've heard him... He was different than he's ever been with me. Still gruff and domineering, but contrite, too. And what he said about me and the boys getting help if we ever feel that way toward our wives and children... It felt like genuine parental concern to me."

Katie crossed her arms, her face set in a mulish expression that told Owen she might not come around right away. That was okay. It had taken him a couple of days to wrap his mind around it. He turned his attention to his mother, who seemed as stunned as Owen had felt upon hearing his father's story.

"I always wondered," Sarah said softly, "how a boy grows up to be that kind of man. He never spoke of his childhood. After the funeral, we never spoke of his father again."

"He said that was the first time he hit you," Owen said.

Her hand covered her left cheek. "Yes. I said something about feeling sorry for his father dying the way he had, and he slapped me across the face, saying his father was exactly where he belonged, in hell with the devil, and I was never to mention that son of a bitch's name again. I never did."

Next to her, Owen noticed Charlie wrestling with his emotions. It was hard for him to hear about the abuse she'd withstood at the hands of her husband.

"The divorce papers should be landing on Dan Torrington's desk any day now," Owen said, sharing the good news now that the harder part was out of the way.

"What?" Sarah asked, wide-eyed.

"He told me if I took his call, he'd give you the divorce. He promised he'd sign the divorce papers and mail them the day I talked to him, which means you should get them soon."

"Oh, Owen," Sarah said as she put it all together. "He convinced you to take his call by telling you he'd sign the papers if you did?"

"That doesn't matter."

"Yes, it does! How can you say that doesn't matter?"

"Because it doesn't. Not anymore. You're getting what you wanted, and we'll all have some closure."

"At what cost to you?" his mother asked tearfully.

"I'm okay, Mom. I swear. I'm fine. Ask Laura."

His wife nodded in agreement. "He was thrown for a loop at first and anxious about telling the rest of you, but he's good now."

Sarah sat back in her chair, seeming stunned by the turn of events. "He signed the papers."

Owen smiled at her. "He signed the papers."

Sarah began to laugh and cry at the same time.

Charlie hauled her into his arms, kissing her square on the mouth right in front of her children and their partners.

Even Katie smiled at Charlie's rare loss of control. She leaned on Shane, her expression softer now that she'd had a few minutes to process what she'd heard.

"We can get *married*," Charlie said in a gruff whisper.

"We can get *married*," Sarah replied, staring into his steel-blue eyes.

Owen glanced at Laura, who dabbed at her eyes. They shared a smile, full of love and relief and optimism for the future now that the past was where it belonged once and for all.

CHAPTER 27

*S*unday night, Big Mac McCarthy called his family together for a meeting to go over the final plans for their trip to Anguilla in the morning. He'd taken great pleasure in planning every detail of the trip on behalf of his kids, their families, his brothers, niece and nephews. How often would an opportunity like this come along now that all the kids were grown and had families and lives of their own? Big Mac wanted it to be perfect for them, especially Evan, who'd arrived at the powwow without his fiancée.

"Where's Grace?" Big Mac asked his son, who'd been smiling from ear to ear for the last week as they counted down to his big day.

"She's running late at work, but she'll be here. Today's her last day at the pharmacy for a while, and she's turning everything over to Fiona."

"You two have so much to look forward to," Big Mac said, embracing his fourth son.

Evan returned the hug. "Yes, we do."

"Love you, son. I'm so proud of you and Grace, and I can't wait to see you two tie the knot."

"I can't wait either, and thank you for all you did to get everyone there."

"It was a pleasure."

Linda came over to greet Evan with a hug, a kiss and a beer that he gratefully accepted.

"Thanks, Mom."

She patted his face. "One last time—mother of the groom. I can't wait."

"Me either. I'm so ready."

"That's because you got it just right."

"I certainly did."

"We can't wait to officially welcome Grace to our family."

Evan blew out a deep breath as he battled his emotions. "I can't believe we're leaving tomorrow. Been a long time coming."

The others began to arrive in waves—Joe, Janey and PJ, Mac, Maddie, Thomas and Hailey, Stephanie and Grant, Ned and Francine, Tiffany, Blaine and Ashleigh, Kevin and Chelsea, who'd decided to accept Kevin's invitation, Riley, Finn, Shane and Katie, Owen, Laura and Holden, Mallory, Frank and Betsy, and finally, Adam and Abby, who were still tanned from the honeymoon cruise Adam had surprised her with.

"Now that the gang's all here," Big Mac said, calling the meeting to order the way he did town council meetings, "let's go over the itinerary."

"Where's Grace?" Stephanie asked as she and the others devoured the pizza he'd bought for them at Mario's.

"She'll be here," Evan said, eyeing the front door. "Any minute now."

"Joseph," Big Mac said to his son-in-law, "you've got the ferry tickets."

"Yes, sir." Joe made a production of handing out tickets to everyone.

"You'll note the time on that ticket is *zero eight hundred*," Big Mac said sternly.

"Freaking butt crack of dawn on a vacation day," Mac said.

"And you'd better get your butt crack to that dock on time or else," Big Mac said.

"When did Dad turn into a drill sergeant?" Mac asked, his mouth full of pizza.

"You be quiet for once and *listen*," Big Mac said, drawing howls of laughter from the others and a scowl from his eldest son.

"We'll be met at the ferry landing in Point Judith by a bus that'll take us to Logan Airport in Boston, where you'll be given your plane tickets," Big Mac continued.

"He don't trust us with 'em," Ned commented to snorts of laughter.

"You got that right," Big Mac said. "From Boston, we'll connect through Charlotte and San Juan before arriving in Anguilla at six o'clock local time. We'll be met by shuttles from the resort and then shown to our beachfront accommodations."

"*OhmyGod*," Tiffany said. "I can't *freaking* wait."

"Freaking is a bad word, Mommy," Ashleigh said.

"I know, baby, but in this case, it's allowed."

"Your mom wants to play naked boy-naked girl with Blaine," Mac said, earning a glare from his brother-in-law.

"Yes, I do," Tiffany replied, sending the others into hysterics.

"I thought we weren't allowed to play that game anymore," Ashleigh said, setting off another round of laughter.

"*You're* not," Tiffany told her adorable look-alike daughter. "But mommies and daddies are allowed to."

"My mommy and daddy play that game a lot," Thomas said. "I seen it."

Maddie's eyes got very big and very round as she covered her son's mouth with her hand while Mac lost his shit laughing. "Oh. My. Sweet. Hell."

The meeting descended into chaos after that, but Big Mac didn't mind. He'd told them what they needed to know, and everything was in place to ensure a smooth trip from one island to another.

His wife slipped her arm around his waist. "Well done, my love. You missed your calling as a travel agent."

"Aw, thanks, but it was only fun because it was for this crew of lunatics."

"It's going to be the best time ever."

He couldn't agree more. The only thing he was worried about now was the weather. You could plan anything but that.

~

EVAN NOTICED OWEN GO INTO THE KITCHEN AND NOT COME BACK, SO while the others razzed Maddie about Thomas's hilarious comment, Evan went to see what was up with his best friend.

Owen stared out the window at the darkness, his arms braced on either side of the sink.

"What's up, O?" Evan helped himself to two of his father's beers. He opened one for himself and the other for his friend.

"Thanks." Owen took the beer from Evan and tipped back half of it in one swallow, which was unusual for him.

"Something wrong?"

"Nah, it's all good. How are you? Ready for this?"

"I've been ready for a year. Thought it would never get here."

"It's gonna be a blast."

"I know I've told you this a hundred times already, but I'm so, so, *so* glad you're coming. Wouldn't have been the same without you guys."

"Yeah." Owen looked down at the floor, his broad shoulders curving inward, the stance reminding Evan of the dreadful weeks leading up to the trial of Owen's father.

"What's on your mind? And don't say it's nothing. I know you better than that."

Seeming surprised by Evan's blunt statement, Owen looked up at him before glancing into the other room, where Laura chatted with Stephanie and Abby. "She shouldn't be going. It's too close to her due date, but she won't hear me when I tell her we should stay home."

"Oh."

"Yeah, last thing I wanted to do was inflict my worries on your good time. That's why I didn't want to talk about it."

"Dude, come on, aren't we past that? Your worries are my worries. That's how we roll."

"Sometimes I think…"

"What?"

"That I never would've survived the nightmare of my family without the refuge of yours."

Evan put his hand over his heart. "My family is your family, and we'll watch out for you and Laura and those babies. Mallory and Katie will be with us, both of them experienced nurses. If there's any problem, they'll be right there."

"So you don't think I'm taking a foolish risk by letting my seven-months-pregnant wife go on a trip like this?"

"Of course I don't think that, and no one else will either. Besides, we all know Laura does exactly what she wants, and no one, even her devoted husband, can talk her out of something once she sets her mind to it."

Owen laughed. "Yeah, that about nails her."

"I go way back with her," Evan said with a grin.

"Like all the way back."

"Yep. I know without a doubt there's no way she'd ever endanger herself or those babies. David said she could go. Victoria said she could go. And how great is it that she feels well enough to travel after being so bloody sick for months at the beginning?"

"It is pretty great," Owen said, his expression softening as he watched his wife talk and laugh with the other women. "So where's your bride-to-be tonight?"

"That's a good question." As Evan withdrew his phone, intending to call her, the front door opened in a gust of cold air as Grace arrived. He'd made sure to save her some pizza and the glass of chardonnay she would need after a long day at work. The minute she came through the door, however, he could see something was wrong. He knew her so well, better than he'd ever known anyone, and her distress was palpable.

"What's the matter?"

As he took her coat, she looked up at him, blinking rapidly as if trying not to cry. Though he had no doubt that she was every bit as committed to him as he was to her, his heart stopped at the possibility that she might be having cold feet. "I… Um… My parents. They're not coming."

"*What?*"

"Th-they said the trip was too much for them, that they'd been trying to find a way to tell me…" She broke down into heartbroken sobs that made Evan want to kill the people who would soon be his in-laws. They'd done nothing but hurt his beloved Grace in big and small ways since he'd known her, and he'd had about enough.

He wrapped his arms around her and guided her into the formal living room his mother kept for "guests," out of the view of the others. "I'm so sorry, honey. I hate that they would do this to you, especially so late in the game."

"It's what they do," she said, sobs hiccupping through her. "Any time I'm really happy, they find a way to ruin it."

"After this, they'll be seeing and hearing very little from you and us. I won't let them hurt you anymore."

"Wh-who will give me away if my dad isn't there?"

Evan's heart, the heart that belonged completely to her, split right down the middle. "My dad will. You know he'd love to."

"H-he's nicer t-to me than m-my own f-father has ever b-been."

"He loves you. We all do. We're your family now. Us and your brothers and all your friends. You're surrounded by people who'd do *anything* for you. Your brothers would give you away, wouldn't they?"

"P-probably, but they'd be aw-awkward and uncomfortable. I think I might rather have your dad."

"You can have anyone you want, and my dad would be delighted to do it."

Because he was holding her so close, he felt her backbone stiffen and her usual fortitude return. "I'm sorry to show up in this condition when everyone's excited."

"Don't apologize. Not to me or anyone else. Of course you're upset, and with good reason, but we can't let them ruin this amazing week that we've been looking forward to for so long."

"I won't let them ruin this for me. No way."

"That's my girl. Your brothers will still be there, right?"

"Oh yes, they wouldn't miss it, but this is it for me with my parents. I can't keep letting them do this to me."

"No, you can't, and I'm glad to hear you say that."

"Because you've wanted me to cut things off with them for a while now?" she asked with the hint of a smile ghosting her lips.

"Something like that, but I never would've said it. You had to get there on your own."

"Well, consider me there."

Evan cupped her face in his hands and kissed her cheeks, brushing away her tears, before turning his attention to her sweet lips. "Focus on me. I'm your family, and I'll never let anyone hurt you ever again."

"I'd be lost without you, Evan. You have no idea how much I need you."

"Yes, I do, because I need you just as much." He kissed her again, more intently this time, before the clearing of a throat interrupted them.

"Sorry to interrupt the early honeymoon," Big Mac said. "I was just making sure you two are okay. Someone said Grace seemed upset." He zeroed in on her tearstained face, his brows furrowing with dismay.

That was what Evan loved best about his dad—he took care of them all, whether they were his biological kids or their friends.

"Who made you cry, and how can I kill him or her?" Big Mac asked. "The offer includes my son, in case you're wondering."

Grace's face lit up with a big, bright smile. His dad had that effect on people, especially the ones who loved him. "Your son is the most wonderful man who ever lived, and he only makes me cry with laughter."

"Then who do I need to see about tears on my daughter-in-law's pretty face the week of her wedding?"

"Grace's parents let her know today that they're unable to make it to the wedding." Evan saved her the trouble of having to say the words again.

His father's face went slack with shock. "They... Well... I'm sorry, honey."

"Grace was worried about who might give her away, and I said—"

"I'll do it," Big Mac said fiercely. "I will do it, and it'll be my honor."

Grace began to cry again, but these were happy tears. Evan knew the difference by now. She released him so she could hug his dad, who wrapped her up in his strong arms. She looked so small and fragile next to his strapping father, and the sight of them together brought tears to Evan's eyes.

"Everything's going to be okay, sweetheart," Big Mac said, rubbing small circles on Grace's back. "I'll make sure of it, and so will Evan."

"I-I've never said this before, but you sh-should know... I love you all so much. Your family... I'm so happy that you're going to be my family."

"You're damned right you're our family." Big Mac raised his hand to invite Evan into their embrace. "Tomorrow, we're going to Anguilla, and we're going to get you two married in the most beautiful wedding you've ever seen. After that, you and Evan are going to have the most beautiful life. And that's just the way it's going to be, you hear me?"

"I hear you," Grace said, sighing.

And so did Evan, because if his dad said it was so, he believed him. Big Mac McCarthy was rarely ever wrong about anything.

CHAPTER 28

On their third night in Anguilla, the guys and girls went their separate ways for bachelor and bachelorette parties for the bride and groom.

Evan's brothers took over a British pub on the resort property, and the beer was flowing a couple of hours into the party.

"What're the ladies doing?" Alex asked as he toked on one of the cigars that Dan Torrington had contributed to the gathering.

"Something about the spa." Mac turned up his nose. "They really know how to party."

"They're getting spa treatments and then going to dinner at the Japanese steakhouse," Evan said. "They're probably finishing dinner by now."

"Ohhh," Adam said. "How *wild.*"

"Well, Tiffany helped to plan the night," Blaine said, "so anything can happen with my wife involved."

"This is true," Mac said. "She's a terrible influence on my sweet wife."

"Whatever!" Blaine said. "Whose idea was it to tell us they'd hired strippers for Jenny's bachelorette party?"

"*Maddie's,*" the guys said in unison.

Mac squirmed. "That was a rare lapse in judgment for my lovely wife. She's been soundly disciplined, and it won't happen again."

"I *sooo* can't wait to tell her you said that," Joe said, laughing and accepting a fist bump from Grant.

"It might be better if you didn't tell her," Mac said, sending the others into hysterics.

"I've only been married a couple of weeks," Paul said, "but even I can predict trouble in your future, Mac."

"Nah." Mac waved his hand, sending cigar ashes flying. "She worships at the altar of Mac McCarthy."

"It just gets better and better," Shane said, grinning as he shook his head at Mac.

"Son, far be it from me to tell you what to do, but if I were you, I'd stick a sock in it," Big Mac said, to howls.

"He'll never stick a sock in it," Frank said. "He's been this way all his life."

"Sad but true," Kevin said.

Slim took it all in, laughing at Mac's antics and enjoying one of the fine cigars Dan had brought. This was usually one of his favorite ways to spend a night—with his best friends, juicy steaks, good vodka and fine cigars, laughing and bullshitting. But on this night, he wasn't able to relax or fully enjoy the party because someone was missing.

Erin would be here tomorrow, but that felt like a lifetime from now. He'd only gotten there himself late that afternoon, in time for the bachelor party, which was why he'd had her come the next day. He knew he wouldn't want to leave her for any reason after she arrived, and he couldn't miss Evan's party.

So he was destined to spend one more night alone and was half out of his mind waiting for her. From the moment she'd said yes to his invitation, time had slowed to a torturous crawl for him. Every minute felt like an hour, every day like a year. The flight from Palm Beach to Anguilla had been pure torture. But once he'd arrived, he'd found the ebullient McCarthy family in high spirits, and it was impossible to be anything other than sucked into their excitement.

Finn McCarthy joined the bachelor party late, having taken part in an all-day scuba-diving expedition that had returned after dark. He was drawn right into the circle of friends and family, given a beer and a plate of food.

"Ran into the ladies on the way over here," he said between bites.

"Where were they heading?" Luke asked.

"I'm almost afraid to tell you guys."

"Now you'd better," Blaine said in his sternest cop voice.

"There was talk of skinny-dipping at the beach."

The boisterous group went silent.

"Like hell," Blaine said, getting up from the table and heading toward the beach.

"Wait! Blaine, *wait!*" Mac called after him. "This is our *chance*."

Blaine stopped, turned back, hands on hips, clearly seething. "For *what?*"

"Revenge," Mac said, drawing out the single word with dramatic flair. "Come back here, and let's make a plan."

"Uh-oh," Finn said, giving his full attention to the steak. "Was it something I said?"

"You just threw gas on a fire, son," Kevin said, chuckling.

Slim sat back, filled with amused detachment, listening to the guys plot against their women and imagining the many ways this could go wrong. As a single guy, he didn't feel he had any place to speak up and suggest they might want to reconsider their plan. What did he know about being married or engaged, or committed, for that matter? He hoped to change that status very soon, but in the meantime, he couldn't resist tagging along on their mission, just to see how it turned out.

They snuck down to the beach, where the women could be heard a mile away, screaming, laughing, splashing. To say a good majority of them were pregnant and sober, they were having one hell of a time. Thanks to the full moon shining down on the white sand, they could easily pick out the piles of clothes that had been left on the beach.

"There," Mac whispered, pointing to the clothes. "Let's go."

"Boys," Big Mac said, "I have to tell you… This is *not* going to end well."

"Oh come on, Dad," Grant said. "It'll be hysterical, and they have it coming after the crap they've pulled on us."

Grant's capitulation surprised Slim, as he tended to be much more mature than his older brother. One thing Slim had to say for Mac, he'd missed his calling as a military commander. He was excellent at getting others to follow his lead. While they crept onto the beach to collect the women's clothing, Slim stayed back with Big Mac, Frank, Kevin and Ned, otherwise known as the actual adults in this group.

"Buncha fools," Ned muttered.

"Ah, yes," Big Mac said, "but they're my fools. I'm just glad Linda, Betsy, Francine and Chelsea offered to babysit tonight so the girls could go out. I'd want no part of digging myself out of this one."

"You know it, brother," Frank said.

"Chelsea would kill me," Kevin said bluntly.

The guys returned, laughing and whispering—loudly—arms loaded with dresses and panties and bras and sandals that they then deposited in a pile on the sand.

"I did this once to Abby," Adam whispered. "I thought she was going to murder me."

"She will this time for sure," Frank said.

"I can't believe Katie is skinny-dipping," Shane said. "She doesn't like being naked in the shower."

"Dude!" Owen said, sending the others into somewhat-silent hysterics. "That's my *sister* you're talking about."

"Sorry," Shane said, chuckling.

"No, you're not."

"I feel your pain," Mac said, using his thumb to point to Joe.

"I only speak the truth," Joe said, "and your sister is one hot mama."

"*Joseph*," Big Mac said. "End it. Now."

"You're talking about his precious princess," Frank said, patting Joe on the back. "Inferring that you sleep with her is grounds for execution by firing squad."

"You're goddamned right it is," Big Mac growled.

"So what happens now?" Slim asked the mastermind.

"Now, we wait for them to notice," Mac said.

The ladies were in no apparent rush to end their nocturnal adventure, and the splashing and screaming continued for another fifteen minutes.

"I gotta pee," Grant said.

"Me, too," Alex replied.

They left to find the nearest men's room while the rest of them waited and waited and waited, so long it was almost as if the women knew they were torturing them by dragging it out. They'd be thrilled to hear later that they'd done that without knowing it.

"Kara is going to kill me dead for this," Dan said.

"But what a way to go," Paul said, grinning.

"We are going to rescue them, aren't we?" Shane asked, sounding nervous. "I was hoping Katie might actually marry me at some point."

"Let me tell you something about revenge, young grasshopper," Mac said, his hand on his younger cousin's shoulder. "It doesn't count until they suffer a *fraction* as much as they made us suffer."

"But, um, Katie's gonna be pissed, and I was hoping to get laid like a lot this week."

"*Dude!*" Owen's roar carried across the beach, resulting in silence from the women.

Uh-oh.

"What was that?" Maddie asked.

"Sounded like Owen," Laura said. "Owen? Are you out there?"

Mac put his hand over Owen's mouth and glared at him.

"I swear to God," Stephanie said, "if they're spying on us, I'm going to neuter Grant."

"Okay, I'm out," Grant said as he returned from the men's room without Alex.

Mac grabbed his arm before he could bail. "No one's out. We're all in this to the finish now."

"She said the word *neuter*," Grant hissed at his brother.

"All talk," Mac said, releasing his brother. "Stay strong."

Wary now, the women got out of the water and walked up the beach to discover their clothes were gone.

"*Those sons of bitches!*" Tiffany's howl could be heard for miles.

"What?" Katie asked. "What's wrong?"

"Our clothes are gone."

The screaming started in earnest at that point.

"Adam McCarthy!" Abby yelled. "Bring me my clothes, or *I'll divorce you.*"

Adam whimpered and tried to pull free of Mac's iron grip.

"Stay strong," Mac said to his brother. "She'd never actually divorce you."

"I'm not so sure," Adam muttered.

"Can we get a group rate on divorce?" Stephanie asked.

"How could they do this?" Katie asked, sounding slightly hysterical. "What'll we *do?*"

"Dan Torrington!" Kara's voice echoed through the night. "Bring me my clothes, or you'll never see your favorite parts of me again! *Ever!*"

"I'm out." Dan took Kara's dress off the pile and headed for the beach.

"Don't look at my wife." Blaine grabbed Tiffany's dress and followed Dan. "I'll fucking shoot anyone who looks at her."

"Oh come on, you guys," Mac said as the others followed Dan and Blaine, intending to rescue their women.

"Mac McCarthy, if you can hear me, you'd better get over here right now with my dress, or you're never, ever, *ever* having sex again. *Ever!*"

"Well," Mac said with a sheepish grin, "this was fun, but might be time to call it a ball game."

Slim rocked with silent laughter. This was the funniest thing he'd witnessed since naked boy-naked girl, and it just got better when the guys arrived with the women's clothes, and much screaming ensued as the wrong guy saw the wrong woman naked.

"Someone poke my eyes out right now," Evan said. "I just came face-to-face with Janey's boobs."

"I should get to see Grace's," Joe said. "It's only fair."

"Not the same thing," Evan argued. "Those were *sister* tits. They don't even count as tits."

"Oh *yes* they do," Joe said.

"*Joseph!*" Big Mac bellowed.

"I'd like to say for the record that this wasn't my idea," Luke said to Sydney as he handed over her dress.

She yanked it out of his hand. "You're still in big trouble, mister."

"Uh-oh," Luke said. "What does this mean for vacation nookie?"

Sydney's glare answered for her.

"*Where's Alex?*" Jenny screamed.

"He had to go pee-pee," Paul told her.

"Oh my God! Don't look! I'm going to kill him!"

"I'll help you," Stephanie said, using her hands to cover the important parts until her clothes were located.

"I'm not looking," Paul said to Hope. "I only have eyes for my wife."

"Who will poke your eyes out of your head if you so much as glance at one of my naked friends," Hope said.

"Awww, baby, come on. You gotta admit it was funny."

"Hilarious," Hope said dryly.

"One of my *brothers* had better bring me my clothes, or you're going to see more of your new sister than you ever wanted to," Mallory said.

"Got 'em right here," Grant said.

"Ladies," Maddie said, beating off Mac's hands as he tried to help her get dressed. "This means *war*. No sex for any of them for the entire time we're here. Who's in?"

"*Me*," every female voice, except for one, said at the same time.

"Not me," Grace said as she pressed her naked body against Evan and kissed him. He scooped her up and carried her away while the other women called her a traitor and the guys begged them to change their minds.

But the women weren't budging, and the guys were shit out of luck, much to Slim's amusement. How do you spell *backfire*?

"Told them it was a bad idea," Big Mac said, shaking his head. "They never listen to their old man."

"Especially your oldest one," Frank said.

"True, but I think his wife can handle him." Big Mac gestured to

Maddie, who was marching Mac off the beach with his arm bent behind his back.

"Looks like she won't be worshiping at the altar of Mac McCarthy this week," Joe called after them.

"*Did you say that?*" Maddie smacked Mac's shoulder with her free hand.

"You might want to step up the discipline, too, bro," Adam called after them. "Seems to be working out real well for you."

"I'm going to kill you," Maddie growled.

"Come on, baby," Mac said, walking on tiptoes as she wrenched his arm even higher on his back. "It's all in good fun."

"Don't you *baby* me."

The poor bastard was in for it, but Slim had to give him credit. He was one funny son of a bitch who sure knew how to get himself into deep shit with his wife.

CHAPTER 29

$\mathcal{T}$he ride to the airport in the resort shuttle the next afternoon was the most torturous part of a torturous six days since Erin accepted his invitation to come to the wedding. An accident on the single-lane road had them sitting still for fifteen minutes. Slim was about to get out and start jogging through the thick humidity if that was what it took to be there when she came through the door from customs.

He didn't want to miss a single second with her, even if that meant showing up sweaty and winded.

Before running became necessary, the shuttle began to move—far too slowly for his liking—going around the accident to continue on.

When they pulled up to the curb, Slim bolted from the van before the driver could come around to let him out. He jogged into the airport and straight to the reception area, where others milled around, waiting for family, friends, loved ones.

Erin was all three to him, Slim realized. One phone call at a time, one text, one FaceTime conversation and every blissful hour in her arms had made her essential to his future happiness. It all hinged on her. He didn't want to be alone anymore, but that was only because not being alone meant being with her.

That made her different from anyone else he'd ever been with. He'd never considered changing his life for any other woman. He'd never even come close. Perhaps that was in part due to what he went through with his high school girlfriend, but it was more than that. It was Erin. She fit him in every way that mattered, and if the longest weeks of his life were any indication, living without her, even for a short time, was going to be nearly impossible.

After her flight was announced, he nearly lost his mind waiting for her to clear customs. And then there she was, wearing a gorgeous floral dress and a wide-brimmed hat. Her dark hair was long around her shoulders, her smile brightening when she saw him waiting for her.

They moved toward each other, him working against the crowd, dodging families, suitcases and even a dog on a leash to get to her. He picked her right up off her feet and crushed her to him, drawing a squeak of surprise and then laughter from her that was smothered when he kissed her, mindless of the people all around them or that her hat had flown off her head.

What did he care about any of that when he finally had her back in his arms where she belonged?

He could've stood there all day kissing her, but she pulled back from him, looking up with laughter dancing in her gorgeous eyes. "Fancy meeting you here."

Bending to retrieve her hat, he said, "How was the flight?" He'd worried endlessly about her being afraid without him there to calm her.

"Half a Xanax and first-class service took the edge off."

"Told ya."

"How're things here?"

He'd taken great pleasure in relaying the details of the prank gone wrong to her on the phone the night before. "Tensions were running high at breakfast. The guys are contrite, and the women are determined to make them suffer."

"They have it coming."

"I gotta say I agree with you in this one case. Normally, I'd side with my bros. This time, they got what was coming to them. I'm just glad you weren't here yet, so I wasn't tempted to participate."

"You'd be sleeping alone for a long, long time if you did that to me."

"Good to know."

Slim took her suitcase handle in one hand and wrapped his free hand around hers to lead her out of the terminal to the resort shuttle. The heat of the late-day sun was in stark contrast to the air-conditioned building.

"Oh wow," Erin said, taking in the blue sky, the palm trees, the heat. "Doesn't that feel good?"

"Nothing beats the Caribbean when it's snowing at home."

The driver took her bag to put it in the back while they got into the vehicle.

Slim kept his arm around her, his lips sliding over the silk of her hair. "I thought today would never get here."

"Me, too. I've been on pins and needles."

"Because of the flight?"

"That was only a small part of it. The rest was you. I couldn't wait to see you."

Slim raised his hand to her face and turned her toward him so he could kiss her again. This, right here... This was love, as pure and as simple as anything had ever been. Over the last few years, as his friends had fallen like dominoes, he'd had cause to wonder what the hell was wrong with them. Why would they shackle themselves to one woman when they could have *all* the women?

Well, he got it now. He couldn't imagine ever again wanting to hold or kiss or make love to any woman but the one currently in his arms. And the thought of her with any guy but him made him positively murderous.

They barely came up for air on the ride to the resort. The poor driver was probably used to it with all the honeymooners he transported, but Slim couldn't be bothered with caring what the driver thought. Not when he had the woman he loved back in his arms. He had no idea how much time they'd have together. Would it be just this week, or would she take him up on his offer to come to Florida? Not knowing what the future held made him even crazier than he'd been for the last week spent waiting to see her again.

A lot was riding on this week. More than she knew. He was determined to make a go of this relationship, and he wasn't leaving this island until she was on the same page.

HE'D SWEPT HER OFF HER FEET—LITERALLY. THE BREATHLESS GIDDY feeling had never been stronger than when he greeted her at the airport and kissed her all the way back to the resort. Upon arrival, they'd gone directly to his room, walking along beautifully landscaped sidewalks that she barely noticed as she struggled to keep up with his long-legged stride.

That he was in an all-fired rush to be alone with her only added to her anticipation, which was already off the charts. Her OCD had been epic this week, while she waited for something to go wrong, to disrupt the excitement his invitation had stirred in her.

Like in Philly, the second the hotel door clicked shut behind them, he had her pressed against the wall, devouring her with deep, drugging kisses. Erin was so happy to be with him again that she surrendered completely, willing to go anywhere he wanted to take her. And apparently he planned to take her right there.

"Another wall," she said, gasping as he lifted her skirt and ripped her panties in his haste to get them off.

"Can't wait," he said, sounding as desperate as she felt.

Then he was inside her, filling her so completely that she could barely breathe, let alone speak.

"God, I missed you," he said gruffly, his lips brushing against her ear and setting off a chain reaction of sensations that she felt everywhere, especially in the place where they were joined.

With her arms around his neck, she held on tight as he took her on another wild ride. "Missed you, too. So much."

"Gonna be quick."

"Fine by me."

He reached down to coax her to the finish line, right ahead of him. His head dropped to her shoulder while he tried to catch his breath.

Erin ran her fingers through his hair, soothing him as their bodies quaked with aftershocks.

"Just when I think it can't get any better…"

"Mmm," she said, laughing softly. "If it gets any better, I might not be able to walk."

"I was rough with you."

"And I loved every single second of it."

Raising his head, he looked into her eyes for a long moment before he kissed her softly and withdrew, setting her down on her feet and waiting to make sure she was steady before letting her go. Then he began unbuttoning her dress, until it fell into a billowing cloud of fabric at their feet. Her bra soon followed, leaving her naked before him.

He kept his gaze fixed on her as his shirt, which was covered in palm trees, disappeared over his head. He took her by the hand, led her to the bed and turned down the covers for her, kissing her when he tucked her in. "Be right back."

After he disappeared into the bathroom, Erin took her first look at the gorgeous room that had been decorated in shades of white and tan. It included a kitchen, sitting room and deck that overlooked the crystalline blue water. But the view had nothing on him when he emerged from the bathroom, having removed the rest of his clothes.

She took a greedy, hungry look at his muscular body, and the cock that was hard and heavy once again.

He crawled into bed and reached for her. They came together in the middle of the king-size bed, arms and legs intertwined, lips hungry for more. "What've you done to me, Erin Barton?"

"The same thing you've done to me," she said, smiling up at him.

He kissed her everywhere, reducing her to a quivering mess of nerve endings—all of them on fire for him—before he made slow, sweet love to her while watching over her with the eyes that saw her in a way no one else ever had.

Afterward, they lay on their sides, facing each other as the sun set over the Caribbean in a fiery ball. He ran a finger from her shoulder to her hand and then back up again.

She had so much she needed to tell him, so many things she wanted him to know, and the long days of counting down the minutes until she could see him again had made her realize that the time for hedging was over.

"The last time I saw my brother," she said, breaking a long silence, "we had a rare argument. Mitch and I had rented a place in the Hamptons for a weekend with Toby and Jenny, two weeks before Toby died. Mitch was asleep on the beach—well, passed out, I should say. Jenny had gone to shower, and Toby asked me to take a walk with him. We went down to the water and walked along the shore, talking about law school and his job and his and Jenny's wedding, which was a month and a half away. And then he told me he had something he'd wanted to say for a while by then—that I could do better than Mitch." She paused before she continued. "I was so angry with him for saying that, for putting those thoughts in my head, because he knew how important his opinion was to me. I was more furious with him that day than I'd ever been before. I'd gone out of my way to make Jenny feel welcome in our family, which was certainly no hardship. I loved her from the first time I met her, and I thought he owed me the same courtesy."

Slim continued to stroke her arm as he listened to her, watching over her as she shared her pain with him.

"I'd just moved in with Mitch and had made this huge commitment to him, and here was my brother, my best friend, the most important person in my life, telling me I'd made a mistake."

"Did he know you were pissed?"

"Uh, *yeah*," she said with a laugh. "He knew. I walked away from him, and he ran after me. When he caught up, he took me by the arm to keep me from storming off again. He said, 'Mitch is not a *bad* guy, but *you can do better*. Don't settle for him, Erin. Hold out for something better.'"

"Yikes. That must've gone over like a fart in church."

She smiled at his choice of words. "You could say that. Things were tense between us for the rest of the weekend. Mitch asked me what was up. Jenny asked. But I never told them, and I don't think he did either. And when it came time to leave on Sunday, he hugged me, told me he loved me best of all and that he didn't want me to leave mad. I said if he didn't want me to be mad, he should've kept his opinions to himself."

"What did he say to that?"

"He laughed and hugged me again as tight as he had in years, and he said, 'Someday, you'll know exactly what I mean, and you'll thank me.'"

"Cocky bastard, huh?" Slim said, grinning.

"Not usually, but in that case, yeah, seriously cocky." She linked their hands and looked up at him. "Every time I've thought about that weekend since then, I've been annoyed with him for trying to sabotage my relationship with Mitch, but now I know he was one hundred percent right. Now I know exactly what he meant, and I'm indeed thanking him."

"Yeah?" he said, his brows raised in question.

She nodded and took the plunge. "My Toby was telling me to wait for you, and as usual, he was right. I love you, Tobias Fitzgerald Jackson Junior."

He blinked a couple of times, as if trying not to cry, before he reached for her, bringing her close enough to kiss. "Marry me," he whispered gruffly against her lips.

Erin gasped. "What?"

"You heard me. Marry. Me. Erin. Please, marry me. Be my wife, my love, my everything. I love you more than I ever thought I could love anyone. Will you please, please, *please* marry me and let me teach you how to fly in every possible way?"

She was so stunned that she could barely think.

"We could have it all, baby. Winters in Florida, summers on Gansett. Together every day. Maybe even a little Slim or Erin tossed in there, too, if we get really lucky. You're the only thing I need to be happy. You're it for me. Say yes."

She loved him, her parents loved him, her friends loved him, and she had no doubt, no doubt whatsoever, that her beloved brother would've loved him, too. What was left to think about? Absolutely nothing. "Yes."

"Really?" he asked, his expression priceless.

"Really."

"Oh my God," he said on a deep exhale. "You're really going to marry me?"

"I really am, and I'll let you teach me how to fly, too."

"I'd love to." He kissed her then with a kind of desperation he'd rarely shown her, and she returned the desperation, the intensity, the desire. "I need to get up for a second, but I'll come right back."

Erin reluctantly released him, and true to his word, he returned a minute later and put a stunning diamond ring on her left hand. Tears filled her eyes and spilled down her cheeks. "W-what? When… When did you get this?"

"The day before I left West Palm. I hadn't planned to blurt out a proposal the second you arrived, but after what you just told me about Toby… It was the perfect time, the perfect woman." He kissed the back of the hand where his ring now resided. "If you don't like it, we can return it."

Laughing through her tears, she said, "I love it. We're not returning it." She was filled with every kind of emotion possible, including one she'd never expected to experience so fully again—joy. "Who'd have thought that spraining my ankle and getting a flat tire on a dark road would turn out to be the best thing that ever happened?"

"I did. I knew from that first night that you were going to ruin me in the best way possible."

"You did not know then!"

"Yes, I did. I really did. And you know how I knew?"

"How?"

"Me, who made a career out of never, ever spending a night with a woman, slept in that uncomfortable chair in your living room so I could be there if you needed me during the night. That was the first sign of trouble where you were concerned."

"Trouble, ha! I haven't been any trouble to you."

"Are you *kidding* me? You've been nothing but trouble to me, disturbing my focus, plaguing my dreams, keeping me awake at night, forcing me to jack off in the shower more than I have since I was a kid. If that's not trouble, what is it?"

Laughing at his recitation, she said, "It's love."

"Yes, it is, and I want all the trouble you can dole out for the rest of our lives."

"You got it. Thank you so much for taking on all my issues and helping me find a way to be happy."

"Baby, being happy with you is like breathing—the easiest thing I've ever done."

EPILOGUE

$\mathcal{T}$here had been a time, not that long ago, when Grace Ryan had been convinced she'd never have a boyfriend, let alone a husband. Lap-band surgery had transformed her body, but Evan McCarthy's love had transformed her soul. Seeing herself through his eyes, she felt beautiful for the first time in her life, and standing before the full-length mirror in the resort's bridal suite, she took in the sight of herself in her wedding dress and could see for herself, for once, that she was indeed beautiful on the most important day of her life.

From one of the most embarrassing incidents ever had come the love of a lifetime. Sometimes it seemed like minutes rather than more than a year since the night she'd been abandoned by a date on Gansett Island and rescued by Evan, who'd been playing a gig with Owen at the McCarthy's marina.

Evan had taken the time to find out why she was sitting by herself, crying. The guy she'd come to the island with had taken off on his boat with her purse, her money and her clothes, all because she'd refused to have sex with him after finding out their "relationship" had been yet another in a series of jokes about the "fat" girl.

She refused to think about him. Not today. She'd much rather focus on the man who'd taken her home to his parents' house, put her up for the night and paid for her ferry ticket home to Connecticut the next day. The single best thing she'd ever done in her entire life was return to the island the following week to reimburse Evan for the ferry ticket. He hadn't wanted her money, but much to her surprise, the handsome, sexy, ridiculously talented musician who could've had any woman in the world had wanted her. They'd been together pretty much ever since, and she'd ended up giving her virginity to a man who truly loved her and always would—her first and only boyfriend, the love of her life.

A knock on the door drew her out of the trip down memory lane. "Come in."

The door opened, and in came Linda McCarthy. She shut the door behind her and crossed the room to Grace. "Oh, honey," Linda said, her hand over her heart. "You're stunning. Evan won't know what hit him when he sees you."

"Thank you," Grace said, fortified by her soon-to-be mother-in-law's reaction. Her hair was long and shiny thanks to the efforts of the resort's salon. She wore the same makeup she wore most days, which wasn't much, and her dress, which her friend Tiffany had helped her to special order, was a simple white, floor-length gown with a beaded bodice and a long, flowing skirt. The bicep curls Grace had been doing every day for six months had brought new definition to her arms that she was damned proud of.

She would carry a bouquet of red and hot pink tropical flowers and had a red hibiscus bloom tucked behind her right ear.

"Is there anything I can do for you?" Linda asked.

"I think I'm good. You can send the girls in if they're ready."

"They're outside. I'll get them for you, but before I do... I just wanted to say, Mac and I are so thrilled to welcome you into our family. If we could've handpicked the perfect partner for Evan, we couldn't have found anyone better suited to him than you are. Thank you for making him happier than he's ever been."

"Oh, Linda, don't make me cry." Grace reached for her hand. "Your son is the finest man I've ever known, except for maybe your husband, and it's the greatest honor of my life to become a McCarthy. All this time, in the back of my mind, I think I've been waiting for something to go wrong. Something always goes wrong."

"Not today, sweetheart. Today will be perfect, and at the end of it, you'll be Evan's wife and he'll be your husband. Just the way it was always supposed to be."

Grace risked wrinkles to hug Linda. "Thank you so much for coming to check on me. It means so much to me to know you and Mac are happy for us."

"We're delighted. We love you both very much." Linda hugged her, carefully, kissed her cheek and stepped back. "I'll send your girls in."

"Linda."

She turned back, her brow raised in inquiry.

"Thank you for knowing that I could use a little mothering right now."

"Of course, honey. This mother is available to you any time you need her."

"I'll probably be needing her a lot."

"That's fine with me." Linda left her with a smile, closing the door behind her.

Grace took a deep breath, battling the emotions stirred by Linda's generosity. She had fallen in love with Evan's family almost as quickly as she'd fallen for him, and knowing they would be part of her life forever made this amazing day that much sweeter. In her opinion, she'd done a rather admirable job of forgetting her own parents weren't there. She'd enjoyed the time with her brothers, Evan's family and their wonderful friends. It wasn't just enough. It was more than enough.

After a quick knock, the door opened, and in came Grace's tribe of bridesmaids—Abby, Stephanie, Janey, Maddie, Laura and Tiffany, along with Ashleigh, who was their flower girl. Each of them wore dresses made from the same floral material, but all in different styles that they'd chosen for themselves.

Not only had meeting Evan led to her first real boyfriend, it had also led to deep and meaningful friendships with the most incredible group of women who would serve as her attendants.

"You look amazing," Tiffany said, giving Grace a critical once-over. "I wouldn't change a thing."

"That's high praise from the empress of style," Maddie said, "and I completely agree with my sister. You're beautiful."

"Thank you," Grace said, blinking back tears as she brought them in for a group hug. "Thank you all so much for being the best friends I've ever had."

EVAN HAD EXPECTED TO BE NERVOUS, BUT HE WAS TOO EXCITED TO BE nervous. Today he got to marry his amazing Grace, and he couldn't wait to make it official. They'd been counting down to this date, the eighteenth of January, for what felt like forever.

And now that the day was finally upon them, Evan wanted to push the clock ahead an hour so he could see her. Because she was superstitious, they'd spent the night apart, and he hadn't yet seen her today. He was losing his mind waiting for the magical sunset hour they'd chosen for their wedding. They should've done it at sunrise so he wouldn't have had to spend most of the day without her.

"Are you with me?" Owen asked from his perch on the stool next to Evan's.

"Oh, yeah, sorry."

Owen laughed in his face. "You're a mess."

"I'm anxious to get on with it."

Owen looked over his shoulder to see the sun heading toward the horizon in a fiery ball that gilded the surface of the crystal-blue water. "Won't be long now, and from the looks of things, it'll be worth the wait."

"Means a lot to me that you're here, and singing with me, and everything."

"I'd be so bummed if I were at home missing it."

"Does that mean you've come around to enjoying the getaway with your wife?"

"Well, except for the part where she's giving me the deep freeze thanks to your stupid brother and his big ideas."

Evan tossed his head back and laughed. "I've got the most pissed-off and horny group of groomsmen."

"I'm never listening to Mac again. *Ever*."

Still laughing, Evan said, "Let's go through it one more time."

Playing ukuleles, they went over their rendition of Israel Kamakawiwo'ole's "Over the Rainbow/What a Wonderful World" medley, singing in perfect harmony, as always. They'd practiced as often as they could over the last few days, and exchanged smiles as it came together just the way Evan had envisioned. Grace had left the music to his discretion. He wanted it to be special for her, and having Owen there with him made it special for him, too.

When they finished that, they practiced Evan's number-one hit song, "My Amazing Grace," before declaring themselves good to go. The rehearsal had been a formality, something to kill the time. He and Owen could play together in public on a moment's notice without so much as a minute of rehearsal.

They stashed their instruments and went to make sure the other guys were getting ready on schedule. On the way to the villa where they were meeting the others, they ran into Big Mac. Evan's dad wore the same white linen shirt and khaki pants as the guys in the wedding party.

"Was wondering where you two had gotten off to," Big Mac said.

"One last sound check on the beach," Evan said.

"Owen, would you mind giving me one minute with my son?" Big Mac asked.

"Of course not. I'll see you back at the house."

"We'll be right along," Big Mac said. "And Owen? It wouldn't have been the same for Evan without you here."

"I'm glad Laura manipulated me into coming," Owen said with a grin before he left them.

Evan stood with his dad on the expansive boardwalk that looked out over the water. "You're not going to make me cry like a little girl or anything, are you?"

"Would I do that?" Big Mac asked.

Evan laughed at his indignant reply. "Yeah, you would."

"I just wanted the chance to say how happy I am for you and Grace and how proud I am of the man you grew up to be."

Sure enough, Evan blinked rapidly. "You know how much your opinion means to all of us."

"I'm also proud of you for pursuing the music when it would be less complicated to let go of the dream and take the easy road. You always would've wondered what might've been if you hadn't taken this chance, but you should know how much we'll miss you. We'll be waiting for you when it's time to come home."

Evan nodded and smiled at his dad. "That's good to know. I'd hoped you would approve."

Big Mac put his arm around Evan's shoulders. "I approve, and I love you, son. More than you'll ever know."

Evan battled his emotions to find the words he needed. "I've always known I was lucky to be born into our family, but after seeing what Grace has been through with hers, I appreciate it so much more than I ever have before. You and Mom are the heart of us, and I hope to be able to give my kids a fraction of what you've given me."

"And you thought *I'd* make *you* cry."

Evan hugged him, holding on tight to the man who'd been his true north his entire life.

"Let's go get you married, shall we?"

AFTER PUTTING EVAN IN CHARGE OF THE MUSIC, GRACE HAD BEEN prepared for just about anything, but listening to him and Owen on the ukuleles singing a song he knew she loved, Grace couldn't contain her smile or the tears that filled her eyes. It was perfect, just the way he'd said it would be.

They sang that song as their guests were seated and as the wedding party came together in couples, Mac and Maddie, Joe and Janey, Grant and Stephanie, Adam and Abby, Tiffany and Blaine, and Laura as her matron of honor, who'd join Owen as Evan's best man.

While waiting to hear if Laura would be able to convince Owen to come to the wedding, Grace had held off on asking anyone else to be her honor attendant. As Laura headed down the sandy path to the spot they'd chosen for their wedding, Grace was so happy everything had worked out and they'd been able to come. Even the location was perfect after being moved from the resort they'd originally chosen in Turks and Caicos, which had been damaged in a storm.

"Ready, honey?" Big Mac asked, extending his arm to her.

Grace slid her hand into the crook of his elbow. "Ready."

Through highs and lows and ups and downs, through his absences on the tour and everything else they'd been through together, she and Evan had become closer than ever. And as she took Big Mac's arm and heard Evan switch to a solo version of "My Amazing Grace," she followed the sound of his voice down the path just as the sun touched the horizon, firing the sky with brilliant colors, the same way Evan had filled her life with magic.

He locked his gaze on her as he sang the song he'd written for her, and never looked away as she made her way toward him on the arm of his father. When Evan's voice faltered, Owen picked up the slack, finishing the song while Evan put down his guitar and stepped forward to meet her, hugging his dad as he delivered her to him.

Grace handed her flowers to Laura as Owen took his place next to Evan.

Grace would never forget the way Evan looked at her when he took her hands and brought them to his lips, kissing the back of each one. "You take my breath away," he said softly.

This man, this extraordinarily handsome, sexy, talented, sweet man, was going to be her husband. He'd shown her his heart the first night she met him, and nothing she'd seen since then had altered that unforgettable first impression.

The resort had provided a celebrant who led them through the recitation of traditional vows and the exchange of rings. Then he turned to the groom. "Evan?"

Evan smiled down on her and gave her hands a reassuring squeeze. "From the first time I saw you in the crowd at the marina, I couldn't look away. While I was having a blast playing with Owen, you'd had a rough night. Something drew me to you, and that same thing has been drawing me to you ever since. You are the sweetest, sassiest, sexiest woman I've ever known, and I can't wait to hit the road with you and see where life takes us. I can't wait to see you pregnant with our babies. I can't wait for everything with you. Thank you for taking this amazing ride with me. I promise you'll never be bored."

Grace laughed as she cried and tried to collect herself so she could respond.

Evan released her hands long enough to wipe the tears off her face and then reclaimed her hands.

"You've been my hero since that first night when you came to my rescue at one of the lowest points in my life and showed me that decent men still exist. You took care of me that night, and you've been taking care of me ever since. The best thing I ever did in my life was return to the island to reimburse you for the ferry ticket you bought me—money you've consistently refused to take from me, I might add. It took me about five minutes to fall head over heels in love with you, your amazing family and your beautiful island. I can't wait to hit the road with you, to be with you every day, no matter where life may take us, and then return home to the island we both love to raise our family." Her voice dropped to a whisper. "I love you so much."

Evan leaned his forehead into hers. "I love you just as much."

The celebrant declared them husband and wife and told Evan to kiss his bride. But he didn't need to be told.

Their friends and family cheered as he kissed her with the same desperate passion he'd shown her from the beginning. As she held on to her gorgeous new husband, Grace didn't care who might be watching or what they might be thinking. For once, she had everything she'd ever wanted, and Evan by her side for the rest of their lives.

~

Thanks so much for reading *Desire After Dark*! I hope you enjoyed it.

Check out *Light After Dark*, Mallory and Quinn's story, available now. Turn the page to read Chapter 1!

LIGHT AFTER DARK

Chapter 1

The slap, slap, slap of running shoes on pavement was the only sound in the otherwise tranquil morning on Gansett Island. No cars, no bikes, no mopeds, no airplanes overhead. Nothing but wide-open road before her as Mallory counted down the miles on her usual circuit around the island.

Slap, slap, slap. *Laid off.*

Escorted from the premises after twelve years.

Disposed of like yesterday's hazardous waste.

Galling.

Humiliating.

Infuriating.

It'd been ten days since Mallory Vaughn, RN, director of emergency nursing, had been given a pink slip. With hindsight, the handwriting had been all over the wall for months, with every management meeting focused on the hospital's increasingly dire budget situation.

Naturally, they were cutting the highest-paid employees and in many cases not replacing them at all or with people so new they were still trying to tell the difference between an ass and an elbow. Oh to be a fly on the wall the first time the Emergency Services Department didn't have enough nurses on duty to cover a shift. She hoped it was utter chaos. That was the least of what the hospital deserved after treating her like a common criminal when she'd given them everything she had for a big chunk of her professional life.

Thanks a lot for nothing.

Although, the severance package *had* been generous, she'd give them that much. They'd given her a year's salary, a one-time, lump-sum payment for all her accrued sick and vacation time and health insurance coverage for a year. It definitely could've been worse, but it would be a very long time, if ever, before she got over being escorted from the building by security as if she were a common criminal rather than a faithful, dedicated employee.

She understood why they had to do that. Disgruntled employees had been known to leave with a flourish by deleting critical files from computers along with other malicious activities, but did they honestly think *she* would do something like that? The incident was particularly galling in light of the fact that she'd sacrificed so much for that job, including any semblance of a personal life. Who had time for a personal life while working eighty hours a week, doing a job that needed two people to get it done properly?

Good luck finding some other schmuck willing to work like a dog.

More than once since it had happened, Mallory had thought the layoff might turn out to be a blessing. The tight knot of stress in her gut that she'd lived with for years was gone. She woke up now unencumbered, with the whole day ahead of her to do with as she pleased. It'd been years since she'd had a real vacation with no one calling or texting or emailing for answers only she could provide.

And best of all was unlimited time on the island that had become her second home in the last year, since a letter from her late mother had finally given Mallory the name of her father and told her where to find him.

Big Mac McCarthy.

All she had to do was think about him and she smiled. After she'd lived her entire life with a giant question mark where her father should've been, Big Mac had more than made up for lost time by wrapping his big, burly arms around her and welcoming her into his life. He and his wife, Linda, had made her feel like a part of their family from the minute they learned she existed.

Like everyone else who knew the big, jovial, generous, affectionate man who'd fathered her, Mallory was madly in love with him as well as with Linda and their amazing family. Mallory had gone from being completely alone after her mother died to having parents, five siblings, four sisters-in-law, a brother-in-law, two nephews and a niece, as well as uncles and cousins she already adored and the wide circle of friends that came with the McCarthys. Sometimes she still couldn't believe the twisting turns her life had taken since she lost her mother.

Over the last year, she'd tried to reconcile and make peace with the secret her mother had kept from her and her father for nearly forty years. She'd run the gamut of emotions from anger over what she'd missed, to sadness for what could've been, to elation over her new family.

Though she knew that raging against her late mother wouldn't change the past, anger simmered just below the surface of her newfound happiness. Her mom had sacrificed a lot to bring her into the world, including her own parents and siblings, who'd turned their backs on her when she became pregnant out of wedlock.

Diana had done her best to give Mallory every advantage in life, and the two of them had made a happy family together. But when Mallory thought of what might've been with the other half of her family, she simmered with outrage that had no outlet. Mallory had loved her mother and was trying to forgive her for the secrets she'd kept. Forgiveness was a work in progress, as was her hard-won sobriety, which had been tested in the last year.

Mallory was ashamed to admit that she'd had a few sips of beer and wine here and there while trying to fit in with her new family. Those few sips had her back to Alcoholics Anonymous meetings for the first time in many years. The tastes of alcohol she'd allowed

herself during a particularly stressful time in her life hadn't derailed
her recovery, but they'd scared her straight into daily meetings.

Sobriety, she'd learned, was a journey with many destinations. The
drinks she'd relied upon when meeting her Gansett Island family had
been the first she'd had in more than ten years. When she realized
what she'd allowed to happen during a particularly stressful and
emotional time, she'd been unnerved by how easily she'd put aside all
her hard work with almost no thought to the consequences. That
couldn't happen again.

She was beginning to get tired and thought about turning around
to head back to Big Mac and Linda's house when a motorcycle came
flying around the curve behind her, just missing her as it passed in a
flash of metal, the roar of an engine and the stink of exhaust.

Ugh. If that idiot only knew the injuries she'd seen thanks to
motorcycles, he'd never go near one again.

Mallory had turned toward home when a sickening sound of metal
scratching against pavement had her reversing course and heading in
the direction the sound had come from. Though her legs were tired,
she sprinted with everything she had toward the man she saw
sprawled in the street, his bike on its side about ten feet from him.

From the other direction, another jogger came toward them,
arriving a second after Mallory squatted next to the man on the road
to assess his injuries. Blood was pouring from an abrasion on his face,
and his leg was resting at an awkward angle that indicated a possible
femur fracture.

"What've we got?" the other runner asked when he stopped next
to her.

Mallory filled him in on what she'd seen so far. "Do you have a
phone? I never bring mine when I run."

"Yeah, I'll call it in." He withdrew a cell phone from the pocket of
his running pants and made the call. "I'm at the scene of a motorcycle
crash with a single rider unconscious and bleeding from abrasions to
the head and bleeding profusely from what appears to be a compound
fracture of his femur." He recited the other details in a methodical way
that indicated medical training. Bending low to the ground, he peered

at the growing pools of blood under the unconscious man. "Dispatch a chopper. We're going to need it." He ended the call and then pulled his T-shirt over his head to make a tourniquet for the man's leg.

"Are you a doctor?" she asked, trying not to notice his ripped chest and abdomen or bulky arm muscles. In addition to his medical abilities, he also apparently spent a lot of time in the gym.

"Trauma surgeon. You?" Still bending at the waist, he worked the man's wallet out of the back pocket of his shorts and flipped it open.

"ER nurse."

"Despite how it seems, this might turn out to be our friend Michael's lucky day." He sighed. "Twenty-four years old. From New York."

In the pearly early morning light, they stayed by the side of their victim, watching over him until help arrived. Though she was conditioned to senseless injuries after a career as an emergency nurse, it never got any easier to see a young person's life possibly changed in a matter of seconds or to think about the frightening call an unsuspecting family was about to get.

"I'm Mallory Vaughn," she said after a long silence.

"Quinn James."

No other words were exchanged between them as they listened to the sirens get closer to their location on the island's north end. Though he was unconscious, Michael's heart continued to beat and his breathing was regular, if shallow. It remained to be seen if he had suffered life-threatening damage.

EMS arrived and took over in a whirlwind of activity and shouted orders.

Mallory recognized Gansett Island Police Chief Blaine Taylor in the crowd of first responders. Blaine was married to her sister-in-law Maddie's sister, Tiffany. He walked over to her with another man who had to be six and a half feet tall.

"Hey, Mallory," Blaine said. "Did you see what happened?"

"Hi, Blaine. He was driving like a maniac and crashed after he just missed taking me out as he went by. Dr. James and I did what we could."

"You might've saved his leg," the tall guy said. "Mason Johns, fire chief."

"Oh, hi," Mallory said, shaking his hand. "Mallory Vaughn, ER nurse." Or former ER nurse, she should say, but since she hadn't yet told her own family she'd been laid off, it probably wasn't the best idea to tell someone she'd just met.

Mallory stuck around until the Life Flight helicopter arrived and took the young man to a level-one trauma center in Providence. Dr. James offered to go with him, which Mallory thought was nice of him, but the paramedics said they had it covered. As soon as the chopper left, the doctor took off running back the way he'd come, still shirtless after donating his to the cause. Mallory watched him go, noticing a slight hitch in his gait and wondering what his story was.

"Can I give you a lift home?" Blaine asked when the police and firefighters had cleared the site of debris and gotten traffic moving again.

Her muscles were rubbery from standing around, and the sun was now shining down on them, so his offer would save her the trek home, and it would allow her to make her meeting in town. "Do you have time?"

"Sure do. Hop in."

"Good to meet you, Mallory," Mason said as she walked past with Blaine.

"You, too, Mason."

Big Mac and Linda were eating breakfast when she came in the front door.

"There you are," her father said. "We were beginning to wonder if you'd jogged off the bluffs."

"I witnessed an accident and stuck around until the Life Flight came."

"Oh, we heard that and wondered what was going on," Linda said. "Anyone we know?"

Mallory shook her head and helped herself to a glass of ice water. It'd taken a few months to make herself at home here, but they'd insisted often enough that she finally relaxed and helped herself to whatever she wanted. "Tourist from New York on a motorcycle."

"Ugh," Linda said. "I hate those things, especially the one Mac bought from Ned when he was in high school. I was so sure he'd kill himself, and now Evan's got it." She shuddered. "The best part about him being away on tour is no one riding that horrible thing."

Big Mac chuckled at her tirade. "Tell us how you really feel, dear."

"I just did."

As always, Mallory giggled at their banter. They had the kind of marriage she'd once hoped to have herself, but fate had made other plans for her.

Since she had time before her meeting, she took her ice water to the table and sat with them. It was time to tell them what'd happened at work.

Big Mac gave a look she'd seen him use on the others, inquisitive, concerned, paternal. Now it was directed at her, and she loved that. She loved having a father, and she especially loved that *he* was her father.

"What's on your mind?" he asked.

"I've been meaning to tell you that I got laid off about ten days ago."

"*What?*" Linda said. "Are you kidding? You run that department!"

"I know, and I'm sure by now they know it, too." She told them the whole story, about being escorted from the building and how it made her feel, to the generous severance package that would buy her time to figure out her next move.

"It's an outrage," Big Mac declared. "How can they treat loyal employees that way?"

"You and I agree, but that's the way it goes. I was one of the highest-paid nurses in the building, and they're having major financial problems, so the pink slip wasn't a total surprise."

"Still," Big Mac said, "it must've been upsetting to have it go down that way."

"It was, but I'm better now. Thanks for letting me hang out here for the last few days. I'll figure out my next move and get out of your hair soon."

Linda reached over to put her hand on top of Mallory's. "You're not in our hair. We love having you, and you're welcome to stay for as long as you'd like. It's boring around here this time of year. It's nice to have the company."

"I agree," Big Mac said. "Our home is your home for as long as you want to stay."

"Thank you." Mallory swallowed hard, determined not to break down in front of them. They would never know what it meant to her to have them on her side now that her mom was gone. She'd felt so alone in the world until she came to Gansett and found Big Mac and his brood. Now a big, boisterous family surrounded her, and they would get her through this latest challenge.

Light After Dark is available in print from *Amazon.com* and other online retailers, or you can purchase a signed copy from Marie's store at *shop.marieforce.com*.

OTHER BOOKS BY MARIE FORCE

Contemporary Romances

The Gansett Island Series

Book 1: Maid for Love (*Mac & Maddie*)

Book 2: Fool for Love (*Joe & Janey*)

Book 3: Ready for Love (*Luke & Sydney*)

Book 4: Falling for Love (*Grant & Stephanie*)

Book 5: Hoping for Love (*Evan & Grace*)

Book 6: Season for Love (*Owen & Laura*)

Book 7: Longing for Love (*Blaine & Tiffany*)

Book 8: Waiting for Love (*Adam & Abby*)

Book 9: Time for Love (*David & Daisy*)

Book 10: Meant for Love (*Jenny & Alex*)

Book 10.5: Chance for Love, *A Gansett Island Novella (Jared & Lizzie)*

Book 11: Gansett After Dark (*Owen & Laura*)

Book 12: Kisses After Dark (*Shane & Katie*)

Book 13: Love After Dark (*Paul & Hope*)

Book 14: Celebration After Dark (*Big Mac & Linda*)

Book 15: Desire After Dark (*Slim & Erin*)

Book 16: Light After Dark (*Mallory & Quinn*)

Book 17: Victoria & Shannon (Episode 1)

Book 18: Kevin & Chelsea (Episode 2)

A Gansett Island Christmas Novella

Book 19: Mine After Dark (*Riley & Nikki*)

Book 20: Yours After Dark (*Finn & Chloe*)

Book 21: Trouble After Dark (*Deacon & Julia*)

Book 22: Rescue After Dark (*Mason & Jordan*)

The Green Mountain Series

Book 1: All You Need Is Love *(Will & Cameron)*

Book 2: I Want to Hold Your Hand *(Nolan & Hannah)*

Book 3: I Saw Her Standing There *(Colton & Lucy)*

Book 4: And I Love Her *(Hunter & Megan)*

Novella: You'll Be Mine *(Will & Cam's Wedding)*

Book 5: It's Only Love *(Gavin & Ella)*

Book 6: Ain't She Sweet *(Tyler & Charlotte)*

The Butler Vermont Series

(Continuation of the Green Mountain Series)

Book 1: Every Little Thing *(Grayson & Emma)*

Book 2: Can't Buy Me Love *(Mary & Patrick)*

Book 3: Here Comes the Sun *(Wade & Mia)*

Book 4: Till There Was You *(Lucas & Dani)*

The Treading Water Series

Book 1: Treading Water

Book 2: Marking Time

Book 3: Starting Over

Book 4: Coming Home

Book 5: Finding Forever

Historical Romances

The Gilded Series

Book 1: Duchess by Deception

Book 2: Deceived by Desire

Single Titles

How Much I Feel

Five Years Gone

One Year Home

Sex Machine

Sex God

Georgia on My Mind

True North

The Fall

The Wreck

Love at First Flight

Everyone Loves a Hero

Line of Scrimmage

Erotic Romance

The Erotic Quantum Series

Book 1: Virtuous (*Flynn & Natalie*)

Book 2: Valorous (*Flynn & Natalie*)

Book 3: Victorious (*Flynn & Natalie*)

Book 4: Rapturous (*Addie & Hayden*)

Book 5: Ravenous (*Jasper & Ellie*)

Book 6: Delirious (*Kristian & Aileen*)

Book 7: Outrageous (*Emmett & Leah*)

Book 8: Famous (*Marlowe*)

Romantic Suspense

The Fatal Series

One Night With You, *A Fatal Series Prequel Novella*

Book 1: Fatal Affair

Book 2: Fatal Justice

Book 3: Fatal Consequences

Book 3.5: Fatal Destiny, *the Wedding Novella*

ABOUT THE AUTHOR

Marie Force is the *New York Times* bestselling author of contemporary romance, romantic suspense and erotic romance. Her series include Gansett Island, Fatal, Treading Water, Butler Vermont and Quantum.

Her books have sold nearly 10 million copies worldwide, have been translated into more than a dozen languages and have appeared on the *New York Times* bestseller more than 30 times. She is also a *USA Today* and *Wall Street Journal* bestseller, as well as a Speigel bestseller in Germany.

Her goals in life are simple—to finish raising two happy, healthy, productive young adults, to keep writing books for as long as she possibly can and to never be on a flight that makes the news.

Join Marie's mailing list on her website at marieforce.com for news about new books and upcoming appearances in your area. Follow her on Facebook at www.Facebook.com/MarieForceAuthor and on Instagram at www.instagram.com/marieforceauthor/. Contact Marie at marie@marieforce.com.

Made in the USA
Middletown, DE
07 July 2020